Gray Skies

Sherryl D. Hancock

Published by Vulpine Press in the United Kingdom in 2017

ISBN 978-1-83919-244-9

Cover by Claire Wood

Cover photo credit: Tirzah D. Hancock

www.vulpine-press.com

For everyone out there who's looking for love, NEVER stop searching, it will happen! It just has to find you, be open to it!

Prologue

In Los Angeles, things at The Club were in their usual swing. Jet made her way through the crowd, with beers for her and Skyler, a Baileys for Devin, and a soda for Fadiyah who finally had a free evening to spend with her wife. Jericho and Zoey were there, as were Quinn and Xandy. There'd been the usually flurry of excitement about Xandy Blue being at The Club but it had finally calmed down which meant Quinn could relax. Natalia and Raine were at The Club as well. Natalia had met a friend there that wanted to talk about putting together a dance studio.

The bois in the group had admired the newcomer, a redhead with green eyes, and a body that was definitely worth the time to admire if nothing else. At five four, Jazmine Collette was a definite showstopper with her waist-length red hair that fell in loose curls, her sweetheart-shaped face with a perfect California tan and smooth skin, and wide green eyes that sparkled when she talked. She worked as a dancer for hip-hop videos and the like and had been rumored to have dated a number of hip-hop stars. It was for that reason that everyone was shocked when the girl had no problem dancing with the random butches that asked her or moved up to her out on the floor. The redhead was definitely a party girl.

Tyler and Shenin arrived at The Club shortly after everyone else and rounds of hugs were exchanged. Shenin joined the girls on the dance floor, and Tyler took her beer and stood with Quinn, Jericho,

Jet, and Skyler who were all leaning on the raised bar that surrounded the dance floor watching their girls dance. Even Fadiyah had been persuaded to dance, and Natalia was showing her how.

"So what do you think of the new girl?" Quinn asked Tyler.

"The redhead?" Tyler asked.

"Yeah, not your redhead, the other one," Quinn said, winking.

Tyler chuckled, then took a good long look. "Nice... She looks... ah... friendly..." she stammered. "Who's she here with?"

"Well, she came to meet Nat," Jericho said, "but she didn't show up with anyone."

Tyler nodded, her look considering. "Looks like she'll have lots of options when she leaves..." she said, as yet another woman moved in on the girl.

As the song ended, the DJ said she was taking a break, and put on regular music. The girls all headed for the group, except for Natalia and Jazmine, who headed to the bathroom.

Everyone was standing and talking, when Natalia came running back to the group.

"Raine! Jericho! It's Jazmine! Hurry!"

Raine, Tyler, Jericho, Quinn, Jet, and Skyler all followed Natalia to the back of The Club where there was a scuffle going on. As they stopped to figure out what was happening, the girls all ranged out in a line.

There was a black guy yelling at Jazmine who was backing away from him with her hands up in front her.

"Hey!" Jericho yelled, distracting the guy for a moment.

Jazmine saw her opportunity and started to walk away but another black man, bigger than the first, appeared and grabbed her. She screamed.

Quinn was about to react when a woman from behind the black man stepped in. She was every bit as tall as the man, standing about six foot, and she snatched him up by two handfuls of his jacket and threw him a good three feet from Jazmine. Jazmine had fallen to the floor in the melee. As the group watched, the woman took a knee leaning down to Jazmine and saying something.

Everyone was shocked when Jazmine looked up at the woman and promptly fainted. The woman was close enough to cradle her head, then moved to pick her up easily. Turning around, her eyes scanned the crowd.

"Ray?" Tyler queried suddenly.

The woman's eyes, that looked almost black, moved to Tyler.

"Ty," the woman said, nodding. "Good to see ya, where can I put her down?" she asked, a grin on her lips.

"Ah." Tyler looked over at Jet who nodded for the woman to follow her.

The rest of the group trailed after, having to know what the story was here.

In the office, the woman strode over to the couch and once again went down to one knee to lay Jazmine down gently. She stood then, turning to look at the women who were all watching her with fascination. The woman was tall, but the two inch heeled boots she wore made her seem taller, with a strong handsome face that was tanned with black brows and lashes. Her hair, pulled back in a long thick braid hung half way down her back and was jet black. She had the look of an American Indian that was confirmed a minute later when she introduced herself.

She grinned showing a set of very white, very straight teeth, her dark eyes sparkling with a knowing look.

"Rayden Black Wolf, at your service," she said inclining her head as her grin widened.

With that Rayden walked over to Ty and shook her hand.

"How've you been, Ty?" Rayden asked, smiling.

"Good, good," Ty said and nodded. "Shen's here, she'll be thrilled to see you."

"We haven't met," Jericho said, moving to shake Rayden's hand, her eyes on the new comer, "but we've talked, I'm Jericho Tehrani."

"My new boss…" Rayden said, grinning as she nodded. "Good to meet you, ma'am," she said, inclining her head respectfully.

"Call me Jericho," Jericho replied. "Nice save there," she said, nodding toward Jazmine.

"Not the first time I've rescued that particular redhead," Rayden said, grinning.

"Really now?" Jericho said, raising an eyebrow.

Rayden chuckled. "I'm lucky she passed out when she saw me instead of smacking the shit out of me," she said jokingly, but the look in her eyes told Jericho she was not kidding.

"You're rather handy to have around," Quinn said as she walked over and put out her hand. "Quinn Kavanaugh, good to meet ya."

Rayden canted her head. "Irish?" she queried, referring to Quinn's accent.

"Yup," Quinn said, nodding.

"Quinn's a bodyguard; we're trying to convince her to come work for your program, actually," Jericho said.

Rayden paused for a moment, assessing Quinn. . "Might just have to see about that," she said, smirking.

"Not gonna happen," Quinn said, smiling. "I like freelancing."

"Ray, this is Skyler Boché and Jet Mathews," Tyler said, gesturing to the other two women standing in the room. "They're DOJ too. As a matter of fact, Shenin's working with DOJ at the moment."

"Yeah?" Rayden asked, looking surprised. "Still Force though, right?"

"So far," Tyler said, grinning.

Just then Jazmine started to stir. Jericho and the rest of the group moved to check on her, whereas Rayden stood back, wondering if disappearing right now might be the best idea.

"Rayden!" Jazmine exclaimed as she sat up.

Rayden winced, knowing this wasn't going to go well.

Chapter 1

"What the hell are you doing here, Ray?" Jazmine asked, not for the first time that evening. Her tone was accusatory, as if Rayden was there just to annoy her.

Rayden Black Wolf had just rescued her from two men who had been trying to accost her at a local gay club. As she had long ago, Rayden had come in and handled the situation with her usual use of force. Jazmine, who hadn't seen Rayden in ten years, had been stunned to see a woman who'd haunted a lot of her dreams for years appear and be the amazing protector she'd been years before.

Unfortunately, the shock of being attacked by two thugs, and the shock of seeing Rayden after so many years had been too much and she'd passed out. When she'd awoken, she'd seen Rayden trying to essentially sneak out of the room. She'd stopped her, but it hadn't gone well after that. In the end she'd followed Rayden out to her car, a low-slung Copperhead Edition Viper, which just screamed Rayden's style, still screaming at her.

Rayden had ordered her to get in the car if she felt like she needed to continue to bitch at her. Jazmine had done that without a second thought, not even noticing the surprised look on Rayden's face. Now Rayden was driving down the freeway and Jazmine was still trying to get something out of this woman but not getting anywhere.

Rayden grinned, shaking her head, ever amazed at the stubborn redhead.

"What was that about back there?" Rayden asked, not for the first time either.

Jazmine narrowed green eyes. "It's none of your business," she said, her tone snide.

Rayden nodded, dark eyes staring out the windshield as she drove.

"Well, could you at least tell me where I'm dropping you?" Rayden said mildly.

Jazmine was silent then. Rayden glanced over at the girl and saw actual fear on her face.

"Jaz?" Rayden queried.

"I can't go back there," Jazmine said, shaking her head, as the realization hit her again.

Reaching up she put her hands to her face. "Oh, God… I'm so fucked right now, it's not even funny…"

"Okay, what's going on?" Rayden asked, her tone authoritative.

Jazmine blew her breath out slowly, swallowing convulsively as she thought about what she was brave enough to tell Rayden. There was so much history between them, none of it really that good, at least not the last part of it. It had been so many years, but Jazmine remembered it like it was yesterday.

Jazmine couldn't figure out what it was about guys like Tony, but they always turned into assholes at the most unexpected times! He always told her what a rocking body she had, and would enjoy that she wore clothes that revealed her body, but tonight he'd decided she'd overdone it. As far as Jazmine was concerned, he'd overstayed his time in her bed now. He'd practically dragged her out of the club as was yelling at her in the alley. What scared her was that he was getting more and more pissed off.

"You can't embarrass me like this in front of my boys, Jazmine!" he yelled.

"You always want me to look hot…" she began again, trying to remind him that he'd always said this to her.

"You look like a fuckin' slut Jazmine!" he yelled, fingering the tassels at the bottom midriff top she wore.

"Well, that's really sweet, Tony. Fuck this!" she shouted, throwing her hand into his face. "I'm out."

She started to walk away from him, but he grabbed her arm. She stumbled on her heels and fell. What she expected was that he'd be sorry he'd gotten violent. Instead, she suddenly realized that he was yelling at her.

"Think you're gonna fucking walk away from me? I don't fucking think so bitch…" he growled, reaching down and hauling her to her feet.

"Tony!" Jazmine yelled, trying to get through to him. "Stop!"

He grabbed both of her arms then, shaking her violently. Jazmine tried to reach out to grab his arms to try to stop him, but he kept shaking her and yelling expletives at her. When he finally let her go, she stumbled away from him. She leaned against the wall hoping he was done, but he started to stalk toward her. She put her arm up over her head.

That's when Tony suddenly stopped, and Jazmine looked at him, trying to figure out why he had such a strange look on his face. Then she saw the woman standing behind him, and saw that the woman had grabbed him by a handful of his jacket and was holding him back.

"I think that's just about enough of that," the woman said, her tone mild.

"What the fuck?" Tony yelled struggling against her hold on his jacket.

"I think you owe the lady an apology," the woman said then, her dark eyes looking over at Jazmine.

Jazmine stared back at the woman, unable to believe what she was seeing. Tony wasn't really a big guy, only about five seven, but this woman was taller than him. And she was definitely strong. Tony was stocky but the woman was holding him with what didn't look like too much effort on her part.

"I think I'm gonna fuckin' kill you bitch!" Tony yelled, increasing his struggle and managing to get free of her grasp.

He spun around, ready to attack and that's when he laid eyes on the woman. It made him pause for a minute, but then she started to grin, her eyes sparkling with laughter at his hesitation.

"Cunt!" he yelled and charged at her.

To Jazmine's shock, she put him down with one punch to the jaw. She looked at the woman again, this time with more respect. She was dressed in jeans, a black tank top, with three black corded necklaces with various silver pendants on them, a long jacket that fell to her mid-thigh, and black heeled leather boots.

"How did you do that?" Jazmine asked her tone awed.

To her surprise the woman casually pulled out a cigarette and a lighter, flicked the lighter open, and lit her cigarette.

"Wasn't hard," she said simply as she leaned back against the wall and smoked, putting a booted foot up on the wall behind her.

Jazmine walked over to the woman, stepping carefully around Tony lying on the ground.

"Do you do that kind of thing a lot?" Jazmine asked, gesturing to Tony.

"Only when I see some guy mistreating a woman," the woman replied, her dark eyes looking back at Jazmine. "I think you should probably upgrade your taste in dates."

"Should I?" Jazmine asked, smiling brightly. "To someone like you?"

The woman looked back at her, grinning. "Nah," she said simply.

Jazmine was surprised, and her green eyes reflected it. "Who are you?" she asked then.

"No one," the woman replied, shrugging lightly.

"You obviously learned to fight somewhere," Jazmine said, moving closer to the woman to gauge her interest.

The woman's dark eyes narrowed slightly at her approach. She took a long drag off her cigarette assessing Jazmine and wondering what her intentions were. Finally, she nodded.

"U.S. Navy," she said simply.

Jazmine nodded slowly. "That makes sense," she said, then she extended her hand to the woman. "I'm Jazmine," she said, her eyes looking directly into the other woman's.

The woman regarded Jazmine's hand for a long moment, then shifted her cigarette to her left hand as she extended her hand to take Jazmine's. "Rayden."

"Rayden?" Jazmine repeated.

"That's the name they gave me," Rayden replied with a grin.

"I like it," Jazmine said, smiling flirtatiously.

Rayden looked back at her, once again evaluating this woman, then her gaze shifted to Jazmine's arms as she noticed they were already showing signs of bruising from where Tony had grabbed her. Putting her cigarette between her teeth, she shrugged out of her jacket and put it around Jazmine's shoulders. Jazmine was pleasantly surprised by the gallant gesture.

"Your arms are bruised," Rayden said by way of explanation.

"Thanks," Jazmine said, smiling again, then she looked down at Tony who had started to stir. "We should probably go," she said, nodding toward the street.

Rayden looked surprised, but nodded and followed Jazmine out of the alley.

"Where's your car?" Jazmine asked as they reached the street, her green eyes staring up into Rayden's.

Rayden dropped her cigarette, blowing smoke out as she did, her eyes looking amused by the question.

"Over there," Rayden said pointing to the parking lot across the street. "Why?"

"Tony has a lot of friends inside the club, you probably don't want to go back in there, and I know I don't."

"Tony's friends don't scare me," Rayden said, her tone even.

"Well they scare me, so could you please get me out of here?" Jazmine said, her tone tremulous suddenly.

Rayden looked back at her, her dark eyes searching the girl. Finally, she nodded and led the way over to the lot. As they walked through the parking lot Jazmine tried to figure out which car would be this woman's. She was not completely surprised when the lights to a green Mustang lit up and Rayden walked over to it.

Jazmine admired the Mustang; it was a tough-looking car, with a body kit that dropped it to the ground, and aggressive lines, with black rims and a hood scoop. It also had a thick black racing stripe from the front to the back of the car and a racing spoiler. It was a hot car, and Jazmine found that for some reason it excited her, it seemed to really fit the woman driving it.

Rayden walked over to the passenger door and opened it for Jazmine, who got in smiling. As Rayden got in the driver's side, she glanced over at the girl. She wasn't sure what the hell she was supposed to do with the straight girl, but she hadn't been able to resist the plea to get her away from the club. She had a weakness for girls in trouble, and she knew it. Damsels in distress were her major downfall.

Jazmine felt a thrill go through her as Rayden started the Mustang; the engine had a deep throaty growl to it that had always been an exciting thing for Jazmine. She loved muscle cars!

Rayden caught the look of pure ecstasy on the girl's face, and grinned, at least she appreciated cars; that was a point in her favor. As she pulled out of the parking lot, she looked over at the girl again.

"So where can I take you?" Rayden asked, as she gunned the engine. "Anywhere you want…" Jazmine said suggestively.

Rayden looked over at her sharply. "Uh..." she stammered, having no idea how to handle such a direct come on by someone she was fairly sure was as straight as the day was long.

Jazmine looked over at Rayden, inanely pleased that she'd surprised the woman. She'd never been with a woman before, but she felt her body practically humming with desire and she always listened to her body.

"Doesn't the conquering hero always get the girl?" Jazmine asked then, her look both sly and flirty.

"Not if the conquering hero is gay and the girl is straight," Rayden replied, having regained her composure.

"Who says I'm straight?" Jazmine asked.

"The guy I had to put down for manhandling you pretty much said that," Rayden said.

Jazmine bit her lip, breathing heavier suddenly. The vision of Rayden punching Tony played through her head, and imagining what else Rayden could do with all that strength was likely to drive her crazy.

"You've never heard of bi-sexuals?" Jazmine asked, seizing on the idea.

Rayden looked over at her again, her eyes narrowed slightly. "Yeah, I've heard of them," she said. "Don't usually deal with them though."

"Why?" Jazmine asked.

"Not my thing," Rayden said simply.

"What is your thing?" Jazmine asked her eyes heated.

Rayden didn't answer at first, trying to figure out what this girl was really looking for. Did she just want someone to save her, or was she

13

really as hot for it as she was acting. As it happened, Rayden had just gotten back from a three-month stint in the South Pacific so it had been a while since she'd been with a woman. This girl was definitely hot, but the last thing Rayden needed was to have to deal with extra drama.

"I prefer my sex drama free," Rayden said simply.

"I can understand that," Jazmine said, nodding.

"Can you?" Rayden asked, looking doubtful.

They stopped at a red light at that point, and Jazmine shocked Rayden by unbuckling her seat belt and moving to straddle her lap, her slim body easily able to fit between Rayden and the steering wheel. She leaned to kiss Rayden's lips without hesitation, putting her arms around Rayden's neck, and pulling her closer as she pressed her body against Rayden's. By the time the light turned green, Rayden was convinced that this girl wasn't just hot, but more than ready to go. Jazmine moved back to her seat as Rayden gunned the engine.

Fortunately, her apartment wasn't far and she made it there in record time. She parked the car and strode around to the passenger side to open the door, putting her hand out to help Jazmine out of the car. Continuing to hold Jazmine's hand, Rayden turned and led her to the elevators. After hitting the button for her floor, she turned to Jazmine, and backed her up against the side of the elevator, her dark eyes staring down into Jazmine's, but not touching her.

Jazmine could feel her body vibrating with excitement; this woman definitely had an animal magnetism that was impossible to ignore. She didn't think she'd ever been so excited in her life. When the elevator stopped, Rayden led the way to her apartment. Rayden held the door open for Jazmine, who admired the nice apartment as she walked in. It had dark furniture, beige walls, and wasn't overly decorated. Not girlie in the slightest.

Inside, Rayden dropped her keys on an entry table, her eyes fixed on Jazmine. She was curious if the girl was going to back down now. It had happened before; she wouldn't have been surprised in the least. She leaned back against the front door, her look assessing as Jazmine looked around the apartment, and then finally back at her.

Jazmine turned to see Rayden watching her. Rayden leaned against the door, her left hand twisting the ring on her right middle finger, her look speculative. Rayden was a very hot-looking butch and Jazmine couldn't help but admire her strong features and long ebony hair. Then there were the dark eyes, almost black with long thick black eyes lashes surrounding them, framed by black eyebrows. Jazmine's look fell on Rayden's lips, currently slightly pursed in consideration.

Jazmine recognized that Rayden was waiting for her to make a move. 'A gentleman never pushes' was the thought that went through Jazmine's mind. She walked straight over to Rayden, pressing against her, her eyes staring up into Rayden's eyes and reached up to pull her head down to hers. When their lips met this time, Rayden was doing the kissing and Jazmine instantly felt the difference, she felt weak in the knees almost immediately. She wound her arms around Rayden's neck out of sheer desperate desire. She was beyond excited when Rayden picked her up in her arms and carried her into the bedroom.

Rayden laid her down on the bed, moving over her, kissing her lips, pressing her body close, but keeping her weight off of the girl. She could feel the girl trembling and clamped down on the desire to move as fast as she would with another lesbian. She knew this was the girl's first time with a woman, no matter how brazen she'd tried to be. The last thing she intended to do was scare her. Instead, Rayden took the time to excite the girl to such a heated state, that it only took the slightest movement of her hand sliding up the girl's inner thigh, and the lightest brush over already wet panties to have her coming.

Jazmine thought she was going to go insane with the desire screaming through her body. Rayden's lips, even though she hadn't removed either of their clothes, seemed to burn her skin and make it tingle at the same time. The way she pressed her body to hers, suggestively, moving it against her, made her gasp and moan softly, her hands grasping at Rayden's shoulders.

Then Rayden shifted her body slightly to one side, and Jazmine understood why a moment later when she felt Rayden's hand on her thigh. As it moved upward, Jazmine could feel her body going taut with expectation. When Rayden's thumb brushed against her, even though the material of her underwear still covered her, she lost all control. She was screaming and holding onto Rayden, writhing as Rayden kissed her again. Rayden continued to kiss her, as her thumb moved aside the material and touched her again. Jazmine groaned and came again, feeling like her body was going to explode.

In the end, Rayden eventually removed all of Jazmine's clothes and brought her to multiple orgasms, so many that she couldn't even count, or think to count anymore. Afterwards, she lay completely drained, breathing heavily as Rayden moved to lie on her back and pulled Jazmine onto her side, so she could wrap her arm around her shoulders. It was then that it occurred to Jazmine that Rayden still had all of her clothes on, with the exception of her boots, which she'd kicked off at one point.

Levering herself up on her elbow, Jazmine looked down at Rayden.

"Why am I completely naked and you're not?" Jazmine asked.

Rayden grinned. "Well, that's because I removed your clothes."

"But none of your own..." Jazmine said.

"I see your confusion," Rayden said, her eyes alight with amusement. "Unlike a man, I don't have to remove my clothes to make a woman come."

"Well, I can testify to that sister," Jazmine said, grinning. "But how do I make you come?" she asked, her eyes widening on the last phrase.

Rayden looked back at her. "That's up to you," she said simply.

Jazmine bit her lower lip, heat burning in her eyes once again.

"You're not going to tell me," Jazmine said.

"Nope," Rayden said, her dark eyes inscrutable.

Jazmine narrowed her eyes. "Alright."

She moved to straddle Rayden's waist, staring down at her as she slid her hands up under the tank top Rayden wore. Their eyes stayed connected as she moved fingertips over hard nipples. She watched as Rayden's lips parted and she knew she was on the right track. Reaching down she pulled the tank top up and off over Rayden's head, leaning down to put her mouth where her hands had been. She was excited to feel Rayden's hand slide into her hair.

At one point, she pulled back and looked down at Rayden's torso. The woman was undeniably toned, and then she saw the tattoo on her mid-torso; it was the SEAL Trident, the logo for the Navy SEALs. She looked back at Rayden, shocked.

"You're a Navy SEAL?" she asked, stunned. Women were rarely, if ever, taken into the SEALs, even Jazmine knew that.

17

Rayden nodded. "I told you Navy," she said simply.

"You didn't say SEAL," Jazmine said.

Rayden shrugged. "Same difference."

"Not really," Jazmine said.

"Weren't you doing something?" Rayden asked, her look pointed.

Jazmine narrowed her eyes, but then nodded, and moved to unbutton Rayden's jeans. Once she had the woman naked, she took her time, touching, tasting, and teasing. It took a bit, but eventually she had Rayden pulling at her and telling her to "come here." She held back, and could see that it was working to do just that. Rayden became more and more insistent, and Jazmine thoroughly enjoyed holding back, and making Rayden absolutely insane with desire. At one point, she looked Rayden dead in the eye and said simply, "Beg."

Rayden's dark eyes narrowed at her, her breath came in ragged gasps and she slowly shook her head.

Jazmine pressed her body closer, her body pressing in exactly the right places, and slid her hand up over Rayden's breasts. Rayden gasped, and moved her body with Jazmine's, but then Jazmine stopped, letting her body hover above Rayden's. She knew that Rayden had the strength to take what she wanted, but she could also sense easily that Rayden wasn't that type.

In the end, Rayden did beg, and Jazmine very happily brought her to release, reaching her own again too, excited by Rayden's cry of pure ecstasy. Afterwards she moved to lie on her back. Rayden surprised her completely by turning onto her stomach, putting her arm and leg across Jazmine possessively, and putting her face against the side of her head, her lips at Jazmine's temple. Jazmine liked the feeling of this woman

18

against her, and the idea that the woman wanted to possess her this way. They fell asleep lying that way.

"Are you going to tell me what's going on?" Rayden asked, her look pointed.

"Can we just not right now?" Jazmine asked, her tone tired.

"Not if you're gonna end up at my place we can't," Rayden said, suddenly sounding like the Rayden she'd known before.

Jazmine stared back at her, and could see that Rayden was serious and she knew she really didn't have a choice.

"Those two guys at the bar were friends of my ex," she said.

Rayden nodded. "And the ex is…"

"He's a rapper," Jazmine said.

"He," Rayden repeated with a snide look. "Still trying to play it straight, huh Jaz?"

"Well, the lesbian I tried kind of ruined me for that lifestyle," Jazmine snapped.

Rayden's lips twitched at that statement. Jazmine wondered if that meant Rayden actually felt bad about the way things had ended with them.

"Too bad, you seemed like a natural," Rayden said, her tone even.

"Fuck you Rayden!" Jazmine snapped.

"You did," Rayden said simply.

"Fucking… let me the fuck out of here," she said, reaching for the door handle blindly as tears sprang to her eyes.

Rayden saw her action and veered the car over to the side of the road.

"Jaz!" she yelled, reaching across the car to grab Jazmine's hand and keep her from opening the door. "I'm sorry, okay? I'm sorry," she said, her tone strong

Her right arm was across Jazmine's body to keep her in the car, her left hand holding Jazmine's wrist. Jazmine started to cry then, bowing her head and sobbing as tears fell from her eyes. Then she was in Rayden's arms, and Rayden was holding her as best she could across the console of her Viper.

When Jazmine had calmed down, Rayden let her go, and pulled the Viper back onto the road. It was another five minutes before either of them spoke.

"I'm sorry, Jaz," Rayden said. "I was a stupid kid, and I didn't know how to deal with ending things with you."

Jazmine nodded, reaching up to wipe her eyes delicately.

Rayden looked over at the girl; she was still damned beautiful, actually more so now. Ten years had done her a lot of good.

"So what do you want to do?" Rayden asked after another few minutes.

Jazmine shrugged, shaking her head. "I don't have any place to go right now," she said. "I'm so embarrassed... I'm still such a fucking mess..."

"Why did this guy send his friends after you?" Rayden asked, switching lanes and taking the onramp to another freeway.

"Because he's trying to intimidate me into not testifying against him," Jazmine said.

"Jesus, what are you testifying against him for?" Rayden asked.

"Well, besides the fact that he put me in the hospital six months ago, I saw him shoot a guy."

Rayden held her hand up. "Wait, he hurt you?"

Jazmine smiled sadly. "Always worried about the girl, huh?"

"Yeah, it's a weakness," Rayden said, grinning. "What happened, Jaz?"

"I was going to leave him, and he knew it, and he didn't want me to…" she said, shaking her head as her voice trailed off.

"Always trying to get away from some guy…" Rayden murmured.

Jazmine looked over at her sharply, and Rayden immediately held her hand up.

"Sorry," she said, "but you certainly do get yourself into trouble with men…"

Jazmine blew her breath out, nodding her head in agreement.

They made the rest of the ride in silence. Jazmine had time to look Rayden over. She looked absolutely amazing, better than she had ten years before, dressed in all black in a collared shirt that look crisp and wrinkle free. At her throat she wore a thick linked gunmetal chain with a silver and black pendant that was a set of four interconnecting swirls. Jazmine didn't know what the symbol meant, but was sure it was a Cherokee symbol; most of the jewelry was related to her tribe. Her black hair was back in a braid as it tended to be, even Jazmine had rarely seen Rayden's hair down and they'd lived together for six months. She was so caught up in looking at Rayden, before Jazmine knew it they were pulling into a garage.

"Is this your house?" she asked.

"I hope so," Rayden said, grinning.

"Wait!" Jazmine exclaimed as Rayden turned off the car.

"What?" Rayden asked.

"Are you married?" Jazmine asked, having just noticed the black band on Rayden's left ring finger. Rayden glanced at the black band, as if seeing it for the first time. In truth, she never thought about the fact that it was there anymore. It was part of her and it would never leave her finger.

"No," she said, her tone somber.

"But…" Jazmine said, gesturing to the ring.

"No," Rayden repeated.

Jazmine could see she wasn't going to get any more of an answer. Rayden got out of the car, and walked around to open Jazmine's door, putting out her hand to help the girl out, since the car was so low. Rayden led her into the house, and stopped to turn off the alarm. Jazmine looked around at the new-looking townhouse. They were just outside of West Hollywood in a nice area. Jazmine wondered how much this place had set Rayden back.

"What exactly are you doing these days?" Jazmine asked, as Rayden walked into the kitchen and opened the refrigerator.

Rayden looked at her as she took a beer out, holding it up to her in askance.

"Sure," Jazmine said, thinking it might settle the nerves that were suddenly very jumpy again.

Rayden twisted open the bottle and handed it to Jazmine, who pulled out a barstool and sat down. She watched as Rayden pulled out another beer for herself and took a long drink.

"I'm about to start a new job," Rayden said, moving to lean against the counter on the opposite side from where Jazmine sat.

"Are you still in the SEALs?" Jazmine asked.

"No, I haven't been for four years now," Rayden said.

"So what were you doing before this then?" Jazmine asked.

Rayden looked back at her for a long moment. "Protecting the President," she said simply.

"Of what?" Jazmine asked.

Rayden grinned. "The United States," she said.

"Bullshit," Jazmine said, laughing, but the she saw that Rayden was looking at her seriously. "You're not kidding, are you?"

"Sorry," Rayden said, shrugging.

"No lie?" Jazmine asked, her face reflecting her awe.

"No lie, baby girl," Rayden said, her eyes sparkling with amusement.

Jazmine couldn't control the shiver that went through her, it happened every time Rayden called her "baby girl." It was what she'd called her years before, and it had always thrilled her. No one else had ever affected her the way that Rayden had, no woman or man.

"So where is your new job?" Jazmine asked, trying to distract herself from the fact that she was in a house alone with her singular obsession.

"At the Department of Justice actually," Rayden said, straightening from the counter and moving to stand near where Jazmine sat, leaning with her hip against the counter.

"You're going to be a cop?" Jazmine asked.

Rayden chuckled. "Well, actually, I'm going to be a Special Agent in Charge, but yeah, it's a cop I suppose."

Jazmine looked at her for a long moment. "I guess that makes sense," she said finally, "you're always the hero somehow."

Rayden laughed at that one outright. "I don't think I'd go that far."

"Why not?" Jazmine said. "You're always rescuing me, and I'd bet all the money I have that you've saved lots of other women too."

Rayden looked back at her for a long moment as a look of sadness crossed her face. It was a look Jazmine didn't understand at all, but one that made her ache to fix it.

Rayden was headed for her barracks on the base in Iraq, when she happened upon an interesting scene. A man was talking to a woman, which ordinarily wouldn't be interesting to her. The problem was the way the man was standing, his arm up over the woman's head, in a somewhat threatening manner. The woman he was talking to seemed to be doing her best to stand up to him, but at around five four and maybe 120 pounds, she wasn't having much luck. He looked like he was far from put off. Rayden slowed her pace, stopping a few feet away, trying to keep from interfering unless she had to do so, but listening intently to the conversation.

"You know you want to…" the man was saying. "You don't have to pretend that you don't."

"I'm not pretending," she was telling him. "I just not interested, I'm sorry."

"Come on honey…" he said, moving closer to her.

She backed up, and he grabbed her arm to stop her.

"I said I'm not interested," the woman said sharply.

"And I think you are," he said, pushing her up against the wall forcefully.

"Okay, enough," Rayden said, stepping up behind the man.

"What the hell?" the man asked, turning around.

His eyes widened when he saw the size of the woman he was now addressing.

Rayden was an imposing woman; one hundred percent Cherokee Indian with the strong build of a Navy SEAL. She had the ability to intimidate most people, even men.

"Yeah, you need to listen when a woman says she's not interested," Rayden told him evenly.

"You need to butt out of conversations that don't involve you, bitch," he said, trying bravado to stave Rayden off.

"One last warning," Rayden said flatly, but her eyes sparked with malice. "Leave the lady alone and walk away."

"Make me," he said, his eyes challenging.

One hand whipped out and grabbed him by the throat, turning and slamming him into the nearest wall, lifting him a half a foot off the ground in the process.

He struggled against her hold, and she tightened it until he calmed down.

"If I ever see you manhandle a woman like that again," she growled, "I'll break your fucking neck, do you hear me?"

When he didn't answer, she banged his head against the wall.

"I said, do you hear me…" Rayden queried.

"Yeah, yeah, fuck!" the guy snapped.

With that Rayden let him go, and he dropped to the ground with a thud. She turned on her heel and casually walked away.

Two hours later Rayden was lying in her bunk, with one well-muscled arm over her eyes.

"Excuse me?" said a tentative female voice.

Rayden lifted her arm, her dark eyes falling on the girl from earlier. She was cute, petite with honey-blond hair and slate-blue eyes. She was wearing Air Force BDUs, her name patch read Comstock, and she had the wings patch signifying that she was a pilot. That actually surprised Rayden; she hadn't expected that at all. Though now, taking a second look over her, she seemed to ooze the confidence of a pilot.

"Yeah?" Rayden asked, her tone even.

"You didn't let me thank you," the woman said, her smile warm.

Rayden grinned, and put her arm back over her eyes. "Wasn't looking for a thank you," she said simply.

"Okay, but…" the woman said, her voice trailing off as she stepped closer to Rayden's bunk.

Rayden felt a soft hand on the underside of her upper arm. She lowered her arm, an indulgent grin curling her lips as looked at the woman.

"I'm Grayson Comstock," she said, smiling down at Rayden.

"You also don't give up easily," Rayden said.

"Not usually, no," Grayson said, shaking her head and smiling.

Rayden chuckled. *"Rayden Black Wolf."* Grayson's eyes widened.

"Which tribe?"

"Tsalagi," Rayden said, grinning.

Grayson turned her head slightly, detecting that she was being given a hard time.

"Which translates to...?" Grayson began, her look pointed as her voice trailed off.

Rayden smiled, showing very white and perfectly straight teeth.

"Cherokee," Rayden said.

"Ah," Grayson said, nodding. *"So how can I thank you?"*

"You can't," Rayden said.

"I'll bet you I can," Grayson said, smiling, her eyes sparkling mischievously.

Rayden smiled in spite of herself. *"It's not necessary."*

"Well, see, that's the thing..." Grayson said, running her finger over Rayden's bicep. *"I wasn't interested in him, but I'm definitely interested in you... So while thanking you may not be necessary, going out with you is."*

"Who says I'm gay?" Rayden asked.

"Your eyes say you're gay," Grayson said.

"Do they now?" Rayden asked as she sat up putting her feet on the floor, and turned to face Grayson.

Grayson moved to stand between Rayden's knees, putting her hands on Rayden's shoulders, staring into her eyes directly.

Rayden widened her eyes at the bold move.

27

"Just go out with me," Grayson said, her tone cajoling.

"And if I don't?" Rayden asked.

"I'll bug you till you do," Grayson said, smiling.

"There can't be that few gay women here…" Rayden said, her tone trailing off.

"There's plenty," Grayson said, "but right now I'm interested in you."

"Why?" Rayden asked, her look direct.

"Because of what you did for me," Grayson answered.

"What do you think that proves?"

"That you're chivalrous," Grayson said.

"Maybe it just proves that I like to beat the crap out of men," Rayden said.

"No," Grayson said, her tone sure. "You are a gallant, courageous warrior, and I want to go out with you and you're just going to have to say yes."

"I am, huh?" Rayden asked, grinning now.

"Yes, you are," Grayson said, her slate-blue eyes staring into hers.

Rayden sighed, grinning again. "Okay, you win."

"Finally!" Grayson said, laughing.

"Are you always this persistent?"

"When I want something, yes, I am."

"Does anyone ever say no to you?"

"Sometimes," Grayson said.

"Do they get worn down like me?"

Grayson smiled. "Only when I really, really want something."

"And you think you really, really want me?"

"Yes, yes I do," Grayson said.

It was a hell of an auspicious beginning.

"Ray?" Jazmine queried when Rayden had been quiet for a long couple of minutes. She seemed lost in her own thoughts, and they didn't look like happy thoughts.

"Hmmm?' Rayden murmured, coming out of her reverie.

"You look beat," Jazmine said, seeing how tired Rayden's eyes looked suddenly.

Rayden looked at her watch, a black and gunmetal Movado. "That's because it's like four in the morning in D.C. right now."

"When did you get here?" Jazmine asked.

"Day before yesterday," Rayden answered, stifling a yawn.

"Guess this little adventure wasn't on your agenda, huh?" Jazmine said, her tone self-effacing.

"No, but it's okay," Rayden said, smiling warmly. "Come on, I'll show you where the guest bedroom is." She drained the rest of her beer and set the bottle on the counter.

Jazmine followed Rayden upstairs, pointing to the right. "That's the second bedroom."

"Okay," Jazmine said, nodding.

"It has its own bathroom, so feel free to shower or whatever if you want, there's towels and stuff in there."

"Wow, you're awfully organized," Jazmine said, grinning.

"Don't be too impressed, you can pay people to do this stuff," Rayden said, winking at her. "And I did, 'cause I didn't have time to do it myself."

"Aw," Jazmine said, grinning and nodding.

"See you in the morning," Rayden said, leaning over to kiss her temple.

Jazmine reached up to hug Rayden, feeling really sentimental suddenly.

Rayden held Jazmine in her arms for a few moments with her eyes closed, remembering what it was like years and years before... before everything went to hell. She gritted her teeth managing to keep it together.

Jazmine went into the second bedroom and Rayden walked into the master bedroom, closing the door softly behind her. She walked over to her dresser, taking off her watch, and the chain around her neck. Once again, her eyes fell on the black band on her finger.

"Damnit, Gray..." she muttered, balling her left hand into a fist, feeling fresh pain pump through her, making her heart ache.

She turned on the Bose and hooked up her iPhone, selecting Gray's playlist, knowing exactly the artist to play. Gray loved Adele and played her constantly. As she walked into the master bathroom she took off her clothes, hung up her long jacket, and put her boots back, the rest went into the laundry basket. She turned on the shower and got in, hearing Adele sing about the River Lea.

A half an hour later she lay in bed, Adele still singing. One song ended, and the next song began, and Rayden let the sounds of drums and keyboards roll through her. The song was called "I Miss You" and the words broke her heart over and over as they played on.

When the song ended, Rayden had tears down the side of her head. Fortunately, she was also asleep from pure emotional exhaustion.

In the other room, Jazmine could hear Adele playing and was shocked. Rayden had always been into rock music, for her to listen to Adele was absolutely out of character for her. Apparently, some things had indeed changed in ten years.

It was four in the morning when Jazmine heard her phone buzz. She ignored it the first few times, not that she was really sleeping anyway, but when the phone seemed to buzz constantly, she reached over to pick it up. The text messages were from her ex-boyfriend and it was obvious his boys had gotten back to him about what had happened at The Club. There were all kinds of comments about dykes, and how he was going to "fuck them up." She could tell he was getting more and more angry.

Once again, she had no idea what she'd ever seen in him. Not that she'd been in love or anything, but Jeremy "JJ King" had seemed like a really nice guy, to start with anyway. She was now beginning to wonder if she could tell the difference. There was something she hadn't told anyone, including Rayden, and that was that she'd recently aborted the child she'd become pregnant with who had been fathered by Jeremy. She just hoped that didn't become public knowledge. As she read the messages though, she realized that he had indeed found out and that it had been on TMZ that evening.

The messages took a very deadly turn and he was threatening to kill her and, "that bitch she left the club with in the copperhead

Viper." That had Jazmine up and out of bed and walking into Rayden's room. She stopped, seeing Rayden lying on the bed, one arm up over her eyes. She was wearing a black job bra and black boy short underwear and nothing else, and Jazmine had to calm her libido before she could think straight again. Walking over to the side of the bed, she could see that Rayden had added a few tattoos over the years. They looked very sexy against her dark skin. Jazmine shook her head, trying to make herself focus.

"Ray?" she queried softly.

"Mmm?" Rayden murmured tiredly as she lifted her arm off her eyes. "What's wrong?"

Jazmine held out her phone to Rayden. She reached over and picked up the remote for the Bose, and turned the music off. She then took the phone, blinking a couple of times to try to focus on the lit screen. Jazmine could see her dark eyes scanning the writing.

"Jaz, you don't think they'll really come here do you?" Rayden asked, her tone far from worried.

Jazmine shrugged, looking afraid. Rayden looked back at the girl and sighed. Shifting to the center of the bed, she patted the bed next to her.

"Come here," she said, holding her arm out to Jazmine.

Jazmine didn't need to be asked twice; she immediately laid down and put her head against the hollow of Rayden's shoulder. She was wearing the silk tank top she'd been wearing at The Club and underwear, so she was equally scantily clad as Rayden was.

"I see you've gotten more ink since I saw your body last," Jazmine commented.

Rayden grinned. "Some."

Jazmine levered herself up on her elbow looking back down at Rayden. "So what's this one?" she asked touching Rayden's right shoulder. It was the same symbol she'd seen on Rayden's necklace earlier.

"It's the Tsalagi symbol for strength."

"Okay," Jazmine said, nodding, "that's definitely you... What about this one?" she asked, touching the other shoulder. This symbol had a black sun-like outer circle with a star inside of it.

"It's the symbol for transformation," Rayden said.

Jazmine's eyes fell on the tattoo that was partially covered by the jog bra. Rayden saw her eyes and winced slightly, knowing what she was going to ask.

"What's 'Gray'?" she asked. "And..." She pulled the jog bra down slightly. "What is that symbol?"

Rayden looked back at Jazmine for a long moment, feeling that familiar pain slide through her again. She blew her breath out, closing her eyes in a slow blink. She knew she needed to just say it, she needed to get used to telling people.

"Gray is short for Grayson," Rayden said, her tone tremulous. "Grayson was my wife."

Jazmine stared back at Rayden, stunned. Rayden had gotten married? Rayden who was terrified of commitment? Who fought every single convention known to man that even hinted at a commitment? What the hell?

"So you are married," Jazmine said, nodding.

"I'm widowed," Rayden said, her voice breaking on the last syllable. "She was a pilot for the Air Force. Her plane went down in the Indian Ocean."

Jazmine blinked a couple of times, unable to believe what she was hearing. Rayden had been married, and her wife had died? What kind of God did that to people? It was obvious from the devastated look in Rayden's eyes that she'd loved her wife very much. Tears came to Jazmine's eyes as she thought about how horrible that really was.

"Rayden…" she breathed, shaking her head slowly.

"Please don't," Rayden said, gritting her teeth as she closed her eyes. "I really can't handle anyone's sympathy anymore."

"How long…" Jazmine began to ask, but stopped as she saw Rayden grimace.

Instead, she lay down, putting her head against Rayden's chest, wanting to lend her strength, but at the same time wanting to cry. Rayden had finally committed to someone and that someone had died. What was the likelihood of her ever committing to anyone again? Right about nil, was Jazmine's assessment. It broke her heart.

Chapter 2

At twenty-four, Dakota Blair was self-assured enough to walk through a crowd of women and have at least half of them interested immediately. It wasn't that she was outrageously attractive; she was good looking in the soft butch, sexy bed hair, slim hipped, hippy meets biker kind of way. Dakota had an air about her that promised hot sex and no strings. It was a combination that made women want to catch her and keep her. The rumor was that Cassandra Billings, an ultra-rich lesbian from the art world, had done both, not that it was evident in the way Dakota moved through the crowd at The Club.

She made her way over to the girls, greeting Natalia and Raine, and nodding to the others that she really didn't know. In truth she didn't really know any of them, but Natalia and Jazmine were working with Cassandra to build a dance studio. Dakota was essentially the person doing the work in the studio, acting as a contractor more or less. One of the few solid things she'd done in her life was getting a contractor's license.

Dakota made her way to the bar, asking the bartender for a Jack and coke with a wink. The bartender gave her the drink with a smile.

"Thanks doll," Dakota said, smiling in return.

As she walked outside, she pulled out her cigarettes and lighter, and sat down at one of the tables, checking out the women. She wore faded jeans and a black leather vest with nothing underneath, motorcycle boots, and a long leather tong necklace with a feather that lay between the slight curve of her breasts. Her blue eyes, lined with black liner, scanned the crowd, picking out the ones that would be quick, easy lays. She had her eye on a brunette when she heard a familiar voice.

"Dak?" Cody asked, her tone stunned.

Dakota turned her head, already smiling as she did. Jumping up from the chair she sat in, Dakota grabbed Cody in a hug.

"Holy hell, Cody!" Dakota said, hugging the other woman and laughing.

When they parted, Cody looked Dakota up and down. "Where the hell did you disappear to?"

Dakota grinned. "Well, got a pick-up, wife wanted a threesome… Guess I was better than he was. He left, I stayed."

"And you're still with her?" Cody asked her tone hopeful.

"Cody, it's been what… nine years. When have I ever fucked the same woman for that long? I've changed women so many times since then, I've lost count."

Cody shook her head. "Still the same, Dak."

Dakota's eyes fell on the blond standing next to Cody who looked back at Cody quizzically.

"Dakota, this is McKenna," Cody said, smiling. "She's my fiancée so don't get any ideas."

Dakota smiled her eyes sparkling mischievously. She extended her hand to McKenna.

"Hi…" she said, her voice husky.

McKenna took her hand, her look saying *really?*

"Hi," she responded, her tone even.

Dakota laughed. "I like you."

"I've known Dakota since I was thirteen," Cody said to McKenna.

"Oh…" McKenna said, her eyes trailing back over to Dakota.

Dakota canted her head at Cody. "She know all that?" she asked in a low voice.

Cody nodded. "She knows all of it."

Dakota looked impressed. "Does she know I was your first?"

Cody laughed. "No, I didn't think to mention the chick that disappeared on me, go figure."

"Disappeared?" McKenna asked, her eyes on Dakota again.

"Yeah," Dakota answered for Cody, "and it doesn't seem that she's done to badly for herself." Her eyes went from McKenna's to Cody's.

Cody's eyes narrowed slightly and McKenna felt her tense.

"Babe, I'm gonna go inside, so you two can talk," McKenna said, sensing that things needed to be said that didn't need her as an audience.

"Okay," Cody said, leaning down to kiss her lips tenderly.

McKenna glanced at Dakota again, her look quizzical, but she smiled and nodded to the other woman, then went back inside the bar.

Dakota watched her go, then her eyes went back to Cody's.

"Nice…" she said, her look somewhat lascivious.

She saw Cody tense and smirked. "Very possessive over that one, huh?" she asked as she moved to sit down again. "Not the smartest play," she said, shaking her head.

"It's not a play, Dak," Cody said, sighing as she sat down across from Dakota and pulled out a cigarette.

Dakota leaned forward to light it for her.

"Thanks," Cody said, slouching back into the chair, assessing Dakota.

"Whatcha lookin' for Cody?" Dakota asked with a wry grin.

Cody narrowed her eyes, chewing on the inside of her cheek.

Dakota laughed, shaking her head. "You haven't changed a bit, Cody, still doin' that shit when you don't want to talk about something…" she said, her look changing as she leaned forward, as if in confidentiality. "If you're looking for my moral compass, I still don't have one," she said, her tone matter of fact, her eyes glittering with a combination of malice and amusement.

Then she sat back, her look considering. "I see you got yourself a nice big one though," she said, her lips curled in derision. "I hear you're a cop now."

Cody looked surprised, but then grinned sardonically. "I guess I shouldn't be surprised that you kept tabs on me."

Dakota shrugged. "I always looked out for you Cody, when I could," she said simply.

Cody nodded, a grimace flickering across her face. "Who looked out for you?"

Dakota gave a humorless laugh. "I did, babe."

Cody wet her lips, swallowing in sudden discomfort.

Dakota noticed Cody's discomfort and canted her head. "You feel guilty that you got a life, Cody?"

Cody looked surprised.

Dakota gave a snort of laughter. "You think I can't still read you like a book?" she said, leaning forward to put her hand on Cody's leg, her look intense. "Don't feel guilty. I'm happy that things worked out for you." She sat back, taking a drag off her cigarette. "You weren't cut out for that life; it would have killed you early."

"What about you?" Cody asked, her tone haunted.

"Still here, aren't I?" Dakota said expansively, with a cavalier smile.

Cody looked back at her, nodding, her look circumspect.

"That's always been your problem, Cody," Dakota said her tone knowing. "You always felt way too much." She moved to stand then, stretching as her eyes fell on the brunette again. Turning her head she looked at Cody, "'Scuse me," she said with a wink.

Cody watched as Dakota moved toward the brunette. She saw the girl look up at Dakota smiling. Dakota talked to her for a few minutes, leaning in a few times and whispering in her ear. A few minutes after that, Dakota took the girl's hand and led her to the back area of the patio that was fairly private. Cody shook her head, she couldn't fault Dakota; she had been just as bad with women before she'd met McKenna a few months before. Still, she felt like Dakota was running away from something and it bothered her to see it.

Cody rejoined the group inside. McKenna immediately saw Cody's melancholy look and got her a beer, then reached up to kiss her lips.

"You okay?" McKenna asked, her eyes searching Cody's.

"Yeah," Cody said, smiling softly at her, "just kind of a blast from the past, ya know?"

McKenna nodded.

Dakota was sitting back in her chair a half an hour later when Jazmine walked out onto the patio. Jazmine smiled at Dakota and walked over to her, leaning down to kiss her cheek and hug her.

"How are you?" Jazmine asked.

"Alright and you?" Dakota said, smiling at the hot redhead.

"I'm okay," Jazmine said, nodding with a wistful smile on her face.

Dakota caught the smile. "Sure about that?" she asked, her look pointed.

Jazmine looked back at Dakota, seeing the flirt in her eyes. "Yes, I'm sure," she assured the girl, giving her a sly look.

It had been a week since Jazmine had started staying with Rayden. So far things had remained platonic, but friendly. She'd been careful not to push.

"Is Cassandra here?" Jazmine asked, looking around.

"She doesn't come to places like this," Dakota said.

"Oh," Jazmine said, nodding.

She didn't know much about Cassandra. She'd only met her through Natalia, who had met Cassandra when she'd been dancing professionally. Cassandra had been a supporter of the dance company Natalia had belonged to. Cassandra had recently heard about Natalia's hugely successful dance class at the gym and had started discussing the idea of her own studio with her. Jazmine and Natalia had been talking about it for a few months, having met through their dance background. Jazmine was a dancer and had starred in a number of hip-hop and rap videos. She had a unique look that made her stand out from the crowd. She'd met Natalia when Natalia had choreographed a few of the videos she had been in. They'd hit it off right away. Jazmine was investing some of her own money in the project, her life savings in fact. She knew it was risky, but she also knew that she wanted to get out of doing videos and get into business. She needed more security so she wouldn't get stuck with guys like Jeremy who thought they owned her.

"She doesn't mind you coming here?" Jazmine asked Dakota.

Dakota looked back at Jazmine for a long moment, a slow grin spreading across her face. "I wouldn't know," she said.

"Oh," Jazmine said, surprised.

Dakota chuckled, shaking her head. "She does her thing, I do mine."

Jazmine nodded. "Okay," she said, her tone indicating that she wasn't butting into their business.

Jazmine saw Shenin Devereaux-Hancock then and wanted to talk to her. She glanced at Dakota. "Excuse me," she said, smiling.

"Any time," Dakota said, her eyes alight with innuendo.

Jazmine walked over to where Shenin stood at the bar.

"You're Shenin, Tyler's wife?" Jazmine asked.

Shenin turned around, glancing at the other redhead.

"Yes," she said curiously.

41

"I'm Jazmine. I was hoping I could talk to you about Rayden."

Shenin gave a slow nod, now realizing who this woman was. She was the one that Rayden had rescued the week before and had then taken back to her place.

The bartender handed Shenin her drink and Shenin tossed a twenty on the bar. She nodded her head to a table and Jazmine followed her over to it. Shenin sat down, pulling out a cigarette and lighting it. Jazmine sat down across from her.

"So what did you want to talk about?" Shenin asked.

"You and Tyler know her, right?" Jazmine asked.

Rayden had mentioned that she'd known Tyler from D.C.

Shenin nodded. "Yeah we know her."

"And you knew her wife too, right?" Jazmine asked, looking nervous.

Shenin's eyes narrowed slightly. "Yeah, we knew Grayson too."

Jazmine blew her breath out. "Would you mind if I asked you some questions about her? I mean her wife."

"Did you ask Ray these questions?" Shenin asked, not wanting to talk out of turn.

"I… I can't…" Jazmine said, grimacing. "Every time I see her even think about her wife, it looks like it's painful. I don't want to ask her a bunch of questions that are only going to hurt her more."

Shenin nodded, understanding that concern. "How do you know Ray?" she asked then, having been curious since Tyler had told her about Jazmine yelling Rayden's name that night in the office.

Jazmine blew her breath out again. "I dated her way back when," she said. "She really left a scar."

Shenin looked surprised by that statement. "How?"

Jazmine and Rayden had been together for a month. It had been very casual and Jazmine had sensed that Rayden was keeping her at arm's length. For her, however, she was completely into the dark-haired Navy SEAL and was willing to take anything Rayden gave her. It wasn't something she was used to doing, since men tended to want to be with her. She was young, only eighteen, and that tended to make men very hot for her. Rayden didn't seem to care, other than to ensure that she was indeed eighteen and legal.

"How'd you get into that club that night?" Rayden asked her when she'd admitted to Rayden that she was only eighteen.

"Fake ID," Jazmine replied, shrugging.

"Show me the real one," Rayden said, her tone authoritative.

"You don't believe me?" Jazmine asked, secretly excited by Rayden's commanding attitude.

"Show me the real one," Rayden said again, her tone unchanged, but her eyes narrowed this time.

"Okay, okay, sheesh!" Jazmine said, reaching for her purse.

She took out her ID, the real one, and handed it to Rayden who examined it at length.

"Geeze, you a cop or what?" Jazmine asked, her tone chiding.

Rayden pinned her with a look. "I'm not about to lose my career by fucking an underage girl, Jaz," she said sharply.

"Okay!" Jazmine exclaimed, surprised by Rayden's anger.

Finally, Rayden handed her back her ID.

"Convinced now?" Jazmine asked.

Rayden didn't answer at first, her look saying she wanted to argue the point. Jazmine put aside her purse, dropping her ID inside. Then she moved to where Rayden sat on the couch and straddled her lap, putting her arms around Rayden's neck.

"I'm legal, Ray," she said, her tone a cajoling whisper, "you can fuck me all you want..."

Rayden looked back at her with narrowed eyes. "Don't use that language."

"You did," Jazmine replied.

"I'm in the Navy," Rayden said, her lips curling in derision, "they kick you out if you don't talk like a sailor."

"Do they?" Jazmine asked, smiling.

"Yeah," Rayden said, as a slow smile started on her lips.

"Can I say that you can make love to me all you want?" Jazmine asked then.

Rayden chewed on the gum in her mouth, her look indicating she wasn't fond of that term either.

"Sex," Jazmine said, "we can have sex, okay? I mean, seriously—"

Her words were cut off by Rayden's lips on hers. Minutes later she was crying out in her release and she didn't care what they called what they did. All she knew was that Rayden Black Wolf excited her more than anyone ever had, and she wanted to hold on to the woman with both hands, legs, and feet, whatever it took.

When Rayden stopped calling as often, Jazmine grew desperate. On a particularly bad day when she'd managed to get herself fired from her waitressing job because she'd had such a bad attitude with the customers, she broke down and called Rayden.

"Yeah?" Rayden answered her phone.

"Ray?" Jazmine queried, sniffling.

"Jaz, what's wrong?" Rayden asked, instantly alert.

"I lost my job," Jazmine said, picking at the linoleum on her kitchen floor with her nail.

"Sorry, babe..." Rayden said. "What are you gonna do?"

"I don't know," Jazmine said, fresh tears starting. "My rent is due next week, I don't have it... I think he's going to kick me out this time..."

"I can lend you some money," Rayden said.

Jazmine didn't answer, biting her lip on the other end of the line.

"Jaz?" Rayden queried.

Jazmine sighed. "This place is just too expensive for me, Ray, I can barely make it on my tips... I need to move anyway... Maybe I can find a cheaper place in the Heights or something..."

"You can't live down there, Jazmine," Rayden said, her tone protective now.

Jazmine closed her eyes, feeling that same thrill whenever Rayden became protective.

"Why not?" she asked, knowing exactly why, but wanting Rayden to tell her anyway.

"It's not safe, Jaz, you know that, no, you gotta find another way," she said, her tone deepening.

"There isn't another way, Ray," Jazmine said, knowing she was being manipulative and hating herself for it, but she wanted Rayden so much...

"Yes there is," Rayden said, grimacing at her end of the line.

"What?" Jazmine asked, holding her breath and hoping against hope.

"You could come stay with me," Rayden said, rolling her eyes at herself even as she said it.

"You don't want me to do that," Jazmine said, being completely honest, because she knew it was true.

"I don't want you living in the Heights, Jaz, I'll worry about you all the time," Rayden said, feeling the noose tighten around her neck a little more.

"Maybe I'll just live in my car," Jazmine said then.

"Sure, you are completely safe on the streets of LA in your car," Rayden said, her tone snide. "Just pack your shit, I'll come pick you up when I'm off today."

Just like that she was living with Rayden. It lasted six months, with some serious ups and downs. The final blow, however was dealt when Jazmine came home from work one day to find a note and an envelope.

The note read: "Been deployed to the Middle East, don't know how long I'll be gone. Six months of rent in the envelope. Will contact you when I get settled. Ray"

She didn't see or hear from Rayden again.

Jazmine told Shenin a condensed version of the story, leaving out the part where she'd emotionally blackmailed Rayden into letting her move in with her.

Shenin was shocked by what Jazmine told her.

"Wow, that's not the Rayden I know," she said, shaking her head.

"What Rayden do you know?" Jazmine asked.

"The one who was dedicated to her wife, who did everything in her power to make her wife happy, and who was completely inconsolable when Gray died," Shenin said, her look apologetic, but honest.

Jazmine nodded, looking sad. "It sounds like she was really in love with her. "I mean, I kind of knew that, just by the way Ray talked about her, what little she's said anyway."

Shenin nodded. "I imagine it's still really hard for her."

"How long has it been?" Jazmine asked gently.

Shenin thought about it for a moment. "About a year now."

Jazmine shook her head. "It just doesn't seem right, you know? That she finally committed to someone and God took her away."

"I don't believe in God," Shenin said. "I abandoned that fantasy years ago."

Jazmine looked back at Shenin for a long moment, sensing a lot of undercurrent there.

"How long have you and Ty been married?"

"Almost five years now," Shenin said, smiling fondly. "I had to chase Ty down too, you know."

"You did?" Jazmine asked.

"Oh yeah," Shenin said, smiling cheekily. "I was straight, and Ty was just so incredible, and I wanted her more than anything."

"How did you finally get her?" Jazmine asked, curious.

"Well, she got hurt, really badly over in Iraq, and I flew thirty hours from Alaska to get to her. When I had to leave three days later and she'd just awaken for the second time during that time, I told her I loved her too much to lose her. She showed up in Alaska, the base I was stationed at, about a month later. She'd finally given in and I was so happy…" Shenin's voice trailed off as she saw Tyler walk out of the bar, looking around. "Speaking of the blue-eyed devil…" she said, smiling widely.

Tyler walked over, nodding to Jazmine then turning her very blue eyes to her wife.

"Enjoy that while you can," Tyler said, nodding at the cigarette in Shenin's hand.

"I am," Shenin replied, smiling. She looked at Jazmine. "We're going to start trying for a baby here at the end of the month."

"Oh…" Jazmine said, smiling, "congratulations and good luck!"

"Thanks," Tyler said, smiling. "Jazmine, Natalia is looking for you. She said you need to come dance with her."

"Of course!" Jazmine said, shaking her head. "Thank you," she said to Shenin.

"No problem," Shenin said, smiling as Jazmine made her way back inside.

"What was she thanking you for?" Tyler asked, moving to sit in the chair Jazmine had vacated.

"She was asking about Ray," Shenin said, slipping her feet out of her sandals and putting them on Tyler's lap.

Tyler smiled at the movement, and slid her hands over Shenin's calves, caressing them. "What she want to know about Ray?"

"Well, she really wanted to know about Grayson," Shenin said.

"Why?" Tyler asked, her tone suspicious.

"Relax, babe," Shenin said, "she's got a thing for Ray, they dated years ago, and she doesn't seem to have gotten over it."

"So she was making sure Ray's wife's been dead long enough?" Tyler asked sharply.

"Ty…" Shenin said, her tone chiding. "She thinks it's awful that Ray finally committed to someone and that she was taken away from her. She seems like she really cares about Ray."

"And you're thinking about playing matchmaker?" Tyler asked, frowning.

"She did rescue the girl, Ty," Shenin said.

"She does that kind of shit all the time," Tyler said. "It's that protective thing she's got going on."

"She also took her home that night and Jazmine's been staying with Ray ever since…" Shenin said.

"So, she's a grafter…" Tyler said, grinning.

"Stop it!" Shenin said, laughing. Then she grew serious. "Ray needs someone right now, Ty… She can't keep living her solitary existence without Gray…"

Tyler pressed her lips together. "I know," she said, nodding.

"She was brought here for a reason."

49

"You think fate brought her here?" Tyler asked, knowing how Shenin's mind worked.

"I think fate did, yes," Shenin said, "and I think we need to help her in any way that we can."

Tyler nodded, her look resigned.

"What?" Shenin asked, seeing Tyler's reservation.

Tyler drew in a breath and blew it out slowly. "I guess I've kind of stayed away from her, like her luck could come to me, you know?"

"Oh Ty..." Shenin said, moving to sit in Tyler's lap, and putting her arms around her neck. "No, honey... no... I'm not going any-where."

Tyler kissed Shenin's lips, her hand reaching up to touch her cheek tenderly.

"I wouldn't ever want to live without you," Tyler told her serious-ly.

"You will never have to," Shenin told her.

"My wife, my life," Tyler told her.

"Kinda like me a little bit, huh?" Shenin said, grinning.

"Little bit," Tyler said, smiling too.

It was something they said often, their own private joke. They stared into each other's eyes and no one else existed for a long minute.

Rayden saw it and felt her heart lurch painfully. She had to grit her teeth to force back the lump in her throat.

"Alright, alright, break it up..." she said, grinning as she walked up to the two.

"Hey Ray," Shenin said, grinning up at the other woman.

"Hey Shen," Rayden said, smiling, putting her hand out as Shenin moved to get up off Tyler's lap.

"Thanks," Shenin said, smiling. "Babe, I'm gonna go to the bathroom, be right back."

"Okay, hey, grab me another beer will you?" Tyler asked.

"You got it. Ray, you want anything?" Shenin asked.

"I'm good, thanks," Rayden said, holding up the beer in her hand.

"Okay," Shenin said and walked inside.

Rayden sat down where Shenin had been sitting.

"How's it going?" Tyler asked.

Rayden looked back at her for a long moment. "Are you asking about Jaz?"

"I wasn't," Tyler said, "but since you brought it up…"

"We dated a million years ago," Rayden said, by way of explanation.

Tyler nodded. "It's your business, Ray. We just worry about you."

Rayden chewed at the gum in her mouth, something she did when she was agitated. "I know, and I know that Gray would want you to worry about me, so I'll forgive it."

"Good thing," Tyler said, grinning. "So is there anything there…?" she asked gently.

Rayden drew in a deep breath, then expelled it slowly. "There used to be. I'm just not ready to move on yet, you know?"

Tyler nodded. "Yeah, I know," she said, "but maybe there's a reason she needed rescuing at that exact moment, you know?"

Rayden looked back at Tyler, narrowing her eyes slightly. "Shenin's fate talk?"

Tyler shrugged. "Sometimes she's right."

Rayden blew her breath out audibly. "I don't know, we'll see. Depends on how long she wants to put up with my stubborn, morose ass."

Tyler grinned. Rayden had a way of putting things into perspective.

Inside the bar, Natalia was dancing with Jazmine, Cat, and Jovina. She was annoyed that Raine said she was too tired to dance. Raine had been working a lot lately and it was starting to take its toll on their relationship. Natalia felt like she was always waiting for Raine to come home, and half the time she'd get home and would be too tired to do anything, including making love. Natalia knew that what Raine did for a living was important, she worked as a Special Agent to locate and shut down methamphetamine labs in the greater Los Angeles area, but it didn't keep her warm at night.

She'd been hoping this new opportunity to create her own studio would help fill the void of Raine's absence. Unfortunately, it had polarized it instead. She wanted to share the excitement of planning the studio with Raine, but Raine didn't seem as excited about the prospect. Natalia had been drinking a lot since getting to the bar and Raine, as usual, was late arriving. At one point during the night, Natalia left the dance floor to go to the bathroom. When she came out of the stall, she walked into someone and their hands shot out to grab her to keep her from falling back into the stall.

Looking up she saw she had almost knocked over Dakota.

"Oh my God, Dakota, I'm so sorry," Natalia exclaimed. "Are you okay?"

Dakota grinned, seeing that Natalia was very drunk. "I'm okay," she said, her tone solicitous, "but you don't look like you are…" She could see how glassy Natalia's eyes were.

"I'm okay," Natalia said, nodding.

"You sure?" Dakota asked, her thumbs rubbing Natalia's shoulders gently.

"Yes, yes…" Natalia said, her lower lip trembling at the show of concern.

"Okay doesn't usually involve crying, Nat…" Dakota said softly.

Natalia knew the alcohol was causing her to be weepy. She did her best to wipe away the tears that had gathered in her eyes. Unfortunately, she also wiped makeup into her eye.

"Oh God…" she murmured.

"Ow," Dakota said, seeing how red her eyes were getting. "Okay, easy, let's get you to the sink…" she said, putting her arm around Natalia's shoulders and guiding her to the sink. There she helped her get paper towels and did her best to get the makeup out of her eyes.

"Thank you," Natalia said, shaking her head. "I'm okay now, it's okay."

Dakota grinned, reaching up with her thumb to rub one little bit of makeup away from the corner of Natalia's eyes. Their eyes connected at that moment and Dakota's hand moved to the back of her neck and pulled her forward. Their lips met in a heated almost frantic kiss and they both moaned softly.

Dakota took Natalia's hand and led her back to the far stall, the handicapped one that had more room. Inside she closed and locked the door and turned to Natalia, her lips capturing Natalia's again. Natalia refused to think about what she was doing, her body wanted this; it had been so long since she and Raine had made love. She felt Dakota's hand sliding down her hip, and then up under her skirt. She knew she should stop her, but she didn't. Suddenly Dakota's hand was against her bare skin, and one finger slid against her heat and she groaned against Dakota's mouth. Dakota pressed closer, her lips hungry on Natalia's, and then Natalia was coming and grasping at Dakota's shoulders, doing her best to be quiet as she orgasmed.

Afterwards, Natalia suddenly realized what she'd just done and felt sick. Dakota stepped back, and Natalia sunk to the floor, pulling her knees up to her chest. Dakota knelt down, but Natalia waved her away, her lips trembling as tears began to stream down her cheeks. She was shaking her head as if trying to deny what had just happened. Dakota tried to reach out her hand to offer some kind of support, but Natalia threw her hand up blocking Dakota's hand.

"Please, just go," Natalia said, her voice muffled because her face was now pressed against her knees in shame. "Please…" she pleaded tearfully.

Dakota hesitated. This wasn't some strange girl she'd just met, but then again if word got out to Cassandra that she'd fucked Natalia, she was done for. Finally, she got up and walked out of the stall, leaving the bathroom a few moments later.

It took Natalia a few long minutes to regain her composure. She stood up unsteadily, taking halting steps to get out of the stall and over to the sink. She was wiping at her eyes again when Raine walked into the bathroom.

"Babe!" Raine exclaimed, seeing how red Natalia's eyes were. "Are you okay? What happened?"

Natalia shook her head, feeling horrible. "I... I got sick... I drank too much... Raine, I'm so sorry... I'm so sorry... I love you..." she said, her words disjointed as she cried.

Raine pulled her into her arms to hold her.

"Okay, honey, it's okay. Let's get you home, okay?" Raine said.

Raine tried to help Natalia walk out of the bathroom, but it quickly became evident that Natalia had really had way too much to drink. Raine picked her up and carried her out of The Club.

Dakota watched the couple leave. She felt like shit for leaving Natalia in the bathroom like she had. When someone at the table had mentioned Natalia, Dakota had volunteered the information that she'd seen her in the bathroom earlier. That's when Raine had gone to check on Natalia.

Cody noted the look on Dakota's face when they'd all seen Raine carrying Natalia out of the bar. She knew guilt when she saw it. Cody went to stand next to Dakota and bumped her shoulder, nodding her head to indicate that Dakota needed to come with her.

Outside, the patio was somewhat deserted as it was getting late. As they got outside, Cody wheeled on Dakota.

"What the fuck are you thinking?" she asked sharply.

"What are you talking about?" Dakota asked, her voice perfectly calm as she pulled out a cigarette and lit it.

"You know what I'm talking about, Dak," Cody said.

When Dakota simply looked back at her blankly, Cody shook her head, laughing sarcastically.

"You probably don't," Cody said. "Did you fuck her Dak?"

Dakota took a deep draw on her cigarette, her eyes narrowing as she did. She blew the smoke out a full minute later.

"Answer me," Cody said, putting on her cop tone in the heat of the moment.

Dakota looked back at her, not really wanting to answer. Finally she blew her breath out, dropping her head and nodding it slowly.

"Jesus Christ, Dak…" Cody said her tone sharp. "I get it, you have no moral compass…. But you just fucked with a real relationship here…" Cody blew her breath out, looking disgusted. "Natalia's not some fucking score, Dak. She's in love with Raine, and now you may have screwed that completely up… for what? So you could?" She shook her head again. "I don't know you anymore… and I don't know that I want to." With that she walked back into the bar.

Dakota moved to sit in a chair, staring at the door Cody had gone back through. She blew her breath out shakily. She hadn't been called to task like that in many, many years. Part of her wanted to write it off, because it was only Cody, but the part of her that still felt things said *but she was your only friend…* She took the lit cigarette and pushed it into the skin of her forearm, closing her eyes as she felt the searing heat on her skin. She could smell the burning skin, and finally her shaking hand dropped the cigarette. She clenched her fist flexing the tendons to force blood through the area, causing more pain. After a couple of minutes, she pulled another cigarette out with shaking fingers and lit it, turning her forearm over, and pressing it against her jeans.

Twenty minutes later McKenna walked outside. Dakota was still sitting where she had been.

"What happened between you and Cody?" McKenna asked, her tone even.

"Why?" Dakota asked, her look blank.

"Something happened, Dakota, what was it?" McKenna asked, her tone sharper this time.

"I fucked up, okay?" Dakota said angrily.

"What did you do?"

"It doesn't matter."

"Well, it does to Cody because she's now in there getting drunk and I don't like it," McKenna said her voice strident.

"Take her home," Dakota said, her voice hoarse suddenly. She cleared her throat. "Take her home; derail her drinking by taking her home."

McKenna looked back at Dakota, plainly seeing that the woman was hurting, but right now her main concern was the woman she loved.

"If this is the kind of influence you're going to have on her, I really don't want you around her," McKenna said, her tone flat.

With that she walked back inside, shutting the door behind her.

Dakota stared after her, her mind churning, her heart aching. The waitress walked out then and Dakota looked at her. "Give me a bottle of Jack," she told the girl.

The waitress returned with the bottle a few minutes later. Dakota sat on the patio and drank until closing. The waitress helped her to a cab, and Dakota got her off in the back of the cab on the way to Cassandra's house as a thank you.

"What the hell happened to you!" Cassandra screeched at her three hours later.

Dakota was lying on the bed, face down, fully clothed, and passed out cold. Cassandra's screech rang in her ears for a full minute.

"Holy hell, Cass, calm down," Dakota muttered.

"What time did you finally drag yourself in?" Cassandra queried just as loud.

"Dunno, wasn't lookin' at my watch…"

"Where's the Bugatti, Dakota?" Cassandra snapped.

"Uh…" Dakota stammered. "Oops."

"Oops?" Cassandra snapped. "You don't know where you left a three point four million dollar car!"

"Don't be ridiculous, I know where I left it," Dakota said.

"Where?" Cassandra snapped.

"With the valet at The Club," Dakota said, grinning.

Cassandra stared at her openmouthed. "Are you insane?" she asked, as if she thought it was highly likely.

Dakota looked back at her for a long moment, trying to focus on the conversation, although she was still very drunk at that point.

"It's insured, right?" she finally asked.

Cassandra screamed, throwing her hands up and stormed out of the room.

Dakota chuckled, inanely pleased that she'd managed to really piss Cassandra off. She knew she'd pay for it later, but it was still worth the look on her face. Dropping her head back to the pillows, she drifted back into unconsciousness.

***

Natalia woke the next morning, with an aching head and needing to throw up endlessly. Raine was right there, doing her best to help. It just made her guilt worse. That was right up until Raine got a page and had to report to the office on her Saturday off. Natalia had canceled class calling in "sick" and now Raine was gone again. Natalia lay in bed, thinking about what she'd done. She knew that Dakota was a player, even though she was supposed to be with Cassandra. Natalia also knew that Cassandra was far from faithful to Dakota, so she didn't feel too badly about that. She didn't know how she felt about how excited she'd gotten. She figured it had everything to do with all the alcohol she'd drunk. Raine had excited her that way many times, but recently things were just so messed up between them that nothing seemed to be exciting anymore. Part of Natalia knew that she was just justifying her bad behavior, but the part of her that felt abandoned and hurt overrode that other voice in her head.

***

By that evening, Dakota finally felt human again. It was fortunate since Cassandra was dragging her to some black tie bullshit event. Dakota wore all black, with a shirt that was unbuttoned just enough to display the curve of her breasts with her usual black leather tong necklace, this time with a platinum dragon wing pendant. She walked around the art show, bored out of her mind. She'd already downed numerous glasses of champagne and was feeling a decent buzz, but it wasn't enough. She knew what kind of buzz she really needed. Glancing around she saw that Cassandra was deep in discussion with the artists whose work was being featured that night. Another pretentious asshole as far as Dakota was concerned.

She started walking the rooms, looking for the perfect prey. She wanted a challenge. She spotted the uptight looking wife of a banker type but discarded her because she looked too much like Cassandra. Then her eyes fell on the girl sitting in one of the chairs off to the side of a display. She looked like she was about eighteen, maybe nineteen. She looked bored. Dakota quickly located who had to be the girl's parents. *Holy parental nightmare, Batman,* Dakota thought to herself grinning. Mom was fat and stuffed into a dress two sizes too small and dad looked like he was likely a closet case, probably into bondage or some type of kink.

The girl... now the girl had potential, even if the dress she was wearing was a nightmare too, her mom must have picked it out. It was pink, the kind of pink you see on a twelve-year-old, not an adult. It was too long, but when the girl crossed her legs, the skirt hiked up enough to give a flash of nicely shaped legs. She had a pretty face, and if she got her hair out of that horrible ponytail she could probably look pretty hot. The body looked like it had potential too, even if the dress was too big. *All the better to get it off of her...* Dakota thought to herself.

She walked over and sat down in the chair next to the girl, glancing over and smiling.

"You bored too?" she asked.

The girl looked over at her surprised, then rolled her eyes, nodding her head.

"We could find something else to do…" Dakota said, smiling.

"Like what?" the girl asked, her brown eyes on Dakota's.

"Well, getting out of here to start with," Dakota said, grinning. "The kitchen is always where it's happening."

"Yeah?" the girl asked, her eyes shining with the idea of getting away from her parents.

"Oh yeah," Dakota said, nodding. "Come on." She held her hand out to the girl.

The girl looked around surreptitiously and then took Dakota's hand. Dakota pulled her gently out of the chair and led the way to the kitchen. There they stole a couple of pastries and a bottle of champagne, and made their way to the back area that was deserted, and sat amongst the bags of flour and sugar.

Dakota opened the bottle of champagne and took a long swig, then handed it to the girl.

"I can't, I'm only eighteen," she said, shaking her head.

"I won't tell," Dakota said, grinning.

"Okay," the girl said. She took a drink and handed the bottle back.

Dakota looked at her for a long minute. "Do you like your hair like that?"

"Like what?" the girl asked.

"In that thing," Dakota said, gesturing to the ponytail and ribbon.

"It's looks stupid, I know, but my mother…"

"Fuck your mother," Dakota said, reaching over and undoing the ponytail, tossing the ribbon away from her as if it was offensive.

The girl reached up shaking her hair out.

"That's hot…" Dakota said, grinning.

The girl looked at her for a long moment. "Are you a lesbian?"

"Yes, I am," Dakota said proudly.

"I've never been with a girl before," the girl said.

"I can fix that," Dakota said, moving to kiss the girl's lips.

Ten minutes later, she had her naked and screaming on the bags of flour. It turned out to be a better evening than she'd expected.

Later, on the way home in the reclaimed Bugatti, Cassandra looked over at Dakota who was driving.

"So where'd you get off to in there?" she asked, her tone slightly accusatory.

Dakota had to fight the urge to say, *I wasn't the one getting off, but thanks for asking* but instead she grinned. "Just wandered around looking at the boring shit."

"Boring shit?" Cassandra repeated, even as she reached over and brushed a white powder off Dakota's sleeve.

Dakota grinned, but didn't answer. She wasn't in the mood to banter with Cassandra.

When it was obvious Cassandra was awaiting an answer, however, she felt the need to add.

"You know, while you were jerking off that artist guy," she said, with a sly grin.

"Good Lord, Dakota, must you be so crass?" Cassandra asked.

Dakota looked over at her. "You like that I'm crass, babe, you like that I fuck you whenever and however you want. Let's not pretend that isn't why you're with me, okay?"

Cassandra stared back at her, attempting to look shocked, but Dakota could see that what she'd just said had made Cassandra hot. To prove it, to herself and to Cassandra, she reached across the console, pushed Cassandra's dress up, and, noting that she wore no underwear, slid her finger inside her immediately. Cassandra gasped, but moaned a moment later and was coming moments after that.

As Cassandra leaned back against the expensive leather racing seats, Dakota held her finger, still glistening, to Cassandra.

"This is why you're with me," Dakota said, "don't fucking forget it."

Cassandra said nothing, but nodded as she continued to try to catch her breath. Back at the house, however, she'd gotten her balls back. They had a very loud and raucous round of sex, things were broken, clothes were ripped; it was very physical.

Afterwards, lying in bed, Dakota reached up and touched blood on her neck. Cassandra had bitten her in her heated state. *Great another scar,* Dakota thought to herself as she drifted to sleep. She knew it was Cassandra marking her territory on her, but she was too tired to care at that point.

Later that week, Cody walked out of the building at DOJ and saw Dakota sitting on an insanely expensive sports car. She was smoking, clearly waiting for her.

"What are you doing here?" Cody asked.

"Wanna take a ride?" Dakota asked, her grin wide.

Cody grinned too.

In the car, Dakota got on the freeway, got clear of other traffic, and punched it. Breaking Benjamin was on, and Cody could see that Dakota liked the song that was on by the way she cranked it. The song was called "Follow." The lyrics were harsh and angry.

"So what's up, Dak?" Cody asked when the song ended and Dakota turned it down.

Dakota glanced over at Cody. "Look, I'm sorry, okay? I don't want you pissed at me."

"Dak, you can't just do shit like that," Cody said, shaking her head. "These are people's lives you're fucking with."

"I know, I'm sorry, I really didn't... I didn't think, I just... I'm so used to doing what I want, taking what I want... I didn't think, and I'm sorry."

Cody looked over at Dakota and she could see that Dakota was really trying to apologize. She didn't feel like she was just saying it.

"It isn't like I don't get it, Dak, I do," Cody said. "Before I got together with McKenna, I'd go through two or three women in one night too. But Natalia isn't some random chick at the bar. She's in a relationship with someone, and no matter what's going on with them that let her make such a huge mistake... sorry," she said when Dakota gave her a sharp look. "But screwing someone outside of your relationship is a pretty big mistake, Dak. Anyway, no matter what, you shouldn't have been the one that happened with, okay?"

Dakota nodded. "I get it."

Cody nodded too. "Good."

Two days later, things went from bad to worse. Natalia's class was going on, and for once Raine had made it in time. Cody was there, as were most of the girls and a lot of the bois. Dakota walked into the gym as the class was in full swing. She had a meeting with Jazmine afterwards. Jazmine had made the meeting time, and was just going to grab Natalia for the meeting after class. She had no idea what had happened between Natalia and Dakota.

Cody saw Dakota first, but as soon as she had, she looked over and saw that Natalia had spotted her as well. Natalia froze for a moment, shock written all over her face, which was quickly replaced with embarrassment. Raine too had watched as Dakota walked into the gym. She frowned as she caught Natalia's reaction, then followed her line of sight to Dakota.

"Fuck..." Cody muttered under her breath.

Natalia had gotten her focus back by that time, but even so, Cody waited until she came by and reached out to touch her shoulder.

"She knows," Cody told her, nodding toward Raine.

"What?" Natalia asked looking shocked.

Cody shook her head slowly. "She's a cop, we read people, she knows, trust me."

"How?" Natalia looked askance at Cody, unsure of how Cody knew.

"Doesn't matter, does it?" Cody asked.

Natalia shook her head and moved on with the class. During the quick water break, Raine made her way toward Quinn who was standing nearby on the other side of the half wall.

"Hey, Quinn," Raine said.

"Yeah?" Quinn answered.

"Wanna go a round after?" Raine asked.

Quinn shrugged, looking a little puzzled, but nodded. "Sure."

Cody watched the exchange and shook her head, thinking *Great!* As everyone headed back to the floor, Cody strode over to Dakota.

"You need to get out of here," Cody told her.

"What?" Dakota said, looking surprised.

"Raine knows..." Cody said.

"So maybe I should just let her take her shot then," Dakota said, shrugging.

"Don't underestimate her," Cody said, "she's a helluva lot tougher than she looks. She'll kill you in the mood she looks like she's in."

Dakota glanced over at Raine and saw that the other woman was watching her. She didn't look away. Raine's eyes narrowed slightly, then she looked away.

"Dak, just leave," Cody told her.

"Nope," Dakota said, crossing her arms over her chest, and leaning back against the wall.

Cody went back to the class then, but warned Natalia that Raine had challenged Quinn. The next time she got to the half wall, Natalia looked seriously at Quinn.

"If you hurt her, I'll kill you."

Quinn raised an eyebrow at Natalia. "And if she hurts me?"

"Then Xandy will feel sorry for you," Natalia said, her tone conciliatory.

Quinn chuckled, shaking her head. Natalia moved away then and continued the class. She tried over and over to get Raine to look at her, but Raine wasn't having it. Natalia could see from the look on her face that she was controlling her anger and channeling it into her movements. Natalia had a rough time finishing the class. Raine left as soon as the last song ended, and before they stretched. Natalia rushed the stretching and ran straight into the other part of the gym, to the ring where most of the bois did MMA fighting.

Quinn and Raine were in the middle of a skirmish when she got into the room. Quinn had Raine in a hug from behind; it looked like the match was going to go to Quinn, but then Raine shocked everyone by giving a yell of pure fury. She broke Quinn's hold, and jammed her elbow back, making Quinn jump back or take the chance of getting a cracked rib. Raine turned and rushed Quinn, who rallied back, but Raine just kept pushing forward, even when Quinn landed a blow to her shoulder. Raine just dug in and kept moving forward, kicking out, making Quinn jump back, and block her. When they reached the edge of the ring, Raine gave another yell and drove her fist forward. Quinn ducked and Raine's fist slammed into the cushioned side. She stood breathing hard. Quinn stood looking at Raine, wondering what had sparked all that rage.

Raine turned and climbed out of the ring, stripping off her gloves. Natalia intercepted her as she turned to walk out of the room. Raine's hands went up defensively and she pulled her head back when Natalia tried to touch her face.

"Raine!" Natalia exclaimed.

"Get away from me," Raine said, her tone even and low.

Natalia was stunned. She stepped back and Raine strode past her. As Raine went through the doors Natalia looked over at the group, her look alarmed.

"I'll go," Jet said.

"Me too," Cody said. They'd both watched the exchange and knew something was seriously wrong.

Both women strode after Raine, knowing she was heading for her motorcycle, and since both of them rode bikes that morning, they knew they were the only ones that were likely able to catch up to her.

Raine ran them at breakneck speeds for half an hour. Finally, they managed to corral her and slow her down, getting her to pull off on an exit. Raine turned off her bike, climbed off, and yanked off her helmet before heading straight for Cody.

"What the fuck did your friend do to Natalia!" she yelled, her eyes blazing in fury.

Cody held her hands up. "Raine, I had nothing to do with that," she said shaking her head.

Raine stared at her, her jaw jumping as she gritted her teeth. Finally, she turned on her heel and got back on her bike. She jammed her helmet on then she took off, this time at a more reasonable speed.

"That went well," Jet said, her tone wry.

Cody gave Jet a dirty look.

Jet grinned. "Lesbians, ya gotta love 'em."

Chapter 3

Dating while in the military on a base in the middle of the Iraqi desert had its challenges. Rayden and Grayson ended up at the officers' club, which due to its military clientele meant they could do little more than talk.

"So where did you grow up?" Grayson asked Rayden, lifting a beer to her lips.

"In North Carolina, near the Smoky Mountains. On the res," Rayden said.

"Really?" Grayson said, surprised. "I didn't think people still lived on reservations anymore."

"Well, they do," Rayden said, grinning. "What about you?"

"I grew up in Boston," Grayson said. "My dad's a doctor, my mom is a professor."

"So how did you come to be in the Air Force?" Rayden asked.

"I wanted to do something else," she said, grinning. "And being a pilot sounded really cool."

"And is it cool?" Rayden asked.

"It's awesome," Grayson said, beaming.

"How long have you been one?"

"About a year," Grayson said, grinning. "I'm pretty new."

Rayden nodded.

"And how did you become a Navy SEAL?" Grayson said.

"Wanted to get off the res and figured I'd see the world while I was at it. I joined the Navy, the SEALs was an afterthought."

"Yeah, 'cause pretty much everyone in the Navy does that, right?" Grayson said, her slate-blue eyes sparkling humorously.

Rayden gave her a narrowed look. "No smart-ass, it was actually because some stupid Sergeant told me there was no way I could do it."

"So you proved him wrong," Grayson said, smiling.

"Yep," Rayden said.

"And how often do you go about rescuing damsels in distress?" Grayson asked then.

"Any time I need a date," Rayden said, winking at her.

"Well, if that's the case you're doing it wrong," Grayson said, smiling.

"I am?" Rayden asked.

"Yeah, you're supposed to hang around for said rescued female to thank you profusely."

"Awww," Rayden said, nodding. "I can see where I'm going wrong now, yes, I see."

"Now who's the smart-ass?" Grayson said, grinning.

Two guys nearby were getting loud, yelling at each other.

Rayden watched for a few moments, then looked over at Grayson. "Wanna get out of here?"

"Sure," Grayson said, moving to stand.

They walked out into the chill of the desert night, and Grayson shivered. Rayden took her jacket off and put it around Grayson's shoulders. Grayson smiled at the gesture and put her arms into the arms of the jacket.

They walked along the perimeter of the camp, ending up out to the flight line.

"Which one is yours?" Rayden asked.

"Over there," Grayson said, pointing down the flight line.

"Show me," Rayden said, smiling.

"Okay," Grayson said, smiling.

She led Rayden down the flight line, stopping at her aircraft. She pointed out various things on the aircraft and Rayden watched as she talked. Grayson noticed the smile on Rayden's face and stopped talking for a minute.

"What?" she asked.

"Nothing," Rayden said, her eyes sparkling.

"Bullshit, what?" Grayson said.

Rayden chuckled, moving closer to Grayson, putting her hand up on the underside of the wing they stood under.

"You light up when you talk about your plane," Rayden said.

"I do?" Grayson asked happily.

Rayden nodded, smiling. "Yeah you do," she said, "it's kinda sexy…"

"It is huh?" Grayson said, biting her lip as her eyes sparkled.

"Uh-huh," Rayden said, leaning down to put her lips next to Grayson's ear. "Very sexy actually," she said her voice husky.

Grayson drew in her breath at the thrill of desire that ran through her. She turned her head and Rayden's lips captured hers in a long kiss. Grayson slid her hands up Rayden's chest, wrapping her arms around her neck, deepening the kiss as she moved closer.

Rayden moaned against her lips, her hands sliding around Grayson's waist, pulling her body closer. Grayson happily pressed closer. They kissed until they were both breathless.

"Wait, wait..." Rayden said, as Grayson's hands reached up to unbutton her over shirt.

"What?" Grayson said, her voice breathless.

"Not here..." Rayden said, gesturing around them.

"Where?" Grayson asked, putting her forehead against Rayden's chest.

"I don't know, somewhere... proper," Rayden said, not believing she was saying this and trying to figure out what the hell was wrong with her. She'd had sex with women in more conspicuous places before.

"Proper?" Grayson queried, lifting her head to look up at Rayden. "We're in the middle of a desert, Ray," she said, her tone amused now.

"I know that," Rayden said, her look narrowed. "But... Fuck, I don't know..." she said, shaking her head.

Grayson did her best to subdue her smile. She thought it was really cute that Rayden seemed so old-fashioned. Little did she know Rayden was far from old-fashioned. She actually found out a few weeks later. A nurse passing through happened to hear Grayson tell someone else that she had a date with Rayden later.

"Rayden Black Wolf?" the nurse queried.

"Yeah, why?" Grayson asked, surprised by the woman's interest.

"Oh, she's hot…" the nurse said, smiling.

"Really?" Grayson queried. "And you know this how?"

"Well, no offense honey, but she's not exactly a nun," the nurse said.

"Oh, do tell…" Grayson said.

By the time she got to the date with Rayden that evening, she had a thing or two to discuss with the woman who'd been holding out on her.

"I met someone today…" Grayson told her as they sat out on the flight line. Rayden's back was against the flight gear of Grayson's Raptor and Grayson sat with her back leaning against Rayden's chest.

"Okay…" Rayden said, lifting her beer to her lips. "I assume there's more to that story."

"Oh yeah," Grayson said.

Her tone should have warned Rayden, but she didn't catch it.

"So, do you remember a nurse named Marcie?" Grayson asked.

Rayden immediately choked on her beer. She coughed as she did her best to clear her lungs.

"Um," Rayden stammered, "yeah?"

"Uh-huh," Grayson said, half turning to look back at Rayden. "Yeah… Marcie told me a thing or two about you, E5 Black Wolf…"

"Oh, this doesn't sound good…" Rayden said, rolling her eyes heavenward.

"You had sex with her in the main ward?" Grayson asked, her look pointed.

"To be fair, there were screens…"

"Oh my god!" Grayson said, turning to face Rayden. "You really did that, but you won't have sex with me out here?"

Rayden looked back at her for a long moment considering the question, then she shook her head. "No," she said simply.

"Why!" Grayson cried.

"Because you're not some nurse," Rayden said, her look softening.

"I'm some pilot, so?" Grayson asked her look puzzled.

Rayden looked back at her for a long moment, she shook her head slowly. "It's not the same, Gray."

"Ray, I don't understand," Grayson said, "are you saying I'm not what you want…"

"No, god no…" Rayden said. "I just… I want more than that with you…"

"More than what, Ray?" Grayson asked, trying to understand.

"More than just sex," Rayden said, surprising herself as much as she could see she'd just surprised Grayson.

"Oh…" Grayson said, her voice trailing off as she blinked a couple of times.

"Is that…" Rayden began. Then she stopped suddenly feeling incredibly stupid and defenseless, and totally hating the feeling.

She got up and strode away from where they'd been sitting. She surprised Grayson with her abrupt departure, so much so that she couldn't even form a phrase before Rayden's long legs had carried her half way down the flight line. Grayson had to run to catch up.

"Ray, stop!" she yelled as she caught up and stood in front of Rayden.

Rayden stopped, staring straight ahead over Grayson's head. Grayson could see that she was gritting her teeth by the way that her jaw jumped. She reached up, touching Rayden's cheek. Rayden looked down at her then, and Grayson could see vulnerability in the other woman's eyes.

"I want more than sex with you too," Grayson said. "I just didn't think that's what you'd want... Please Ray, please don't go..." she said, her voice desperate suddenly. "Please."

Rayden looked at her for a long moment, then pulled her into her arms. She hugged her close and breathed a sigh of relief.

"Next week, see if you can get leave," Rayden told her.

"Okay," Grayson said, her voice muffled because her face was buried against Rayden's jacket.

Jazmine walked into Rayden's room later that evening after she'd showered and had dinner. Rayden always left her door open unless she wanted to be alone. Jazmine stood staring down at her; she'd fallen asleep reading on her back with her arm up over her eyes. Jazmine wondered at that, she didn't remember Rayden sleeping that way years before.

"Ray?" she queried softly.

Rayden moved her arm. "Mmm? What is it Jaz?"

Jazmine hesitated. She knew she was being kind of a pain in the ass. "Come here," Rayden said, smiling tiredly as she held her arm out.

"Why do you sleep that way?" Jazmine asked, even as she climbed into the bed.

"What way?" Rayden asked.

"With your arm over your eyes, you didn't use to do that."

"Well, when you sleep in a tent for a while, and you catch sleep whenever you can, you learn to block the sun out any way that you can. I used my arm. It became a habit."

"Oh," Jazmine said, nodding, "makes sense."

"Yeah," Rayden said, as she moved to settle more comfortably with Jazmine at her side.

"I'm sorry," Jazmine said. She looked up at Rayden from where her head rested against Rayden's shoulder, feeling Rayden's arm encircle her shoulders. "This whole thing tonight at the gym was just so unsettling…"

"Shit like that happens in the lesbian world, just like it does in the straight one…" Rayden said.

"I know, but it's just heartbreaking," Jazmine said, "and I really can't believe Dakota did that…" She shook her head.

"How well do you know her?" Rayden asked.

"Not really that well. I know she's a major player. It seems like for her flirting is like breathing, you learn to ignore it most of the time."

"She's flirted with you?" Rayden asked. "Isn't she with someone?"

"She flirts with everyone, Ray, and yeah, she's supposedly the girlfriend of the woman who's coming in with half the money for the studio."

"Dakota looks like a kid," Rayden said. "What is she early twenties?"

"Yeah," Jazmine said, "like twenty-four or twenty-five, why?"

"How old is the girlfriend?" Rayden asked.

"Oh, I'd say about forty."

"Aw," Rayden said, nodding her look knowing.

"Yeah, I do get the feeling it's one of those situations where Dakota's kind of a toy for Cassandra."

"Might be why Dakota flirts," Rayden said. "To get back some of her own."

"Maybe," Jazmine said, giving Rayden a sidelong glance. "Did you ever do that?"

"Do what?" Rayden asked, sensing they weren't talking about flirting now.

"Cheat."

"On…?"

"Grayson?" Jazmine asked, her tone gentle.

"No, never," Rayden said. "Never even thought about it, she was it for me."

Jazmine nodded, feeling a stab of jealousy and trying to tamp down on it. "What about when you were with me?"

Rayden looked back at her for a long moment. She'd seen the flash of jealousy in Jazmine's eyes and she wasn't sure how to feel about that. Then she remembered Jazmine had asked her a question.

"No, I didn't cheat on you either," she said. "If I'm with someone, I'm with them. If I want to be with someone else, I end it with who I'm with first."

Jazmine nodded, thinking that it definitely sounded like the Rayden she knew.

"You just weren't with anyone too often, were you?"

"No, not officially, no," Rayden said.

"Officially?" Jazmine asked, grinning.

"Well, making an actual commitment, like moving the person in…" Rayden said, her look pointed.

"Aw," Jazmine said, catching her meaning. "But you really didn't want to do that with me, did you?"

Rayden narrowed her eyes slightly at Jazmine. "It wasn't my first choice, no," she said honestly.

Jazmine nodded, grimacing slightly. "And I really need to tell you that I know I kind of emotionally blackmailed you back then…"

Rayden smiled slightly, nodding. "I know."

"You do?" Jazmine said, surprised.

"At the time I think part of me knew that, but I knew your financial situation was tenuous at best, and I really couldn't let you do anything stupid like move to the Heights… So…" Her voice trailed off as she shrugged.

Jazmine shook her head. "I guess I shouldn't have been surprised when you disappeared."

"I could have handled it better," Rayden said.

"I could have not forced your hand in the first place," Jazmine said.

"Can we just call it a draw then?" Rayden asked, grinning.

"Yes, I think we can," Jazmine said, smiling.

"Good," Rayden said, smiling too.

They both lay silent for a while. Rayden had her left arm up behind her head and Jazmine notice that she was rubbing the right side of her head. It was something Rayden had done years before, and something she recognized. She looked up at Rayden with a humorous grin on her lips. "What?" Rayden asked.

Jazmine licked her lips, smiling. "Can I ask you a really personal question?"

"Uh," Rayden stammered. "I guess…" she said, her tone unsure.

"How long has it been since…?" Jazmine asked, her voice trailing off as she widened her eyes.

"Since what?" Rayden asked, her look pointed.

"You know… since you… um… got some…" Jazmine said.

Rayden looked contemplative, not sure if she wanted to answer that question. Finally, she figured what the hell and shrugged. "About a year."

Jazmine's eyes widened again, this time in surprise. "Really?"

Rayden looked back at Jazmine, her look serious. "My wife died, Jaz. It wasn't at the top of my list of things to worry about."

"I know, I'm sorry…" Jazmine said. "It's just that… Well, the Rayden I remember had a hell of a sex drive…"

Rayden opened her mouth to say something, then shut it, her look quizzical. "So what made you ask now?"

"Well…" Jazmine cringed. "You kind of have this tell…"

"A tell?" Rayden asked.

"Yeah," Jazmine said, nodding, her look contrite.

"And what's that?" Rayden asked, her eyes sparkling with interest.

"That thing you do with your head," Jazmine said, pointing to where Rayden's hand was still on the side of her head.

Rayden's hand stopped moving immediately, and she rolled her eyes comically.

"Didn't realize I did that," she said diffidently.

"Yeah, you do," Jazmine said. "It's how I always knew when whatever fight we were in was over," she said, grinning. "And it was safe for me to approach."

Rayden chuckled. "Living with me was that much fun, huh?"

"Oh I loved living with you Ray," Jazmine said. "I just had to learn to read you."

Rayden nodded. "I see…" she said, her voice trailing off as her lips quirked in a grin.

Rayden's phone buzzed at that moment. She shifted to reach over to the nightstand and felt Jazmine's quick intake of breath as she brushed against her. She said nothing, she just grinned as she checked her phone. She answered an email and then put her phone back on the nightstand.

"So…" Rayden said after a few minutes. "How long has it been since you got some?" she asked, her tone wry.

Jazmine's mouth dropped open in surprise, then she closed it, giving Rayden a haughty look. "It's been a lot less than a year, I can tell you that."

"Uh-huh," Rayden said, her tone dubious.

"It has!" Jazmine said, her voice rising on the last syllable.

Rayden chuckled. "Okay, then let me put it this way… How long has it been since you got some that was really good?"

"Who said it wasn't really good?" Jazmine asked her look arrogant.

"The fact that you just about jumped out of your skin when I brushed up against you a minute ago," Rayden told her.

"I did not," Jazmine said.

"Really?" Rayden replied, her look cocky.

Jazmine laughed at the look on Rayden's face. "Okay, I might have reacted a little..." she conceded.

Rayden nodded slowly. "So answer the question."

"Which question?"

Rayden gave her a stern look.

"Okay, it's been a while since it was really good," Jazmine said, flabbergasted. "But it's just so much friggin' work..."

Rayden blinked a couple of times. "Work?" she asked, her tone derisive.

"Yeah, you know..." Jazmine said.

Rayden turned her head, giving her a sidelong glance. "No... I don't know... What work is it?"

Jazmine hesitated, then blew her breath out, shaking her head. "I just mean... like getting there."

"There?" Rayden said, her look pointed.

"Yeah," Jazmine said, her voice strident. "Don't tell me you've never had to... you know, help things along."

Rayden pressed her lips together, looking a bit puzzled. "We are talking for you to get there, right?"

"Yeah," Jazmine said, grinning at the incredibly weird conversation they were having suddenly.

Rayden closed her eyes for a second, looking like she was really trying to grasp what Jazmine was talking about, and having a really hard time.

"You have to… help it along… yourself?" Rayden said, trying to use her words.

"Yeah you know… fantasizing and… well, you know…" she said, her voice trailing off as she kind of shrugged.

Rayden's mouth opened in shock as she shook her head, unable to believe what she was hearing.

"You're saying they don't get you off, it's actually you that gets you off?" Rayden asked finally sure she understood what Jazmine was saying.

"Right," Jazmine said.

"But they get off at the same time?"

"Well, yeah, they're guys so…" Jazmine said, grimacing as she said that, knowing how it sounded to Rayden.

Rayden made a "pfft!" sound with her lips. "Yeah, no wonder…"

Jazmine gave her an affronted look. "Geeze… way to be a man hater."

Rayden pinned her with a look. "A man that can't get a woman off is no man, honey," she told her simply.

Jazmine pressed her lips together, then shrugged. "I figure it's just me."

A slow grin spread on Rayden's face. "You never had trouble getting there with me… multiple times if I recall correctly."

Jazmine cleared her throat. "Yeah, I know."

"So what makes you think it's you, and not men?" Rayden asked.

Jazmine pressed her lips together, then she gave Rayden a doubtful look. "Just because it was good with you, doesn't mean I should be with women. Maybe it was just you."

"And maybe it wasn't just me, Jaz," Rayden said. "Were you ever with another woman? I mean after me," she clarified.

"Not really, no. Not like that."

"But like something?"

"Not sexually, just like kissing and stuff…" Jazmine said, her voice trailing off knowing she couldn't tell Rayden that it was always at some guy's suggestion.

Rayden looked back at her, seeing that Jazmine didn't want her to ask too many questions, so she left it alone.

"I think maybe you need to explore the girl thing a bit more, Jaz…" Rayden said.

Jazmine didn't say anything. She just put her head back down against Rayden's shoulder, her fingers picking at a loose thread on Rayden's tank top.

"Jaz?" Rayden queried gently.

"Hmm?" Jazmine answered, not looking up at her.

"Hey, look at me," Rayden said softly.

Jazmine looked up at her, pressing her lips together as she did.

Rayden's eyes searched Jazmine's. "What is it?"

Jazmine shook her head, sighing. "I just don't want to take that chance again, Ray…"

"What chance?" Rayden asked.

"Falling in love with someone and opening myself up to that kind of hurt again," Jazmine said, her voice gravelly with emotion.

Rayden grimaced. "Is that what happened with me?"

Jazmine bit her lip, nodding as she looked down.

"Aw, Jaz…" Rayden said, her tone pained.

"I know, I know, I was stupid to fall for you," Jazmine said, "but I couldn't help it."

"I'm sorry," Rayden said. "I didn't see it, and I really should have, shouldn't I?"

Jasmine shrugged.

Rayden sighed, looking up at the ceiling. It was one more reminder of how stupid she'd been ten years before. She'd been living it up, moving from one woman to the next, getting away with murder as it were. She'd been the classic 'sailor on shore leave,' loving them and leaving them. She'd never really stopped to think about the wake she was leaving behind her. Now she was seeing it firsthand.

"What can I do?" Rayden asked then.

"What?" Jazmine asked, surprised by the question.

"What can I do to make it up to you?" Jazmine laughed. "You don't have to make it up to me, Ray. It's the past."

"Yeah… but I feel really lousy about it, and I want to put it right," Rayden said, her look contrite.

"Tell you what," Jazmine said, smiling. "You can do one thing and make it up to me."

"Okay, what's that?" Rayden asked.

"Kiss me," Jazmine said simply.

Rayden canted her head. "That's it?"

"Yeah," Jazmine said, shrugging. "I want to see for myself if I've been romanticizing your effect on me over the years."

Rayden grinned in surprise. "Romanticizing my effect on you, huh?"

"Yeah," Jazmine said. "Maybe I've just been building it up in my head over the years, and you really weren't all that great, you know… romanticizing it."

Rayden nodded, still looking like she thought Jazmine was crazy.

"So you want to see if I can still affect you," Rayden clarified.

"Right," Jazmine said.

"Do you think I can still affect you?" Rayden asked, her tone becoming more direct, as her dark eyes looked down into Jazmine's.

Jazmine's lips parted, but then she pressed them together.

"I don't know," she answered, barely even convincing herself.

Rayden moved her face closer to Jazmine's and she immediately heard Jazmine's quick intake of breath. Rayden's eyes widened slightly, as she grinned. Jazmine felt her entire body become electric in anticipation. When Rayden's lips touched hers, Jazmine almost orgasmed instantly, as Rayden's lips moved expertly over hers, demanding and yielding alternately. Jazmine felt her body explode immediately. She gasped and moaned against Rayden's lips, grasping at her shirt and pressing her body closer.

The kiss didn't end there, however. Rayden slid her arms around Jazmine's body, pulling her closer still, pulling her up and over her, her hand going to Jazmine's face, her thumb stroking her cheek as she continued to kiss her. Before long, Jazmine could feel her body coiling for yet another release. She pressed her body closer to Rayden's, pressing her pelvis against Rayden's, wanting desperately to affect Rayden as much as she was affecting her. She was on sensory overload, her body alive with sensations and shaking with need and satisfaction at the same time.

Rayden's body was experiencing a reawakening as well. She felt Jazmine's body pressing into her and her body responded with a fervor she hadn't felt for far too long. She shoved away the guilt that wanted to come crashing in. She needed this and she knew that with certainty.

Rayden reached up and pulled off Jasmine's shirt, pushing her underwear down as well. Jazmine obliged by kicking them off, then reached out to pull Rayden's shirt off, pushing at the boy shorts too. Rayden levered herself up to remove them, then pulled Jazmine back down against her, groaning at the sensation of skin on skin. Jazmine's skin was smooth and soft in all the right places and it was driving her insane. As she positioned Jazmine beneath her, Rayden pulled back for a moment, letting her eyes trail down Jazmine's perfectly shaped, curvy body. Moving back over her, she explored the expanse of skin with her lips and tongue.

Jazmine closed her eyes, trying desperately to hold back the screams that wanted to come out of her mouth. Finally, she gave up and screamed, moaned, and gasped in pleasure at all the sensations Rayden was causing with her mouth. She grasped at Rayden's head, her shoulders, whatever she could reach at that moment as she orgasmed over and over again. Rayden finally moved upward, lying over her, and pressed her body against her, moving rhythmically. Jazmine reached up to touch hard nipples, and grasped at Rayden's ass, feeling the muscles there flex as Rayden moved against her.

Within minutes, they were crying out in their release, and as usual, Rayden's half yell and groan sending Jazmine over the edge again. Afterward, Rayden moved to lie half over her, with her arm and leg thrown over her possessively. Jazmine closed her eyes, remembering this feeling so well, and reveling in it.

Rayden arrived at the hotel separately from Grayson. They didn't want to make their visit to Baghdad and the Cristal Grand Ishtar Hotel public knowledge. They certainly didn't want to show up together. Grayson had driven a rental car, and Rayden had gotten a ride into the city with one of her teammates. She'd had him drop her off half a mile away so he wouldn't know what was going on. 'Better safe than sorry' was the way Rayden always figured it.

When she arrived in the hallway outside the room, Rayden stood outside the door breathing in deeply. She wanted this to go right, and she had no idea why the whole thing scared the crap out of her. Part of her didn't want to admit that somehow this woman had become so damned important to her in such a short time. That scared her to death. She heard music coming from the room. Rayden guessed correctly that it was Adele. Grayson loved the woman's music. Taking a deep breath and blowing it out, she put the key up to the door and heard it click. She opened the door, and walked inside. The lights in the room were low. She looked around and didn't see Grayson, but the music was coming from the bedroom area. She took off her jacket and set it aside, kicking off her boots as well. She wore jeans and an army-green collared shirt.

Rayden walked into the bedroom and stood staring at the vision before her. There were candles everywhere, flickering, and giving the room a warm glow. Grayson was sitting on the bed wearing a lace and satin nightgown that was fitted in the bodice, but flowed around her legs, sexily revealing her thigh. It wasn't overly revealing, but definitely suggested the incredible body under it. Grayson's tanned skin seemed to glow. Her honey-blond hair fell softly around her face, her slate-blue eyes framed with darker lashes, and just enough makeup to enhance her beautiful face. Rayden couldn't speak for a few moments, simply awed by this woman. She walked over to the bed, moving to sit next to Grayson. She reached out to touch her face, then put her lips to Grayson's ear.

"You take my breath..." Rayden said, her voice the barest whisper.

Grayson turned her head and her eyes connected with Rayden's. She took Rayden's face in her hands, leaning into kiss her lips softly. Rayden slid her hand across Grayson's midriff, grasping at her waist as their lips met over and over again, increasing in pressure.

"Ray..." Grayson whispered against her lips. "Please..." she pleaded softly.

Rayden moved to lie on her side next to Grayson. She slid her hand gently down to Grayson's waist, moving her gown aside so she could caress her bare thigh. Then her lips found Grayson's neck and she kissed and sucked gently, the sensation causing a current to surge through her.

Grayson's hands were at her shoulders, then at the shirt buttons. Rayden reached up and pulled her shirt off over her head, and Grayson's hands immediately touched her corded muscles and smooth dark skin, with her nails grazing Rayden's skin.

"Rayden… Ray…" Grayson whispered heatedly. "Please…"

Rayden brushed her thumbs over hardened nipples through the satin of the nightgown. Grayson gasped and grasped at Rayden's shoulders as she moved her hips, wanting Rayden so much. Rayden slid her hand downward, and then back up Grayson's thigh, her fingers brushing upward, exciting Grayson even more. Then slowly she slid her hand between Grayson's legs, touching the heat and wetness there and Grayson cried out immediately, pressing against Rayden's hand desperately. Afterwards, Grayson lay on her side, resting her head against Rayden's shoulder, breathing heavily. Rayden held Grayson to her, pressing her lips against the top of Grayson's head.

After a few minutes, Grayson started kissing Rayden's shoulder, then moved up her neck. She kissed her lips again next, all the while unbuttoning Rayden's jeans.

"Take these off…" Grayson told her. "Just take it all off," she commanded.

"Yes ma'am," Rayden said, grinning as she got off the bed to take off the rest of her clothes.

Grayson pulled the nightgown off and tossed it aside, making Rayden breathe faster, just seeing how really incredibly perfect Grayson's body was.

"God, you are so beautiful…" Rayden said, as she climbed back onto the bed.

"And you…" Grayson said, sitting up and looking Rayden's body over from head to toes. "Wow…" she said simply, her look awed.

In truth, she'd never seen such a perfect combination of strength and lean muscle. Rayden's body was solid muscle, with just the slightest curve of breast and hip. She touched the SEAL Trident on her abdomen, running her hand over it, while looking down into Rayden's eyes. Her eyes then went to the four cornered swirl patterned tattoo on her shoulder.

"What is this?" she asked, as she touched the tattoo.

"It's the Tsalagi symbol for strength." Rayden told her.

Grayson smiled. "That is for damned sure," she said, her eyes alight.

Rayden chuckled, wetting her lips and reaching up to touch Grayson's skin, tracing her fingers from her shoulder down to her breasts, making Grayson gasp.

"Come here," Rayden said, her voice husky.

"Oh no…" Grayson said, shaking her head. "You're going to let me touch you now."

"Can't we both touch?" Rayden asked reasonably.

"No," Grayson said, smiling, "if you keep touching me I'm not going to be able to concentrate on you…"

She moved to lie over Rayden, lowering her head to kiss her lips. Rayden's hands immediately slid over her skin.

"No…" Grayson said, reaching down to grab Rayden's hands.

"What am I supposed to do with my hands?" Rayden asked.

Grayson thought for a moment, then she took Rayden's hands, still in hers, and put them above her head, wrapping her hands around the rod iron headboard of the bed.

"Hold on to those," she told Rayden, nodding at where her hands were.

Rayden started to grin. "Are you serious?"

"Very," Grayson said, widening her eyes.

Rayden blew her breath out, biting her lower lip as she grinned. "Well, I gotta say this is a first…"

"Good," Grayson said, smiling. "I want to be your first at something…" she said, winking at her.

Grayson lowered her head then, kissing Rayden's lips, then she moved to her neck, biting it softly, then sucking and kissing. Next, she moved to Rayden's nipples, her hands touching and caressing. Rayden's muscles rippled and jumped in reaction to the sensations Grayson was causing. When Grayson moved lower Rayden was beyond excited, and she closed her eyes blowing her breath out in a rush. She felt Grayson's lips on her stomach and her hair brushing her thighs…

"Gray…" Rayden moaned, breathing heavily, her body straining. "Gray…" she groaned again as Grayson moved lower.

When Grayson's mouth touched her, Rayden lost all control. She'd never had such a forceful orgasm in her life and Grayson kept touching her making it go on and on. Rayden yelled, gasped, and moaned over and over again. Finally, she dropped her hands to Grayson's shoulders, and pulled her up over her so she could and kiss her deeply.

Rayden shifted their bodies, putting Grayson under her with an almost animal growl in the back of her throat as she kissed Grayson hungrily.

"Oh my God…" Grayson said when their lips parted for a moment. "I think I just woke the wolf…"

"Yes, you did…" Rayden said.

Rayden proceeded to make love to Grayson with both heated passion and barely leashed aggression and excited Grayson beyond anything she'd ever experienced. There was no moment when she was afraid of Rayden, she knew that Rayden would die before hurting her, so her hunger and strength only served to excite her more.

Afterwards they both lay panting. Rayden moved to her back, pulling Grayson over her. The music was still playing in the background and the song changed as they lay there. The song "One and Only" by Adele came on. As Rayden listened to the lyrics, she felt like they were being sung to her. They talked of letting go of doubt and allowing a person into her heart and asking to be considered her "one and only." She knew that she needed to do just that with Grayson.

As the song ended, Rayden looked up into Grayson's eyes, and she saw her life in Grayson's eyes. She shook her head slowly, a look of wonder on her face.

"What?" Grayson asked, seeing the look in Rayden's eyes but not understanding it.

Rayden touched her cheek, her eyes looking directly into Grayson's. "Tsi a-ya-s-ti-gi u-ga-u-hi-u ne-hi," she said softly, her accent very clear.

Grayson smiled at hearing the way Rayden spoke. "What does that mean?" she asked softly.

Rayden smiled. "You called me a warrior once…" she said. "It means that this warrior loves you."

Grayson's eyes widened. "Ray…" she breathed, shaking her head. "I never believed… or thought… oh God, I love you so much…"

Rayden smiled, her eyes lighting up as they crinkled at the corners.

"Say it again," Grayson said.

"In which language?" Rayden asked.

"Both," Grayson said, smiling brightly.

"Tsi a-ya-s-ti-gi u-ga-u-hi-u ne-hi," Rayden said again, leaning close to Grayson's lips. "I love you, Gray…"

Grayson kissed her then, and they kissed for what seemed like hours. Eventually they fell asleep, with Grayson still lying in Rayden's arms.

The next morning Grayson was awake before Rayden. She lay staring down at this incredible woman and still unable to believe that she'd been lucky enough to not only meet her, but to be loved by her. She looked at Rayden's face, so much like the classic pictures of brave American Indian warriors with the strong jawlines and high cheekbones. Rayden was the perfect Cherokee warrior and Grayson loved her. She hadn't fully realized it until Rayden had said it the day before, but when she had, it had clicked in Grayson's head. She loved this woman.

Grayson had been listening to the lyrics of "One and Only" too, and she was thinking that she wanted Rayden to be willing to be her one and only. She didn't want to share Rayden with any other woman. She hadn't been sure how that kind of request would go over though. It was obvious from the way that Marcie had talked about her encounter with Rayden that Rayden wasn't exactly the 'in it for the long haul' kind of lesbian. So when Rayden had told her she loved her, Grayson had realized that she loved Rayden too.

Rayden stirred. Her head was tilted toward the sun streaming through the windows so when she opened them and looked at Grayson, the gold flecks in them were very pronounced.

"Oh my God..." Grayson breathed at seeing her eyes.

"What?" Rayden asked.

"I've never seen those flecks of gold in your eyes practically glow before... wow..." she said, amazed and dazzled by them.

Rayden laughed softly. "My grandfather used to tell me that I'd played in the Oconaluftee so much as a kid that the pyrite in the water just sank into my skin and ended up in my eyes."

Grayson laughed, nodding. "I think he may have been right."

"Mmmm," Rayden murmured as she stretched, running her hand up Grayson's skin as she did.

"Indeed," Grayson said, smiling.

Rayden pulled her down to kiss her, and minutes later they were making love again. It was a nice long weekend.

Chapter 4

Raine eventually made it back to the apartment she shared with Natalia after a few hours of just riding around. She walked inside, kicked the door closed, and just stood looking around. Natalia still wasn't home. She suspected she was afraid to return.

They'd made the apartment really nice, adding color and artwork that they'd picked out together. There were the two recliners that Raine had bought to contribute to the furniture when she'd moved in, not to mention her bedroom furniture. There was the TV and the stereo system they'd bought together. She gritted her teeth as she walked into the bedroom. It smelled like Natalia's perfume, and it killed Raine just little bit more. Forcing herself to ignore everything she was feeling, she walked into the bathroom, stripped off her sweaty workout clothes, and tossed them in the hamper. She got into the shower, washed her hair, and then used the eucalyptus and spearmint body wash, which was supposed to relieve stress. Not surprisingly, it didn't work this time.

After her shower she toweled off her hair and body, and braided her hair; it hung down three inches past her shoulders. She put on clean clothes and her riding boots. She then put a few things into a backpack, and set it down near the apartment door with her gear bag for work.

She sat down straddling the arm of the couch, her feet on the ground, her hands on her knees, waiting. She figured Natalia would be home soon. Her mind ran over the course of the evening. She'd seen the look Natalia had given Dakota; it had been a shocked look and then she'd seen a flood of guilt and she'd known in that instant that something had happened between them. Raine knew that things had been strained with them, but she hadn't felt they were that bad. Dakota's reaction to Natalia's look had been to grin roguishly and shake her head. That had sealed it for Raine. She'd known then that she was right.

Challenging Quinn to a match was just a way for Raine to try and get rid of the tension and fury she was feeling. She'd really wanted to do damage to the newcomer, but hadn't wanted to give Natalia something else to hate her for at that point. Raine had no idea what to do with all the feelings of betrayal, anger, and downright devastation she was feeling. This was her first relationship ever, and she had honestly believed it would last forever. She had no idea how to handle moving forward, but she also knew that she needed to stay calm.

Just then, there was the sound of the key in the lock. Raine looked toward the door and waited.

Natalia had been frantic after Raine left the gym. She'd talked to Jet who'd told her about the confrontation between Cody and Raine. Jet had told her that Raine had driven off at a milder speed afterwards. Natalia had been worried sick, waiting at the gym and hoping that Raine would come back so they could talk. Jazmine had walked into the locker room and seen Natalia sitting on the bench, her body bent over as she cried.

"What happened?" Jazmine had asked her.

Natalia had shaken her head, not wanting to even say the words.

"They're saying you did something with Dakota?" Jazmine had said, her tone gentle.

Natalia had cried harder, nodding her head.

"Oh God…" Jazmine had said, grimacing. "Why?" she had asked, thinking that Raine was so incredibly nice and they had seemed so in love.

"I was so stupid, so stupid…" Natalia had said, her voice strident. "Estoy muriendo… estoy muriendo…" she had repeated over and over again, saying in Spanish that she was dying.

When Raine didn't come back to the gym, she knew she would have to go home and face her.

Natalia walked into the apartment to see Raine sitting on the arm of the couch. She noticed straightaway that Raine had showered, but was dressed to leave again and the hope she'd had that they could talk dimmed significantly.

Natalia put down her gym bag, and saw Raine's backpack and gear bag by the door. She began crying immediately, moving toward Raine but Raine's stony look stopped her from coming too close.

"Complacer…" Natalia whispered. *Please*.

Speaking Spanish was something she often did with Raine, because Raine not only understood Spanish but could speak it fluently as well. It was something they shared, something Natalia hadn't shared with anyone else. It was one of the many things that Natalia loved about Raine.

Raine shook her head slowly, her look despondent as if she too had just realized one more thing they were losing.

"I need to know," Raine said, her tone grim. "It was Dakota, right?"

Natalia considered trying to lie her way out of it, but she didn't know what she'd say.

Raine saw the look on Natalia's face and her eyes narrowed. "Don't even think about lying to me again," she said, her tone low.

Natalia squeezed her eyes shut, shaking her head, her face a mask of anguish.

"I'm sorry Raine… I'm so sorry…" she said, her voice reflecting her devastation.

Raine swallowed against the lump in her throat, feeling sick. She'd known she was right, but Natalia's admission hurt more than she'd realized it could. She nodded, tears in her eyes, her lips pressed together to keep from crying out. She took a gasping breath to try to control her emotions. She stood up and felt her knees weaken. The desire to scream was overwhelming, but she stood quietly, reigning in her emotions so she could speak without yelling.

"I'll start looking for a place in the morning," she said, forcing her voice to sound calm, even if she couldn't keep the devastation out of it.

"Raine, no…" Natalia said, moving toward her again.

Raine pulled her head back, looking away from her. "I can't stay here," she said, her voice a barely audible whisper. Then her light blues looked at Natalia. "I don't want to stay here…" With that she walked past Natalia, picked up her bags and left the apartment, closing the door softly behind her.

Natalia crumpled to the floor and cried.

Outside the apartment, Raine leaned against the door sobbing quietly. She could hear Natalia crying inside the apartment, and she had to steel herself against it. She wanted nothing more than to comfort the woman she loved more than anything, but she couldn't, not now, not when she'd done what she had. After pushing off the door, Raine strode to the stairs, and ran down them and outside. She got onto her bike, and gunned the engine. She had no idea where to go so she just drove around for a couple of hours. Finally, she stopped at a coffee shop, got some water, and sat at one of the tables. She checked her phone and saw numerous texts from friends. There were texts from Natalia too that Raine deleted without reading. She assured her friends that she was still alive, including her boss, Catalina Roché.

A couple of minutes later Cat texted her back, asking where she was.

"At a coffee shop," Raine texted back.

"You don't drink coffee," Cat replied.

"I'm not drinking coffee," Raine replied.

"Where are you staying?"

"Don't know."

"Come to our place," Cat told her.

When Raine didn't answer for a few minutes, she got another text. "That's an order, Agent."

Raine shook her head, sighing. Being friends with your boss definitely had its downside. She arrived at Cat and Jovina's house a half an hour later.

Cat answered the door and straightaway and took Raine in her arms.

"Are you okay?" she asked after she finally let go.

Raine blew her breath out and shook her head dismally.

"Too bad you don't drink," Cat said, leading Raine over to the couch. "You could probably use one right now."

Raine shook her head. "No, it'll just make things worse."

Jovina walked over to Raine and hugged her too, then sat down on the other side of her on the couch.

"Feeling that match with Quinn yet?" Cat asked, with a raised eyebrow.

"Not yet," Raine said, knowing she would soon.

Cat looked pointedly at Raine's arm that already had a nasty bruise on it. She could only imagine where else the kid was bruised. Cat remembered her own match with Quinn, where she'd been determined to prove to the other butches that she could butch it up with the best of them. She'd had bruises for a week. Quinn was a damned good fighter, just not very good at pulling punches fast enough.

"Well, you look like you need some sleep," Jovina said softly. "I've made up the extra bedroom for you."

"Obrigado," Raine said, smiling feebly.

"Your Portuguese is getting good," Jovina told her, smiling.

Raine nodded slowly, looking really tired suddenly.

"Come on," Cat said, moving to stand. "I'll get you settled."

Ten minutes later Cat walked into the master bedroom. Jovina was sitting on the bed reading a book.

"Is she okay?" Jovina asked.

"I don't think I'd call it *okay*," Cat said, as she lay down on the bed next to Jovina and looked up at her. "I think she's completely shell-shocked."

Jovina nodded. "I can understand why."

"I can too," Cat said. "I know exactly how that feels."

Jovina looked down at Cat for a long moment, her look pained. "I know you do," she said softly.

Cat shook her head. "I don't know what the hell Natalia thought she was doing. All you have to do is look at Dakota and know she's a player. Why would she throw away what she has with Raine for that?"

"I don't know," Jovina said, sighing. "I never would have believed it."

"I'm with you there," Cat said, shaking her head. "I thought they were good for the long haul."

"Raine has been working a lot lately," Jovina pointed out.

Cat canted her head slightly, nodding. "Yeah, she has, but she's been putting in a ton of overtime to try and come up with some money for Natalia to put in on the studio."

"Does Natalia know that though?" Jovina asked.

"No," Cat said. "Raine wanted to surprise her..." Her voice trailed off as she thought about it. "Jesus, that would suck... if it happened because of that..."

Jovina nodded, looking sad.

Later that night, Cody and McKenna were in Cody's room. Cody was lying on the bed while McKenna moved around the room putting things into boxes. They were getting ready to move to their own place. Cody had done some packing, but McKenna had been sure that the way Cody packed was going to cause a lot of breakage, so she was repacking things. Cody let her have her way. It was getting late and she was too tired to protest.

"Well that turned into a big mess, huh?" McKenna asked.

Cody made a sound in the back of her throat. "Ya think?" she asked derisively, grinning to take the sting out of her words.

McKenna shook her head. "How did Raine figure it out though?"

"Natalia would suck at poker, babe. She has absolutely no filter on her face."

"And Raine caught on that way?" McKenna asked.

"Raine's a cop, Kenna, she's trained to read people."

McKenna shook her head. "I just feel so awful for them, you know?"

Cody nodded, understanding completely.

"I still can't believe Dakota did that. What is wrong with that girl?" McKenna said contemptuously.

Cody shook her head. "Don't judge her too harshly babe, I could have so easily been her."

McKenna looked over at Cody sharply. "No," she said, shaking her head. "No you couldn't have."

Cody laughed without a hint of humor. "You have no idea…" she said, shaking her head.

"Cody, you have a conscience, she doesn't. That's a big difference right there."

"I didn't always have one, Kenna," Cody said. "And I was learning from the best how not having one helped you get through the shit you had to do to survive."

"Dakota…" McKenna said.

"Yep," Cody said, "but no one saved her. Not like Lyric and Savanna saved me. And believe me, Dakota has been through a lot of shit in her life, so much worse than me."

"Really?" McKenna asked, unable to believe that anyone could have had it worse than Cody, who'd been forced into prostitution by a street gang as a teenager.

"Trust me," Cody said, nodding.

McKenna drew in a deep breath, then expelled it as she nodded.

"Have you checked on her?" she asked Cody then.

"I texted her," Cody said.

"And she said she was okay?" McKenna asked drily.

"Yeah. I know she can say whatever she wants in text, but trust me, till she's ready to talk about it, you don't want me goin' over there."

"Why?" McKenna asked.

"Because Dakota has a tendency to get really physical when she's pissed and she is pushed to talk about things…"

"Physical?" McKenna repeated, knowing there was a reason Cody didn't use the word "violent."

"Uh-huh," Cody said, grinning.

"Like sexually?"

"Yeah," Cody said then.

"Oh my…" McKenna said, clearing her throat.

"You don't get it, I know," Cody said.

"No, can you try to explain it?" McKenna asked, moving to sit on the bed, looking down at Cody.

Cody sighed. "For me, sex was always a power thing… I had the power so I could control the situation… For Dakota sex is the way she handles things. She's pissed off, she gets some poor girl to come until she's half dead. She's feeling powerless, she seduces some rich bitch and humiliates her sexually. It's power to her, but it's a lot more, it's her… currency. It's how she pays for things. It's how she proves her worth, how she keeps her edge…"

"Jesus…" McKenna said her tone shocked. "And I'm guessing she needs that edge."

"Oh yeah," Cody said, "or she folds, and that's not an option for her."

McKenna shook her head, trying to imagine what life must be like for someone like Dakota. She wasn't even able to begin to fathom it in the slightest.

Dakota lay on the bed in her room, staring up at the ceiling, smoking a cigarette. The girl she'd just had sex with scurried around the room picking up her discarded clothing, occasionally glancing over at Dakota. Tilly was the upstairs maid, and she was terrified that Dakota would tell Miss Billings about their tryst and she'd be fired. Dakota hadn't had to make any assurances when she'd encountered the girl in her room cleaning it. Dakota had come up from behind, and started touching her.

At first, Tilly had been frightened, but then she'd succumbed to the sensations Dakota's hands had been creating. She'd heard a great deal about Miss Billings' girlfriend, and she'd actually been hoping to get a chance to sleep with Dakota, but she hadn't expected this, in the middle of the day when she was supposed to be working. Dakota hadn't cared and hadn't stopped. In the end she'd brought her to orgasm so many times she was still feeling weak in the knees. Her boyfriend, Jorge, hadn't better want sex that night because there was no way she could handle anymore that day.

Tilly left the room without a word, sensing easily that Dakota wasn't interested in talking. A minute later Cassandra stormed into the room, slamming the door so hard one of the paintings on the wall fell off shattering the glass.

"You're fucking the help now?" Cassandra raged, having seen a very flustered Tilly leaving Dakota's bedroom.

Dakota grinned, still staring up at the ceiling. "Like you haven't?" she said mildly.

"I don't know what you mean," Cassandra snapped.

Dakota moved to sit up, her slim, naked body on full display. "You're really gonna go with that one, huh?" she asked, her tone snide.

Cassandra strode over to Dakota and slapped her hard. Dakota's head snapped back, and she let out a gasp that sounded like it was somewhere between shock and excitement. When she looked back up at Cassandra, there was blood on her lip.

"Did that help?" Dakota asked.

"Strapping you down and whipping you might begin to help, you ungrateful bitch!" Cassandra snapped.

Dakota irritated her more by grinning. "We've never tried that..." she said, her tone a sexy drawl.

Cassandra's hand whipped out and she raked her nails down Dakota's chest, drawing blood with her talon-like nails. To her shock, Dakota's hand lashed out grabbing her wrist to draw her hand away from her chest as she hissed in pain. Cassandra tried to pull her hand away from Dakota's grasp but she tightened her grip. Cassandra tried to hit Dakota with her other hand, and Dakota grabbed that wrist as well, kneeling up on the bed, still holding Cassandra's wrists. Cassandra fought her hold, but Dakota was stronger than she looked, and she increased the pressure to the point that Cassandra cried out.

"You're hurting me!" Cassandra snapped.

"And if I let you go, you're likely to hurt me again, so, here we are," Dakota said, her tone matter of fact.

"I'll call the police!" Cassandra snapped.

"And tell them what? That you lost control of your boi toy and she beat you up?"

"Exactly!"

"Uh, yeah, who's bleedin' here?" Dakota said, giving her a wry grin.

"You think they'll believe you?" Cassandra said, her tone snide. "Some little street whore?"

Dakota narrowed her eyes at Cassandra. "Watch your mouth, Cass..." she said, her tone low in warning.

"Or what?" Cassandra jeered. "You'll do what, Dakota?" she asked, becoming really full of herself.

"You don't want to find out," Dakota said, her tone dead serious now.

Cassandra laughed a harsh nasty sound. "Am I supposed to be afraid of you, Dakota?"

"You might want to be..."

"I'm only afraid you'll fuck all of the help and then I'll have to hire more," Cassandra snapped.

Dakota shoved her away then, and Cassandra stumbled into the dresser near the door and fell to the floor. Dakota lay back on the bed, breathing heavily as she tried to reign in her temper. She had her eyes closed in an effort to force away the dark thoughts she was having at that point. That's why she was truly surprised when she felt a sharp burning pain rake down the underside of her right forearm. She felt Cassandra over her then, pressing against her, her hand clamped over Dakota's wrist, holding it down with her weight. As she opened her eyes she saw the shard of glass Cassandra had picked up from the floor and was raking down her arm.

Dakota yelled in pain as the glass dug deeper into her arm. She could see Cassandra was excited by it. Using her left arm, Dakota tried to shove her away, but Cassandra worked out to try and stay young, so she was able to grab Dakota's arm with her hand and force it above her head.

"Get the fuck off me!" Dakota yelled, bucking to dislodge Cassandra.

She felt Cassandra moving against her body, and knew that she was getting off on hurting her. She went into survival mode then. Yanking her left arm out of Cassandra's grasp, she put it to Cassandra's throat. Cassandra had gotten the piece of glass almost down to her mid-forearm, so Dakota was able to shift her arm painfully against the glass to grab Cassandra's wrist. By wrapping her left leg around Cassandra's and using every ounce of strength she had, she was able to force Cassandra over on her back. Keeping her forearm at Cassandra's throat, she lay over her, her eyes burning points as she stared down at her. Cassandra was panting at this point, she was so excited. Dakota curled her lips in disgust. She shook her right arm, dislodging the piece of glass, and heard it clatter to the floor. She then reached down between them, her blood smearing over Cassandra's white suit, yanked up Cassandra's skirt, and shoved her fingers inside Cassandra as roughly as she could. She repeated the action until Cassandra screamed and grasped in her orgasm.

Afterwards Dakota moved off her, rolling to her back, feeling disgusted with both herself and Cassandra. She knew their relationship had just taken an extremely dangerous turn. She'd always thought that Cassandra had some kink to her. There'd been a few times when she'd gotten excessively rough, but never this crazy. Her arm was throbbing wildly and she could feel the blood still flowing from the long cut.

"This suit is Chanel!" Cassandra exclaimed when she saw the blood on it.

"You're fuckin' kiddin' me right now, right?" Dakota said harshly.

Cassandra chuckled. "I guess it was worth it," she said as she got off the bed.

Dakota closed her eyes, shaking her head. She heard Cassandra leave the room then. She grabbed one of the pillows on the bed and yanked off the pillowcase, some ridiculously expensive thread count Egyptian cotton bullshit, and wrapped it around her arm to try and stop the bleeding. After a few minutes she got up off the bed, walked into the bathroom, and looked in the mirror. She had a nasty cut on her lip and there were nail marks from her shoulder halfway down her chest. She carefully unwrapped the pillowcase, seeing that the cut was about three inches long and blood still seeped out. She found an ace bandage in a cabinet and wrapped it tightly around her arm, hoping the pressure would stop the bleeding.

***

Cat knocked on the door to the room Raine was staying in.

"How's it going in here?" Cat asked.

It had been a couple of days since the incident at the gym. Raine had stayed in the room for the most part. Cat had noticed that the door was open, so she'd decided to check in on the girl.

"Hey," Raine said. She was sitting on the bed with her knees up to her chest and her arms wrapped around them.

Cat walked over to the bed and sat down next to her.

"How are you doing?"

Raine shrugged, swallowing convulsively.

"Have you talked to her?" Cat asked.

"What is there to say?" Raine asked, sounding depressed.

"There could be a lot to say," Cat said, her eyes searching Raine's.

"Like?"

"Like asking why she did what she did."

"What difference is that going to make?"

Cat blew her breath out. "It could make no difference at all, or it could make a world of difference."

"How?" Cat looked back at Raine and suddenly remembered that Natalia was the first person Raine had ever dated, had ever had sex with, all of it. She really had no clue how this kind of thing worked.

"Okay, look," Cat said, looking over at Raine. "My ex cheated on me too, and believe me, we'd been through a lot of shit together and I was really in love with her."

"What did you do?" Raine asked.

"Well, in my case the circumstances of her cheating were really bad, and basically she'd been more or less planning it for a while before she actually did it... and that's what made it impossible for me to forgive her completely. There was intent there, she knew what she was doing, and she did it anyway..."

Cat let her voice trail off, seeing Raine's mind churning.

"So you're saying that maybe if the circumstances aren't as bad then I might want to forgive her?"

"I'm saying it's something to consider, unless you're really done..." Cat said gently. "And it's okay if you are, Raine, don't misunderstand me. I'm not telling you what you should do. This is something you need to decide for yourself. I'm just saying that sometimes circumstances aren't really as bad as they seem, you know?"

Raine nodded, looking pensive.

"So is that what broke you and your ex up? Her cheating?"

Cat chuckled. "Well it should have been, since she did it again about a year later… but I don't learn too quickly, apparently."

***

The day after the incident with Cassandra, Dakota was outside on the driveway, listening to music, smoking, and washing the Bugatti. Jazmine drove up in Rayden's Viper; she'd borrowed it to make the meeting with Cassandra. As she got out of the Viper, she heard Dakota whistle.

"Was that for me, or for the car?" Jazmine asked, grinning.

"It's a toss-up," Dakota said, winking at her. "You do look pretty damned good today…" she said, her voice trailing off as she grinned roguishly.

"Well, thanks," Jazmine said, smiling. Then she saw the scratches, split lip, and the bandage on Dakota's arm. "Oh my god, what happened?" she asked her tone aghast.

Dakota grinned. "Long story."

"It wasn't Raine…" Jazmine asked.

"No," Dakota said, shaking her head and making a face.

"Okay…" Jazmine said, hoping that Dakota was telling her the truth.

"Uh, Cassandra's not back yet," Dakota said, rolling her eyes. "I never get why she does this shit…"

"It's okay," Jazmine said. "I'll just wait."

Dakota started rinsing the car, shaking her head.

"What?" Jazmine asked, moving to sit on the raised curb of one of the planters.

"It just pisses me off the way she treats people, like she's too important to show up to her own shit."

"It's no big deal, Dakota," Jazmine said, shrugging.

Dakota didn't say anything else, just continuing to wash the car. They were both quiet for a while. Rock music played and the song "Believe" by Breaking Benjamin came on. Dakota turned it up, it was a hard driving song, and Dakota sang every word. The words were angry and harsh.

Jazmine watched Dakota as she sang, and she started to really wonder what drove this young woman. She could see that there was some serious emotional damage going on there. It made Jazmine want to ask questions, but she guessed that Dakota wasn't likely to answer any of them.

"So how did you meet Cassandra?" Jazmine asked.

Dakota glanced over at her, turning the music down a little bit. She grinned.

"Why you looking for a sugar mama?" Dakota asked.

"Uh," Jazmine stammered, "no… Is that what she is?"

A sardonic grin spread on Dakota's face, her look telling Jazmine she was rather dumb to even ask that question.

"Oh... I... oh..." Jazmine stammered.

Dakota chuckled. "Don't worry about it. I don't think I'm completely insulted."

"So you don't love her..." Jazmine said.

"Oh God no," Dakota said, her tone aghast

"So why are you with her?"

"Uh, she pays the bills," Dakota said, gesturing to the car and the mansion behind her.

"That's all?" Jazmine asked.

Dakota smiled sardonically as the door in the garage opened. "Nah, the bar service is really good too," she said, holding out her hand.

A dark-haired girl in a tight maid's uniform with a really short skirt and high heels walked out and handed Dakota a beer.

"Thanks," she said, grinning at the girl.

"Mmm hmmm..." the girl murmured, her look seductive.

Dakota watched her walk back into the house, biting her lip lasciviously.

"Seriously?" Jazmine asked.

Dakota glanced over at her, seeing her shocked look and she laughed out loud.

"Man you need to relax, Jaz... ya really do."

"Uh-huh," Jazmine said, shaking her head and rolling her eyes.

After a few minutes she looked over at Dakota. "So is that thing fast?"

"Oh yeah… she's really fast…" Dakota said, rubbing the towel over the car's surface lovingly. "You should come for a ride sometime…" she said, winking.

"I should huh?" Jazmine asked.

"Yeah…" Dakota said, her eyes sparkling mischievously. "And I'll give you a ride in the car too."

"Oh my God, you are so bad!" Jazmine said, shaking her head.

"No, not really," Dakota said, her tone insinuating. "I'm told I'm really good."

"I'll just bet you are…" Jazmine said. Her eyes narrowed as she shook her head.

The next day Dakota had called Cody asking if she could get together with her. Cody had agreed. Dakota had pulled up in the Bugatti outside the house and told her to get in.

"Jesus, Dak, what happened?" Cody asked, seeing the scratches and cut lip first. "Did Raine catch up to you?"

Dakota laughed. "Fuck, why does everyone think that? No, this wasn't her."

"Who was it?" Cody asked.

Dakota grinned. "You know how I am…" she said shrugging.

"This was sex related?" Cody asked, her tone cynical.

"In a way, yeah," Dakota said, reaching up to rub the bridge of her nose.

"In what way, Dak?" Cody asked, narrowing her eyes. "Did Cassandra do that?"

Dakota looked considering for a long moment, then she nodded, her mouth twisted in a derisive grin.

"Why?" Cody asked.

"Well, she kinda caught me screwing one of the help..." Dakota said, not sounding the least bit ashamed of herself.

"Okay, I can see that pissing her off, but that doesn't give her the right to do that," Cody said, gesturing to Dakota's injuries. "That's physical abuse, Dak, I could arrest her ass for that," she said, sounding every bit the cop at that moment.

"Technically, there was sex involved," Dakota said.

"Yeah?" Cody snapped. "Did you get off, or just her?"

Dakota widened her eyes at that question, then a lopsided grin pulled at her lips.

"That's fucking crazy, Dak!" Cody exclaimed.

"Holy hell, Cody, relax, I'm not filing any kind of charges officer, so friggin' relax," she said, reaching over to pat Cody on the leg.

Unfortunately, that's when Cody caught sight of the cut on Dakota's arm. She grabbed Dakota's arm before she could pull it back.

"Son of a bitch... Dak!" Cody yelled. "What the fuck did she do to you? I'll fucking arrest the bitch myself..."

"No! Stop it, okay?" Dakota snapped. "This is my business and it's not what I wanted to talk to you about, so just drop it."

Cody blew her breath out, still seething that Cassandra Billings had done that much damage to Dakota.

"Fine, what did you want to talk to me about?" Cody asked.

"I want to talk to Raine," Dakota said.

"No," Cody said, shaking her head.

"Jesus fucking Christ, Cody, will you stop trying to fucking protect me, I can take care of myself. I just need you to tell me when she's in your building, that's all."

"No, Dakota, you don't need to do that, okay? I think you have enough damage right now, you don't need more."

Dakota blew her breath out, her lips twitching with the effort to control her temper. She flexed her hands on the steering wheel, moving her neck around to stretch it.

"I don't need you to mother me, Cody, I just need you to get me that info, okay?"

Cody looked over at her recognizing Dakota's fury. She also knew that she was pushing her luck with the woman's volatile personality. She'd seen Dakota beat the living shit out of another girl for smacking Cody once, so she knew Dakota had a nasty violent streak when her temper was ignited. She was currently sitting in a fast car and Dakota was hitting 150 at that point.

"Okay, okay, I'll get you the information, Jesus! Slow the fuck down!" Cody yelled.

"Good," Dakota said, taking her foot off the gas.

"But I want to be there," Cody added.

"Cody…" Dakota said. "No, this is my shit… I need to deal with it."

"And I'll let you deal with it, but I'm going to be there," Cody said.

"No, you're not."

"Then I'm not going to help you."

"Fucking A Cody! You don't get it, I feel like shit… I need to get this out of me…" Dakota said looking exasperated. "If she kicks the shit out of me so be it, but I can't keep living with it…"

Cody looked back at Dakota. "What would you say to her?"

"I'd fucking apologize first of all, and I'd tell her that Natalia didn't start it, it was all me… I was the dumbass… I don't know, I just know I need to talk to her and tell her how sorry I am and what happens, happens."

"I don't like it, Dak… if she's still pissed…"

"She has every right to be, Cody. I fucked with her girlfriend, and I knew they were together and I did it anyway… so I need to take whatever she dishes out so I can fucking move on from here… Fuck!" she yelled. "I hate this feeling… I just want it out of me…"

Cody grinned. "It's called a conscience, Dak… It seems like yours is finally growing in…"

"That's not fucking funny Cody," Dakota snapped. "Who the fuck wants one of those? Why the fuck would you want one?"

Cody chuckled. "It's the human condition, most people are born with one."

"Yeah, well, it's a damned manufacturing flaw and someone outta fix it," Dakota said, grinning.

"I'll let Mother Nature know," Cody said, grinning. "And I'll get you the info you want."

"And?" Dakota asked.

"And I'll stay out of it," Cody said, not looking pleased with that last part. "Now give me your fucking arm, I want to see it."

Dakota blew her breath out, she'd won at least one round. She put her arm out, underside up. "Jesus, Dak, this is deep…" she said.

"I know, it bled like a motherfucker too," Dakota said, grinning.

"You could have bled out, this is the way people commit suicide you know…" Cody said, then gave Dakota a sidelong look. "You didn't…"

"Fuck no!" Dakota said. "I don't do that, you know me, I always land on my feet."

Cody blew her breath out, nodding. "Yeah, I know."

As Dakota drove them back to Cody's moms' house she let the 1200 horses under the hood of the Bugatti run free a bit. The Queensrÿche song "Spreading the Disease" came on the stereo and Dakota cranked the sound. She and Cody both sang the words to it. It seemed to fit their lives pretty well. The lyrics talked about using drugs to motivate a person to do anything. It also talked about using sex for power. They both knew a lot about that.

"You like Queensrÿche?" Dakota asked Cody.

"Yeah," Cody said, grinning. "Lyric, one of my moms, introduced me to them, in fact Operation Mindcrime was the first album she gave me."

"Cool, need to meet this woman," Dakota said grinning.

"Come into the house," Cody said, as they pulled up outside.

Dakota considered for a moment, then she nodded.

They both got out of the car, and Cody walked up to the front door, opened it, and led Dakota inside. Dakota admired the nice house; Cody really had done well for herself. She followed Cody through the house and then out to the back patio.

A blond sat out on the patio, smoking a cigarette and reading a sheaf of papers in her hand. As Cody walked out, the woman looked up, her blue eyes narrowing slightly when she looked at Dakota. She dropped a booted foot from the chair it had been resting on and stood up.

"Mom, this is Dakota Blair. Dak, this is one of my moms, Lyric," Cody said, smiling proudly.

Lyric looked at Dakota, extending her hand.

Dakota grinned, and took Lyric's extended hand. She shook it, looking directly back into the older woman's eyes.

"Cody tells me you got her into Queensrÿche," Dakota said.

"Among other bands," Lyric said, grinning and glancing at Cody.

"Well, good call on Mindcrime," Dakota said.

Lyric nodded. "Yeah, seemed to fit... ya know?"

"Oh, I know," Dakota said, nodding.

Lyric nodded, her look searching.

"Babe, I don't know where... Oh, hi?" said a redhead from the door.

Cody turned. "That's my other mom, Savanna. Mom this is Dakota."

"Dakota," Savanna said, stepping toward her. Her eyes connected with Lyric's for a moment and then looking back at Dakota. "It's good to meet you. Cody's told us... well, limited stuff about you. Oh my God what happened to your arm?" she asked, her tone horrified.

Dakota chuckled. "That's where Cody got that mother tone from..." she said, grinning.

"This needs stitches, Dakota…" Savanna said, gently touching her arm.

"Its fine," Dakota said, feeling herself emotionally weaken a bit.

"I've got a medical degree, babe. I assure you it's not fine," Savanna said, her tone as gentle as her touch.

Dakota was at a loss for words. She glanced helplessly at Cody and saw that her friend was suppressing a grin, her eyes shining in amusement. Dakota shook her head, as if trying to shake away the warm fuzzy feelings that were threatening to invade her heart. It was no wonder Cody had grown a big fat conscience!

"Mom, can you fix it?" Cody asked, knowing that Dakota wouldn't go to a hospital.

"Well, this really should be looked at by a doctor," Savanna said.

"You said you have a medical degree…" Dakota said her tone suspicious.

"I do," Savanna said.

"She does," Lyric said at the same time.

"I have it because I'm a psychologist, I don't practice medicine," Savanna said, her tone still soft.

"But you could do it, right Mom? You've fixed me up before," Cody said, her look at Savanna pointed.

Savanna received the message, almost telepathically.

"Sure, of course I can," Savanna said, smiling at Dakota.

"It's really okay," Dakota said suddenly anxious to get out of there.

"Sit, relax, it won't take a minute," Savanna said, glancing at Cody, and canting her head toward the house.

"Got it," Cody said, and she headed inside.

She came back a couple of minutes later with a rather imposing looking first aid kit. By this time, Lyric and Savanna had cajoled and harassed Dakota into a chair.

"Holy hell…" Dakota said, when she saw the first aid kit.

"My girls get into a lot of scrapes," Savanna said, grinning.

"I guess…" Dakota said, rolling her eyes.

Savanna started cleaning the cut, and her touch was extremely gentle, so much so that Dakota started thinking that Lyric was one lucky woman. She shook her head, doing her best to focus on the task at hand.

"How did this happen?" Savanna asked conversationally.

"She got attacked by a rampaging—" Cody started to say.

"Piece of glass," Dakota snapped, interrupting Cody.

"Jesus, where do you live that glass attacks?" Lyric asked mockingly, raising an eyebrow.

"The Valley… So…" Dakota said, grinning.

"Aw," Lyric said, grinning too.

"Are those scratch marks?" Savanna asked, then peered at Dakota's lip. "Were you in a fight?"

Dakota opened and closed her mouth considering the question. "Sort of?" she finally said.

Once again, Lyric and Savanna exchanged a look, and then Savanna looked over at Cody who was looking pointedly heavenward.

"Well, all of those need to be tended to…" Savanna said.

"Mom," Cody said, chuckling, "don't give her too much grief, she'll never come back."

Savanna looked back at Dakota. "You don't like people taking care of you either, huh?"

Dakota looked back at Savanna, not sure what to say. Finally, she just shook her head. "Been doing it for myself for too long now."

Savanna grimaced, but nodded. "Cody was the same way when she first came to my house."

"Then I met Lyric," Cody said, smiling.

Lyric smiled fondly. "Yeah, that's when I met both you and your mom. I'd consider that a fairly lucky day."

Savanna smiled, chuckling.

Dakota looked at the three of them, and felt an ache in her heart. The part of her that she rarely recognized wished she'd had a family. One like this one would have been nice. She looked away for a few minutes, forcing her emotions back.

Cody caught the movement and knew that Dakota was feeling affected by Savanna and Lyric. She was happy to see that Dakota still recognized good people when she met them. A little while later Savanna had Dakota's wound properly closed with butterfly closures.

"This way, maybe you won't scar," Savanna said, smiling.

She'd seen other scars on Dakota's arms, one fresh wound from what looked like a cigarette. It broke her heart a little bit for the girl. She truly hoped that Cody could influence Dakota. It seemed like Dakota needed a friend, and people who loved her.

That night Rayden asked Jazmine about the meeting she'd had with Cassandra that afternoon.

"How'd it go?" Rayden asked, laying down on the bed, and leaning her head on her fist.

"Cassandra never showed up," Jazmine said, sitting down on the bed facing Rayden. "I ended up talking to Dakota for an hour and then finally gave up."

"How's Dakota doing?" Rayden asked.

"Oh, she seems fine, except it looked like she'd been in a fight. She had scratches, a split lip, and a bandage on her arm."

"Did you ask her about it?" Rayden asked, rolling to her back and putting her head on the pillows.

"Of course I did," Jazmine said, moving to lie next to Rayden, and putting her hand on Rayden's stomach.

"And?"

"And she said it was a long story and that no it wasn't Raine," Jazmine said, shaking her head. "I don't know, but she was definitely acting like herself."

"What does that mean?" Rayden asked, her tone surprised.

"I mean she was flirting with the maid, she even made a pass at me," Jazmine said, rolling eyes.

"She did, huh?" Rayden said, grinning.

"Yeah, I think that girl would flirt with a tree stump if she thought it was female…" Jazmine said, grinning.

"Oh, you're far from that, babe," Rayden said, smiling. "Maybe you should take her up on it."

"What?" Jazmine asked her look surprised.

"I'm just saying…" Rayden said, seeing Jazmine's look. "You said you aren't sure you're really excited by women…"

"Except for you," Jazmine said her look still surprised.

"Except for me," Rayden added. "So maybe you should give someone else like Dakota a shot to see if they do it for you."

Jazmine looked back at Rayden, she was clearly hurt by the suggestion. Rayden grimaced.

"I'm sorry, babe, I'm not saying… I'm just saying that someone like Dakota isn't going to be a relationship, she's going to be a hot one-nighter and maybe that's what you need to see if you're…" Rayden's voice trailed off as she saw that she was only upsetting Jazmine more.

"And I'm shutting the fuck up now…" Rayden said, moving to kiss Jazmine's lips, trying to take the hurt out of her eyes. "I'm sorry, honey… I'm sorry…" Rayden whispered against her lips.

Jazmine put her arms around Rayden's neck and buried her head against Rayden's shoulder. She hated this feeling of rejection by Rayden. In her heart she knew that she'd never replace Grayson in Rayden's heart. She knew that Grayson had completely possessed Rayden's heart and that in death she hadn't released that hold. It was something Jazmine continually reminded herself, trying desperately to keep from falling in love with Rayden again.

***

Raine walked out of the DOJ building on Friday and was shocked to see Dakota sitting on the hood of an extremely expensive-looking sports car, smoking a cigarette. Raine's lips twitched in irritation, but she turned to walk toward the parking lot.

"Raine, wait!" Dakota said, sliding off the hood and walking toward the other woman.

Raine turned, her blue eyes narrowed. "What do you want?" she asked, her tone even.

Dakota held up her hands in a kind of calming gesture. "I just want to talk to you for a minute, okay?"

Raine looked back at her for a long moment. Finally, she dropped her gear bag on the ground between them, with her lips pursed in irritation.

"Talk," Raine said, her tone saying that Dakota better hurry before she changed her mind.

"First of all I'm sorry," Dakota said. "What I did... it was fucked up, and I'm really sorry."

Raine's look remained unchanged, but her eyes flickered with mild surprise.

"You need to know that Natalia didn't initiate what happened. That was me, it was all me."

"Why?" Raine asked simply.

Dakota blew her breath out, shaking her head. "I don't know... Sometimes I just get on autopilot and I don't stop and think about what I'm doing or to who... It was a stupid ass thing to do, and I really am sorry."

Raine nodded slowly. "You said she didn't initiate it," she said then, her voice tentative, her look pensive. "You didn't force her, did you?" she asked, her tone taking on a dangerous edge.

Dakota was a bit stunned. For someone who looked so easy going and gentle, Raine clearly had a darker side that she was sure she didn't want to see.

"No," Dakota said. "No, no matter what everyone thinks of me, I'd never do that."

"And she didn't tell you to stop," Raine said. It wasn't a question.

"No," Dakota said, "but she was really drunk Raine, and after… she was really upset… That's why I sent you to her, I knew she needed you."

Raine just stared at Dakota, her lips pursed in disgust. "You knew she was with me."

"Yeah, I did," Dakota said, "and I know I really fucked up your relationship, and that's why I feel like shit. I'm really sorry… if you want to deck me, I'd get it," Dakota said, her look indicating that she meant it.

"Yeah, it was a pretty lousy thing to do," Raine agreed, "and you really did screw things up with us. I don't even know where to go with this now."

Dakota nodded, wanting to let Raine have her say.

Cody says you had kind of a shit childhood too," Raine said, shocking Dakota with the sudden change in topic.

Dakota looked back at Raine, then shook her head. "That's got nothing to do with this."

"I grew up in the foster system in New York," Raine said, her tone even. "So I get thinking you gotta prove something to everyone."

Dakota narrowed her eyes. "I don't have to prove anything to anyone," she practically growled.

"No?" Raine asked, her tone derisive. "You just thought you'd fuck someone else's girl and that wouldn't send a message?"

Dakota stared back at Raine, her mouth slightly open. "What message do you think I was trying to send?" she asked, honestly wanting to know, but not willing to show any more weakness than she already had.

Raine curled her lip in a sardonic grin. "The message of *I can take what you have, so what you have isn't what you think.*"

Dakota heard the words, and they struck a nerve. She had to grit her teeth to keep from making a nasty comment in response just to get back some of her own. Raine watched as Dakota's jaw jumped and she knew that she was itching to respond. The fact that she didn't, told Raine that maybe, just maybe, Dakota had learned something. She sincerely hoped that she had. She couldn't begin to fathom a way out of the pit her emotions were in, and Dakota needed to be aware of the damage she'd caused. It was also important to understand the repercussions her actions could have if she pulled that particular stunt again.

"You need to watch who you put your hands on if you're going to be around this group," Raine told Dakota. "If you'd made this same mistake with someone else's girl, like Quinn or Jet, you'd have been bleeding by now."

Dakota nodded, looking belligerent. "And you don't want to take your shot?" she asked, her voice challenging.

Raine gave her a measuring look, then canted her head slightly. "Would it make you feel better?"

Dakota gave a short laugh, her grin wry. "Actually I think somehow it would."

Raine's lips curled in a sarcastic grin. "Then no," she said, her eyes sparkling with pointed meaning. The last thing she wanted to do at that point was to make Dakota feel better.

Dakota laughed shaking her head. "Point made."

Raine nodded, leaning down to pick up her gear bag.

"Hey," Dakota said, putting her hand out to stop Raine's movement, "something you should know…"

"What?"

"Natalia is pulling out of the studio deal," Dakota said, her look chagrinned.

"She is?" Raine asked, surprised.

"Yeah," Dakota said, her lips twitching in a grimace. "Doesn't want to be around me, I guess."

Raine narrowed her eyes as she nodded. "Okay, thanks."

Dakota nodded. "No problem."

Chapter 5

Rayden had been on shift for forty-eight hours and was dead on her feet. She took a shower, dried off, and braided her hair. She'd just pulled on boy short and a tank top to sleep in when she heard the door to the barracks open. At that point she was alone; there were very few women still at the base, so she was in the smallest barracks building by herself with no one else assigned to it.

"Ray?" came Grayson's tentative query.

"Here babe," Rayden said, smiling.

Grayson walked around the corner of the room and Rayden could see immediately that she was crying. The smaller woman threw herself into Rayden's arms.

"Woah…" Rayden said, catching Grayson in a hug. "What is it, babe?"

Grayson shook her head miserably, her hands grasping at Rayden's shoulders, her face buried against Rayden's shirt. Rayden held her, closing her eyes tiredly, wondering if it was possible to sleep standing up. She waited for Grayson to calm down enough to tell her what was going on. Inclining her head, she kissed Grayson's temple.

"You ready to tell me yet?" she asked gently.

Grayson nodded, and Rayden pulled Grayson down to sit next to her on her bunk. She placed Grayson's hands securely in hers for comfort. Grayson looked down at their hands, tears dropping on them as she did.

"I got my orders today..." she said, her voice tremulous.

Rayden winced, having thought that might be the problem. She knew that Grayson had just finished her tour and that she was likely to get new orders soon. They'd both hoped that Grayson would get another tour in Iraq. Apparently, that was not the case.

"Okay..." Rayden said, her tone leading when Grayson didn't continue.

Grayson looked up at her, her slate-blue eyes more gray than blue at that point.

"They're sending me back to the States..." she said, looking devastated.

Rayden drew her breath in, expelling it slowly as she nodded. "Okay."

Grayson's lips trembled. "I don't want to go..." she said.

Rayden smiled ruefully. "I don't think you get a choice here, babe..."

Grayson blew her breath out in a huff. "I know, Goddamned military, I hate this!"

Rayden smiled consoled by the fact that Grayson was so upset at leaving.

"If it wasn't for the military we probably would never have met, you know..." Rayden said.

Grayson sniffed and smiled weakly. "Okay, maybe I don't totally hate them then."

"It'll be okay, babe… You know going home is supposed to be a good thing."

Grayson gave her a foul look. "Not in this case," she said, her tone indignant.

A grin tugged at Rayden's lips, and Grayson saw it. "Don't you dare…" Grayson said, narrowing her eyes.

Rayden laughed instead. "Sorry, babe, you're just really cute right now."

"I am not!" Grayson said, reaching up to wipe at her eyes, careful not to mess up her makeup.

"You really are," Rayden said, smiling lovingly at her.

Grayson blew her breath out, shaking her head. "You're not going to make me feel better about this," she said. "So stop trying."

Rayden pressed her lips together, her eyes still dancing in amusement.

"Seriously, babe, we'll figure it out, okay?" Rayden said, her tone serious.

"How?" Grayson asked doubtfully.

"I don't know, there's email, Skype, texts," Rayden said.

Grayson curled her lips in derision. "It's not the same thing and you know that."

"Yeah, I know that," Rayden said, nodding, "but that's gonna be our only option at this point."

"How much longer is your tour?" Grayson asked then.

Rayden looked pensive for a moment. "About six months," she said grimacing.

Grayson blew her breath out. "And even then, you'll be more likely to stay, because you're in a combat unit," she said, her tone bitter.

Rayden nodded looking resigned. Grayson was right about that, she'd already been in the Middle East for three years.

Grayson put her head down, resting her forehead against Rayden's chest, with her hands at Rayden's waist. Rayden leaned down, kissing her head, her hands on Grayson's arms. They sat that way for a while, each lost in their own thoughts and concerns.

In Grayson's mind she could see what would happen. They'd email back and forth at first, and then little by little the emails would taper off, and eventually just stop. It was the last thing she wanted. She loved this woman so deeply, and she couldn't figure out how they could stay together. And she worried that, in truth, Rayden was relieved by her getting sent home, so she could go back to being with any woman she wanted whenever she wanted to, and that Grayson was cramping her style.

"So when do you have to go?" Rayden asked softly.

"A week from tomorrow," Grayson said, trying not to think that Rayden was anxious to see her go so she could move on to the next woman.

Rayden drew in another deep breath, and blew it out. Grayson didn't see the flash of anguish in Rayden's eyes because her head was still down.

"Can you get a couple of days away before then?" Rayden asked.

Grayson was silent for a moment, but then nodded.

"Good," Rayden said smiling, "tell me when and I'll reserve a room."

"Okay," Grayson said.

They sat silently for a while again, and when Grayson looked up at Rayden, she suddenly saw how tired she looked.

"Oh, God, Ray... I'm sorry, you were just going to sleep, weren't you? I'm sorry, I know you've been on that killer shift. Damn, I'm sorry, I'm keeping you up..."

"It's okay," Rayden said, suddenly feeling everything catching up to her. "When are you on again?" "I've got another twelve hours till my next shift," Grayson said. "When are you back on?"

Rayden looked at her watch. "Oh, in about five..." she said, her voice trailing off as she grinned.

"Oh God! Okay, go to sleep," Grayson said, starting to get up.

Rayden's hand on her arm stopped her and she lay back on her bunk, pulling Grayson down with her.

"Stay here with me," Rayden said tiredly.

Grayson smiled, wanting nothing more than to do just that. She turned over on her side, with her back to Rayden, and Rayden slid her arms around her, holding her and curling her body around Grayson's. She was asleep a minute later, and Grayson could feel her breath on her cheek. Grayson put her arms over Rayden's, wanting to absorb the feeling of Rayden's body so close to hers, wanting to hold on to that feeling. She fell asleep with tears on her cheeks.

As it turned out, the two days Grayson was able to get leave were the last two days she was going to be in Iraq. Rayden told her to meet her at the hotel they'd been to before and gave her the room number. When Grayson got there that evening, there were candles lit and music playing

133

in the room. Rayden had ordered room service, including champagne. They had dinner and talked, and then moved to the bedroom where they made love for hours. They slept for a couple of hours, but then woke and made love again, ordering breakfast at 5 a.m.

They spent that day walking around Baghdad, being careful not to touch too much, because they didn't want to offend the locals. They did some shopping, and had lunch at a street vendor. Then went back to the hotel and made love again. That night they lay together, talking and just trying to hold onto every moment they had.

Music was playing in the room, and Adele's "All I Ask" came on. The words just seemed so poignant at that point, it was hard not to be affected by them. The words talked about pretending that they didn't know what was coming next for them, and asked if they could just do what lovers did for one more night. It was heartbreaking.

As she listened to the music, Grayson became upset by the prospect that they were running out of time. They'd talked about the ways that they would communicate, but Grayson was still convinced that it would only be short term.

"I want you to do something for me," Rayden said her look pointed.

"What?" Grayson asked, sniffling.

They were lying on the bed facing each other. Rayden reached up, unclasping the chain she wore around her neck, a chain she wore all time, unless she was in full uniform. On the chain hung a pendant. Rayden had told Grayson at one point that her grandfather had given her the pendant years before. Rayden talked about her grandfather a lot, it was obvious she loved him a great deal, and that he was very important to her.

"I want you to keep this for me," Rayden said, putting the chain around Grayson's neck.

"What?" Grayson asked shocked. "Your grandfather gave you this, I can't do that, Ray..." she said, reaching up to try and stop Rayden from putting it on her.

The look on Rayden's face stopped her. "I just want you to keep it, until I can come get it back from you, okay?" Rayden said, her look pointed.

Grayson was stunned. It was Rayden's way of telling her that she was serious about them, and that she intended to hold on to their connection.

"Ray..." Grayson breathed, tears in her eyes.

"We will see each other again, Gray," Rayden said, her eyes staring directly into Grayson's. "I'll make sure of it."

Grayson burst into tears then and put her head down on Rayden's shoulder to cry. Rayden's arms went around her, pulling her close and holding her.

"I hate this, I hate this, I hate this..." Grayson said, her voice desperately sad.

"I know, babe, I hate it too," Rayden said, "but we'll be okay." She pulled back, looking down at Grayson. "You believe that don't you?"

Grayson looked up at her, reaching up to touch the pendant.

"What symbol is this again?" Grayson asked.

Rayden smiled. "It's the Tsalagi symbol for peace."

It was a round pendant of black onyx with the symbol carved into the center and filled in with silver. The symbol itself looked like a pool with three curved ridges on four sides and an elongated S shape through the center.

Holding the pendant, between her thumb and forefinger, Grayson looked up at Rayden. "Yes I believe we'll be okay," she said, her tone sure.

"Good," Rayden said, smiling, her eyes crinkling at the corners. "I love you."

Grayson bit her lip, her eyes shining with unshed tears. "I love you."

All too soon it was time for Rayden to drive her back to the base and take her to the flight line where the transport carrier waited. They threw caution to the wind and embraced and kissed right there on the flight line, drawing whistles and cat calls from many of the service men and women on the tarmac. Grayson walked up the ramp, turning back to see Rayden standing watching her. Rayden was wearing her BDUs, and Grayson knew she'd always picture Rayden with her dark hair, dark skin in her BDUs, standing pretty close to being at attention, watching her leave.

Grayson was sure her heart was breaking as she found her seat and stowed her gear. Every fiber of her being wanted to run back down the ramp into Rayden's arms and never let go, but she knew that wasn't possible. She took slow deep breaths to try and calm her heart and nerves as the plane taxied for take-off. In the darkest part of her heart, she was afraid things would never be the same between them again.

Cody called Dakota a couple of days after she'd been to the house.

"Hey," Dakota answered, seeing that it was Cody.

"Hey, Savanna wants you to come by the house," Cody said without preamble.

"Why?" Dakota asked.

Cody chuckled, recognizing Dakota's rolling-her-eyes tone. "Because she wants to make sure your arm is healing okay."

"It's fine," Dakota said automatically.

"Yeah, and she wants to see it," Cody said. "And don't give me a ration of shit, Dak, I'm just the messenger."

Dakota sighed. "Fine, I'll stop by later."

"Good," Cody said, grinning.

Later that afternoon Dakota drove up to the Falco home. As she pulled up, a black Ferrari drove in behind her. Dakota parked on the street, and saw the Ferrari pull into the garage. She got out of her car and saw Lyric getting out of the other car. Lyric walked down the driveway whistling as she looked at the Bugatti.

"What is this?" Lyric asked, her eyes alight with interest.

Dakota grinned, leaning against the back of the car. "A Bugatti Veyron."

"How many horses?" Lyric asked, her tone reflecting the excitement in her eyes.

"Twelve hundred," Dakota said, sounding like a proud parent.

Lyric blew here breath out as she walked around the car.

"What's it clock in at?" Lyric asked.

"It's been clocked at 254. I've gotten up to close to that in the desert a couple of times."

"Nice…" Lyric said, her voice enthusiastic. "What's one of these run?"

"Three point four," Dakota said, widening her eyes.

Lyric looked deadpan at her. "Thousand?"

"Million," Dakota corrected.

"Holy Fuck…" Lyric said coughing slightly. "Guess I won't be asking the wife for this one." She winked at Dakota.

Dakota laughed then walked toward the garage, checking out Lyric's Ferrari.

"What model this?" Dakota asked, recognizing the Stallion Ferrari logo.

"SI 250 GTO," Lyric said, smiling proudly at her car.

"What year?" Dakota asked, running her hand reverently over the rear fender.

"Sixty-two," Lyric said, enjoying that Dakota obviously knew cars too.

Dakota looked pensive for a minute. "There weren't a lot of these made, were there?"

Lyric laughed, shaking her head. "Nope, only thirty-two."

Dakota stepped back, looking at the car with a whole new appreciation. "That's fuckin' awesome…" she said, her eyes bright with admiration. "Cody drives a red Ferrari doesn't she?"

"Yeah," Lyric said, nodding, "we gave it to her for her sixteenth birthday. My family all has Ferrari's, so it just seemed fitting."

"Lucky little bitch," Dakota said, grinning.

"Well, it didn't look like it does now when she got it. It was a project car and we worked on it together. Just like I did with this one with my dad and brothers," Lyric said, touching the hood of her car.

Dakota nodded, looking a little wistful. Lyric caught the look, and thought that Savanna was right about this girl. It was obvious she needed people who loved her.

"Come on in," Lyric said, walking through the garage into the house.

Dakota looked around the garage as she followed Lyric into the house. She spotted the two motorcycles sitting on the other side and sighed. "Van?" Lyric called when they got into the dining room.

"Hey!" Savanna called. "Be right down."

Lyric glanced over at Dakota. "Want a beer?"

"Sure," Dakota said, nodding.

Lyric walked into the kitchen, opened the refrigerator, and pulled out two beers. She opened them up and handed one to Dakota. Savanna walked into the room then. She kissed Lyric, then looked over at Dakota.

"You made it," she said, smiling. "Let's see that arm."

Dakota sighed, then took off her jacket and put her arm out to Savanna.

Savanna took a good long look, her fingers gently touching the edges of the cut, and turning the arm this way and that.

She nodded approvingly. "It's healing really well, you heal fast," she said, smiling at Dakota.

Dakota chuckled. "If you say so."

"I do," Savanna said, smiling again. "Hey, you should stay for dinner, we're barbecuing. Cody and McKenna are coming over too."

Dakota looked back at Savanna, seeing the kindness in the woman's eyes, and thinking that being around these people was really dangerous. She knew she could get far too used to being around such nice people, and she knew that it could be snatched away just as easily. She glanced at Lyric then, and saw that Lyric's blue eyes were narrowed slightly, like she was seeing what Dakota was thinking.

"Come on," Savanna cajoled, "we don't bite."

"Much," Lyric said, grinning.

"And you need to go get changed so you can start the barbecue, my love," Savanna told Lyric.

"Yes ma'am," Lyric said, grinning.

Lyric left the kitchen then, and Dakota could hear her boots on the floor upstairs.

"You are staying, right?" Savanna asked, her tone not really questioning.

Dakota opened her mouth to decline, but she saw the hopeful look in Savanna's eyes, and just couldn't bear to see that change.

"Sure," Dakota said, smiling.

"Great!" Savanna said, her smile wide. "Come on, let's go outside, that way you can smoke off that nervous edge you have," Savanna said, winking at her.

Dakota laughed, wondering exactly how Savanna could tell that she was nervous and definitely on edge. She wasn't used to people who could read her, or who cared enough to try and read her.

They stepped out into the backyard, and Savanna turned on the music. Dakota grinned.

"Lyric needs music, so does Cody," Savanna said, grinning. "Those two are a lot alike."

"I got that," Dakota said, nodding as she sat down and pulled out a cigarette.

Savanna sat down across from her, giving her an assessing look.

"So how are you?" Savanna asked.

Dakota looked somewhat pensive. "I'm okay..." she said, her voice trailing off as she looked perplexed.

"It was just a question," Savanna said, her tone mild.

Dakota nodded.

"Okay, you caught me, I'm being nosey," Savanna said wrinkling up her nose as she smiled. "What I really want to ask is how things are with... the... um... rampaging piece of glass."

Dakota rolled her tongue over her lips, grinning widely as she chuckled. "She's well... fine."

Savanna nodded, her look searching. "And you're still with her?"

Dakota's look flickered as she pursed her lips, but she nodded.

"And does that..." Savanna said, circling her hand in the direction of Dakota's forearm, "kind of thing happen often?"

Dakota's look was abashed as she rolled her eyes. "No, it doesn't."

Savanna looked relieved and visibly relaxed a little in her chair.

They were both silent for a few moments. Dakota smoked and looked pensive as she picked at the threads on her faded jeans. As usual, she looked like the consummate biker chick with her leather jacket and white tank top, faded jeans and biker boots.

"So Cody says you were her first friend in LA when she got here," Savanna said.

Dakota chuckled. "Yeah, she was desperately in need of a friend in those days."

"I imagine," Savanna said.

"I don't think she was in LA for a month and some guy already had his hooks in her, pimping her out…" Dakota said. She shook her head, her eyes narrowing at the memory. "I got her away from him, and I taught her how to be safer…" Her voice trailed off again as she grimaced, remembering that she was talking to Cody's mother and not sure if she'd ever heard this.

"It's okay," Savanna said, her look gentle. "I know what Cody was doing before she came to the group home. I'm glad you at least kept her safe."

Dakota blew her breath out, smiling fondly. "I loved that kid," she said. "She was so damned scared, I just wanted to protect her as much as I could." She looked at Savanna then. "Did she tell you I was her first?"

Savanna canted her head. "No, she didn't," she said, but then nodded. "It makes sense though, it sounds like you were the one person she could count on then."

Dakota looked derisive then. "Yeah, except for that night she got clipped," she said, referring to Cody previously being arrested for prostitution. "I was sick, I told her not to go out, but she did anyway…" She shook her head, her look unhappy.

"It worked out okay," Savanna said. "It was after that that she came to stay in the group home I was running, and when she met Lyric."

"How'd that happen anyway?" Dakota asked, having been curious how a street kid like Cody had met a cop in any positive way.

"Cody had disappeared, and I was worried about her. Like you said, she was always so scared, I couldn't believe she'd just have run off. Lyric was the only police officer that would listen to me and was willing to look for Cody."

Dakota nodded, looking happy about that. "Cody says you and Lyric saved her."

"Well, Lyric did," Savanna said. "She shot the gang member that was holding Cody against her will."

Dakota looked surprised by that information. "Damn…" she muttered.

"Yeah, Lyric's pretty amazing like that," Savanna said, smiling as Lyric walked out wearing jeans and a DOJ t-shirt.

"What?" Lyric asked, having heard what Savanna had just said.

"I was telling Dakota about how you shot that guy to rescue Cody," Savanna said.

Lyric rolled her eyes. "Did you tell her how Cody took a two-story dive to save McKenna?"

"What!" Dakota exclaimed, looking more stunned by the minute. "She did what?"

Lyric chuckled. "Yeah, a few months or so ago. The guy whose brother I shot rescuing Cody when she was fourteen decided to take me out and was trying for Cody too."

"What happened?" Dakota asked.

"Lyric was shot three times," Savanna said her look somber, "and was in a coma."

"The guy took McKenna to lure Cody in, which worked," Lyric said scowling.

"In the end, Cody went after the guy, charging at him and they both went off the second story balcony of a hotel," Savanna said.

"Wow…" Dakota said, her eyes wide. "The girl has definitely grown some serious cahones."

Lyric laughed, nodding. "That she has."

"She takes after her mother," Savanna said, winking at Lyric.

"Which one?" Dakota asked, smiling.

Lyric and Savanna exchanged a look, smiling at each other.

"Both," Lyric said.

"What's goin' on out here?" Cody asked as she opened the door and held it open for McKenna.

"Oh the usual," Lyric said, grinning. "Gossiping about our kid."

"Great…" Cody said, her tone far from enthusiastic.

"They were just telling me about your swan dive," Dakota said, her tone pointed.

Cody gave a short laugh. "Yeah that was… fun."

"And if you do anything like it again, I'll kick your ass…" McKenna put in, smiling sweetly.

"Love you too," Cody said, winking at McKenna.

"So how'd the meet go with Raine?" Cody asked Dakota as she sat down and pulled out a cigarette.

Dakota shrugged. "I don't have any new bruises," she said, smirking as McKenna leaned down to hug her and kiss her on the cheek.

"Do you think she listened to any of it though?" Cody asked.

Dakota shrugged. "Got me."

Cody nodded. "Well, you did what you could, that's what counts."

Dakota laughed sarcastically. "Yeah, after I fucked everything up in the first place," she said, her tone self-effacing.

Cody gave her a narrowed look. "What counts is that you realize you fucked up and you did what you could to make it right. That's all anyone can expect. You need to let yourself off the hook here."

Dakota looked back at Cody for a long moment, narrowing her eyes.

"Is that what happens when you're raised by a psychiatrist?" Dakota asked. "You psychoanalyze your friends?"

Cody laughed. "Or I use the Ph.D. I have in psychology."

Dakota blinked slowly. "You said what?"

Cody laughed, nodding her head.

"Damn…" Dakota said. "I feel even more stupid now."

"You're far from stupid, Dakota," Savanna said.

Dakota glanced over at Savanna, she wanted to ask how Savanna would know, but she saw the incredibly compassionate look in her eyes and once again just couldn't stand the idea of changing that.

Cody caught the look and knew what Dakota wanted to say. The fact that she didn't made Cody hope that Dakota was opening up to the possibility of letting people care about her. Cody was bound and determined to keep Dakota close and do everything she could to help her realize that there was more to life than loveless relationships based on sex and money. Lyric caught the exchange as well and gave Cody a sly wink. Leave it to Savanna to soften up the tough girl.

"Yeah," Dakota said, smiling. "I've got a Ph.D. in women," she said, putting her tongue between her teeth teasingly.

"Oh Lord," McKenna said, shaking her head, but smiling too.

"You're a doctor, too right?" Dakota asked McKenna.

"Almost," McKenna said, nodding.

Dakota looked over at Lyric. "How's that feel? Surrounded by three doctors?"

Lyric laughed. "I'm very careful with what I say."

"Hey!" Savanna said, laughing.

It turned out to be a nice evening, and Dakota left feeling a different kind of ache in her heart. However, she did her best to ignore it. Once back at Cassandra's house, she went to her room and shut the door. Lying on the bed and smoking, she did something she knew she'd needed to do. She sent Jazmine a message.

***

Jazmine was cooking dinner for Rayden when the text message came in. She wiped her hands and picked up her phone. It was from Dakota.

"Hey, heard about Natalia pulling out of the studio deal… I guess I really fucked that up for you too, huh? I'm really sorry, would like to apologize in person if you're willing."

"I'm willing and besides you owe me a ride," Jazmine wrote back, adding a winking emoticon on the end.

"So tempting…" came the reply, which had Jazmine laughing and shaking her head.

"I meant the car Dakota!"

"Damnit!"

"LOL! When?"

"Tomorrow too soon, say 10?" Dakota replied.

"Tomorrow at 10 works," Jazmine replied.

"C U then," Dakota replied.

"Yes you will…"

"Ohhhh…"

Jazmine put her phone down with a grin. She had to admit, even to herself, that it was nice to have someone flirt with her. She knew beyond a shadow of a doubt that Rayden was nowhere near ready to love anyone again, and even if she had been, Jazmine wasn't convinced that Rayden would ever love her. Rayden was very sweet and considerate, but Jazmine always felt her holding back. No one was going to replace Grayson Black Wolf any time soon. Jazmine wasn't sure how much her heart could take with Rayden. Of course, she also knew that someone like Dakota Blair was far from a relationship, but at least it was fun to flirt with the other woman.

The next day, Jazmine was surprised when Dakota showed up right at ten o'clock in the morning. She even got out of the car and opened the door for her. Jazmine admired the car as she got in. The interior was a rich brown and gray, with luxurious leather seats and a wide flat center console. It was a surprisingly simplified dashboard, not overly cluttered with gauges and buttons. She inhaled the rich scent of the leather as she leaned back in the seat comfortably.

"This is one seriously beautiful car," she told Dakota when she got in on the other side.

Dakota smiled fondly. "Yes, yes it is," she said, nodding, her eyes alight with excitement.

As she started the car with a throaty rumble and put it into gear, Jazmine could hear the engine purr like the deep throaty purr of a big panther.

Jazmine nodded. "Okay, I can see why you love this car."

Dakota grinned. "You ain't seen nothing yet, but we gotta get out of the city. How much time do you have?"

"All day," Jazmine said smiling.

Dakota smiled. "Cool."

With that she took off. A few minutes later, they were driving down the 210 freeway, flying down it really.

Dakota reached over and touched Jazmine's hand, glancing over at her as she did.

"I really am sorry if I screwed up your deal with Natalia," she said her tone earnest.

Jazmine could see she was being completely honest, it was written all over face.

"Why did you do it?" she asked softly.

Dakota grimaced. "I don't even know," she said, shaking her head. "Raine thinks I was trying to prove something."

"You talked to Raine?" Jazmine asked surprised.

"Yeah, I apologized to her too," Dakota said, grinning. "It's like some kind of twelve step program to growing a fuckin' conscience or something."

Jazmine laughed at what she said. "Okay. So what did Raine think you were trying to prove?"

"That I could take what she had."

"Is that what you were doing?"

Dakota looked pensive, then shrugged. "I don't know, maybe," she said her tone open.

Jazmine nodded, looking thoughtful.

"Suddenly I'm around all these people who are major in love and… I guess it just… drags at me," Dakota said.

"Drags at you?" Jazmine asked.

"Yeah, like nagging me that I'm stupid for missing the boat or something."

"You aren't very old, Dakota, it's not like you can't find love someday too," Jazmine said.

Dakota laughed. "Yeah, no…" she said, shaking her head.

"What do you mean 'no'?" Jazmine asked.

"I mean, that's not for me, I'm not looking for that." Jazmine narrowed her eyes, it was obvious that Dakota was in some serious denial, but she didn't think that she should push at this point.

"Maybe you've got the right of it though," Jazmine said, sighing.

"Uh-oh," Dakota said, grinning, "what's going on there?"

Jazmine shook her head. "Just thinking in terms of Ray."

"Are you in love with Rayden?" Dakota asked, surprising herself with the question.

Jazmine sighed. "I don't want to be."

Dakota glanced over at her. "What does that mean?"

"Rayden is still in love with her wife," Jazmine said.

Dakota looked shocked. "Rayden's married?"

"Her wife died a year ago," Jazmine said, "but she's still in love with her and probably always will be."

"That does kind of suck," Dakota said, nodding.

"I should have learned last time," Jazmine said, shaking her head.

"Last time?" Dakota asked.

Jazmine rolled her eyes. "Ray and I dated ten years ago."

"Well, alright…" Dakota said.

"Yeah, well, she took off on me that time, so I should have learned then."

"There are plenty of women in the sea, Jaz," Dakota said.

Jazmine laughed. "Yeah, that's funny," she said, shaking her head. "Rayden's the only woman I've ever been with."

"Huh?" Dakota said, looking dumbfounded. "But you said ten years ago…"

"I've only dated men since then," Jazmine said.

"Why?" Dakota asked, sounding disgusted by the idea.

Jazmine laughed at the look on her face. "That's all I've ever dated, but I seem to be a disaster in relationships no matter who I date."

"How so?"

"Every man I date either treats me like shit or gets violent with me. The last guy basically tried to kill me," Jazmine said, rolling her eyes. "And then there's Rayden."

"Did you love any of the guys you've dated?"

"No," Jazmine said.

"Let me get this straight," Dakota said, grinning. "Pardon the pun, but you're looking for love, and you think you love Rayden, the only woman you've ever been with, and have never loved the men you've been with?"

"Well, when you say it that way..." Jazmine said, grinning.

"I think you need to try out some more women," Dakota said.

Jazmine chuckled, shaking her head. "Rayden said the exact same thing."

"See? She's a smart woman," Dakota said, grinning.

"Well, she also said I should sleep with you, so..." Jazmine said with a cheeky smile.

"Now I really like her..." Dakota said, laughing.

"Oh my God!" Jazmine said, shaking her head.

Dakota just chuckled.

By this time they'd finally reached an area where the freeway was wide open. Dakota looked over at her and waggled her eyebrows. "Hold on..." Jazmine widened her eyes as Dakota shifted gears and put her foot to the floor. The Bugatti leapt forward in response. They went screaming down the freeway, and Jazmine could see the elation on Dakota's face. Before long they'd gone a long distance. They passed a sign that read "Las Vegas - 200 miles." Dakota looked over at Jazmine with a wide grin, her blue eyes sparkling at her over the rim of her sunglasses.

"You up for it?" she asked, her tone challenging.

"What?" Jazmine asked, starting to smile. "Vegas?"

"Yeah…" Dakota said, grinning.

"Are you crazy?"

"Sometimes," Dakota said, grinning. "Are you in?"

Jazmine stared back at Dakota for a long moment, and finally nodded. "I'm in."

"Yes!" Dakota said, punching the gas again.

Jazmine pulled out her phone so she could text Rayden to let her know.

"Texting Ray?" Dakota asked, glancing over at her.

"I don't want her to worry," Jazmine said. "What about Cassandra?"

"She doesn't worry," Dakota said, grinning.

Jazmine looked over at Dakota, and that's when she noticed her arm.

"Is that what was under that bandage?" she asked, reaching over to touch the healing cut.

Dakota nodded.

"Did Cassandra do that?" Jazmine asked.

Dakota hesitated, but then nodded, her look chagrinned.

"So the scratches and your lip that day, those were her too?"

Dakota nodded.

"Did she mean to do it?" Jazmine asked looking worried.

Dakota drew in a breath, nodding. "Yeah, she did."

"Did you want her to?"

Dakota gave a short sarcastic bark of laughter. "No."

"Does she do that kind of thing a lot?"

"No, this the first time she got that crazy," Dakota said.

"Why would you let her do that to you?" Jazmine asked, her tone troubled.

"It's a trade off," Dakota said, shrugging.

"A trade off?" Jazmine asked in disbelief.

"You think three point four million dollar cars are given for free?" Dakota asked raising an eyebrow.

"So it's the price you pay?" Jazmine asked her look dubious.

"Pretty much," Dakota said.

"So when is the price too high, Dakota?"

Dakota didn't answer, she just shrugged.

"Is it worth your life?" Jazmine asked.

"I'm still alive."

"This time," Jazmine said, her look pained.

Dakota glanced over at Jazmine and saw the look on her face. She blinked a couple of times, surprised by her being so concerned. She turned her face back to the windshield and kept driving.

After a few minutes, they started talking about various topics. The trip went by quickly, and before Jazmine knew it, they were driving into Las Vegas.

"Pick a hotel," Dakota said, smiling.

"Are you serious?"

"Yep," Dakota said, grinning.

"Ummm…. Okay, how about the Bellagio."

"You got it," Dakota said, speeding down the Strip and turning into the Bellagio.

A half an hour later they were escorted into the Presidential Suite. An incredibly luxurious suite with its own stocked bar, two master suite rooms, fireplaces in both rooms, fifty-five inch flat screen TVs and 24/7 butler service.

"You're crazy!" Jazmine told Dakota, who'd used Cassandra's credit card to reserve the outrageously expensive room.

"Sometimes," Dakota said, winking at Jazmine.

A little while later, they left the hotel and went across the way to Caesar's Palace.

"Now we need clothes," Dakota said.

"Dakota…" Jazmine said, shaking her head.

But Dakota simply shook her head and smiled.

They went first to Diesel where Dakota bought herself jeans, dress boots, a black denim button up shirt, a new black leather jacket with metal studs and buckles at the bottom, a thick banded black leather metal studded watch, a set of metal denim covered dog tags, and a leather bracelet.

"Now…" Dakota said, as she signed the credit card slip for over $1500. "We need to shop for you…" she said, her voice trailing off as she grinned.

"Oh, no… I'm fine…" Jazmine said, holding up her hands.

Dakota grabbed one of her hands and led her down the way, stopping at Versace. She looked inside and nodded.

"Yep, let's go," Dakota said, leading the way.

"Dakota!" Jazmine exclaimed, trying to stop her.

Nothing stopped Dakota. Four stores and what had to be at least eight thousand dollars later, Jazmine had an outfit for the evening. They'd been to Versace, La Perla, Jimmy Choo, and the Mac store for makeup. They had lunch before they went back to the room. To Jazmine's surprise, Dakota didn't make a pass at her even once. She wasn't sure if she should be insulted, or impressed.

In the room they watched movies and talked, getting into a rousing discussion of where was the most public place they'd ever had sex.

Dakota won hands down when she admitted that she'd had sex in a church in a confessional.

"You're going to Hell for that, you know," Jazmine told her, winking at her.

"If I believed in Hell, I'd probably be worried," Dakota responded, lifting her third beer to her lips.

Jazmine shook her head. "You don't believe in Hell… do you believe in Heaven or God?"

"Nope," Dakota said with a shake of her head. "I never saw any evidence of divine intervention, not even when I needed it most… so God and all the rest of them can go fuck themselves."

Jazmine widened her eyes, sensing she was getting very close to the surface at this point.

"When did you need it most?" Jazmine asked softly.

"Which time?" Dakota asked, grinning, the look in her eyes guarded.

"Any time…" Jazmine asked, really curious to find what made Dakota tick.

"Well, could have been pretty much anytime from when I was about two until recently," she answered.

"What happened when you were two?"

"Well…" Dakota said. She got up off the couch and walked over to the bar. She picked up a bottle of Jack Daniel's and sat back down on the couch. "As near as I can figure, that was the first time my mother sold me to the highest bidder to score some crack."

Jazmine looked back at Dakota, her mouth open, part of her praying that Dakota would laugh and tell her she was kidding. She didn't. Jazmine shook her head, tears in her eyes.

Dakota gave a short laugh, opened the bottle, and took a big swig.

"How long were you with your mother?" Jazmine asked, hoping it wasn't long and that some authority had intervened.

"Well, when I was twelve I decided that since I wasn't seeing any of the profits of my labors," she said, grinning sardonically and taking another drink. "I ran away and started doing my own thing, my own way."

Jazmine moved to sit closer to Dakota, taking the bottle out of her hands and taking a swing herself. She winced as the alcohol burned her throat.

Dakota grinned, taking the bottle back and taking another long drink. Then she stood up, glancing at the clock on the wall. She stretched and said, "I'm going to go take a shower. I'm thinking we need to hit the strip here in an hour or so, what do you say?"

Jazmine grinned, nodding. "Whatever you say."

Dakota went still for a moment, a slow grin starting on her lips. "You might want to be careful saying that to me," she said, with a wink. With that she walked off, taking the bottle of Jack Daniel's with her.

An hour later you could have knocked Dakota over with a feather when Jazmine walked out in the outfit they'd bought her. She wore a Versace leather mini skirt with a fitted zip up jacket, under which she wore a La Perla tulle and lace bra that could be seen through the opening in the jacket. She wore Jimmy Choo leather pumps with laser cut leather around the ankle and down the front. With the heels, she was only two inches shorter than Dakota was in her two-inch heels.

Dakota looked like the hot biker chick she usually did, but with a different edge. Jazmine wasn't sure what it was, but she was seeing Dakota differently now. For the first time she wasn't seeing her as just the troublemaker, she was a real person who'd had a shit life.

"Holy hell…" Dakota said, as she took in every inch of exposed skin, practically drooling. "Maybe we should just stay here…" she said, grinning slowly.

"Come on!" Jazmine said, grabbing Dakota's arm and walking her toward the door.

Dakota grinned and let herself be led out the door. Down in the casino Dakota sat down at a high stakes poker table. Jazmine stood behind her chair, just watching. At one point, a couple who appeared to be from the Midwest joined the game and sat next to Dakota. Before long, Jazmine started to hear comments from the couple. At first, she wasn't sure she was hearing correctly, but then she heard the woman say something about disgusting lesbian trash in such a nice establishment.

Jazmine could see that Dakota heard it too by the way her jaw jumped, like she was gritting her teeth. It made Jazmine mad, how dare they judge Dakota, they didn't even know her. They had no idea what she'd been through, nothing, all they saw was the outside. The man had smiled at Jazmine, as had the woman. She heard the woman say, "Such a beautiful girl…"

Jazmine made a point of leaning close to Dakota as she whispered in her ear. "Just go with it…"

Dakota looked up at her, her blue eyes narrowing slightly. Jazmine unzipped the jacket exposing a very nice expanse of bare midriff, her smooth, tanned skin with the slightest amount of definition, just enough. She leaned over and slid her arm across the back of Dakota's shoulder, her long red hair falling over Dakota's shoulder in the process.

"Oh honey, you're doing so good…" Jazmine purred, sliding her hand down the front of Dakota's shirt seductively.

Dakota finished a hand and won a fairly nice size pot.

"Yay!" Jazmine exclaimed, and she unzipped the mini skirt a little so she could slide it up more on her hips and straddle Dakota's lap facing her.

She looked over at the couple who were watching them with wide eyes. Then she leaned in, and captured Dakota's lips with hers. Her hands slid up Dakota's chest and she deepened the kiss to improve the show. Dakota's hands slid up the outside of her thighs, gripping them when Jazmine deepened the kiss.

Jazmine realized she'd outsmarted herself this time, because kissing Dakota was every bit as exciting as kissing Rayden was. In fact, Dakota's hands on her thighs caused electrical currents to rush straight to her very core. She moaned softly against Dakota's lips and immediately felt Dakota's hands pressing her down against her body.

Dakota pulled her lips from Jazmine's long enough to tell the dealer to cash her out and credit it to the room. She then slid her hands under Jazmine's thighs, lifting her up so she could stand. Her lips reclaimed Jazmine's as she set her down on her feet. Then she took Jazmine's hand, and strode toward the elevators. Inside the elevator, she pressed Jazmine back against the wall, kissing deeply and pressing her body against Jazmine.

They made it inside the room and got the door closed just as Dakota's hand slid up the skirt and past the crotch of the La Perla underwear, touching Jazmine's wetness and heat. Jazmine came immediately grasping at Dakota's shoulders and exclaiming loudly. Dakota picked her up, pressing her against the door, her lips on her again. Jazmine wrapped her legs around Dakota's waist and Dakota carried her to one of the master bedrooms. She laid her down, kicked off her boots, and tossed aside her jacket. She then removed Jazmine's shoes and clothes, leaving the matching bra and panties on her, because they looked so damned hot.

Dakota made her come three times, before Jazmine moved to push Dakota over onto her back. It was obvious from the way that Dakota reacted, that she was very surprised by Jazmine's action. Jazmine unbuttoned Dakota's jeans and shirt, pulled off the jeans, and slid the shirt off as fast as her hands would go. She slid her hand up

Dakota's bare chest, making her shudder and gasp, and pull at Jazmine.

"Come here…" Dakota murmured, pulling at Jazmine.

"No," Jazmine said, kissing down Dakota's flat stomach.

One hand was in Jazmine's hair, with the other still pulling at her, trying to get her to move back up to her lips. Jazmine moved lower, and Dakota shifted, trying to get away from her. Jazmine's hands held her fast, as she looked up at her. Dakota stared down at Jazmine, her sparkling green eyes making her groan.

"Come here…" Dakota said, her tone stronger, her hands pulling at Jazmine in earnest.

Jazmine finally relented, moving her body up over Dakota's, sliding skin against skin, her mouth moving to Dakota's lips again, her hands roaming over bare skin. Dakota's lips on her were hungry and Dakota started to move over her again, but Jazmine stopped her, moving over Dakota instead. Jazmine pulled off Dakota's bra and pushed her panties off as well while Dakota did her best to keep that from happening, but Jazmine's hands on her kept distracting her.

When they were both naked, Jazmine pressed her body between Dakota's legs, leaning down to slide her mouth over very hard nipples. Dakota's breathing was becoming ragged, and she was grasping at Jazmine's hips, but Jazmine could tell she was still resisting her.

She lowered her head and put her lips next to Dakota's ear. "Come for me, Dakota… come…" she whispered, her voice ragged with heat and desire.

It was all Dakota could take, and she came with a loud shout that extended into a long throaty yell. Jazmine's scream joined hers as she came too. Afterwards, Jazmine lay over her, both of them panting.

"Holy hell…" Dakota said breathlessly.

"What?" Jazmine asked, her voice barely audible, as she glanced down at Dakota.

"That's… that hasn't happened in years…" Dakota said.

"What hasn't?"

"A woman making me come," Dakota said surprised.

"Really?" Jazmine asked, shocked. "As often as you have sex?" She was in disbelief.

"They get off, I don't. At least not with them," Dakota said.

"So you take care of that yourself?" Jazmine asked.

"Yeah, alone," Dakota said. Though she wasn't sure why she was admitting this to Jazmine. She figured it was post orgasm afterglow talking.

"Well, if we do this again," Jazmine said, grinning. "I don't go in for that, you'll get off with me, or no one's getting off."

Dakota widened her eyes, grinning. "Really now?"

"Believe it," Jazmine said her tone strong.

Jazmine moved to lie on her back blowing her breath out. Dakota found that she wanted to keep her close. Turning on her side, Dakota put her arm over Jazmine's stomach, her hand grasping Jazmine's waist gently. Jazmine turned her head, looking at Dakota, her eyes half-lidded and looking sleepy. Dakota closed her eyes, feeling quite sated and for once not feeling the need to escape. She attributed it to the orgasm and that because of it she was too lazy to move. They fell asleep that way. During the course of the night, Dakota moved closer to Jazmine, putting her left leg between Jazmine's and her arm across Jazmine's upper torso.

It was the first thing Jazmine noticed when she woke up the next morning. Dakota was holding her in a similar way that Jazmine found so endearing when Rayden did it. She smiled and slid her hand over Dakota's arm, snuggling a little closer, and fell asleep again.

When Dakota woke later that morning, it was with the strangest sensation of a body next to her on the bed. It wasn't something she was used to at all. She insisted she had her own room at Cassandra's so she could go back to her room after sex, or Cassandra could go back to hers. She normally didn't want to cuddle or any of that with women she slept with. She wanted to get them off and then have them go away so she could get off. Part of her knew it wasn't 'normal' but it was how she was and how she liked things. Waking up next to Jazmine was, therefore, very strange to her.

Her eyes took in the sight of the other woman, her dark red lashes around her closed eyes, her rich red hair flowing around her face and over Dakota's arm. She noticed how smooth Jazmine's skin was, there was literally nothing unattractive about the woman. Dakota's eyes moved down her body. She had a dancer's body with lean muscle, but a good amount of curve as well. Dakota noticed a couple of healing scars on her side and wondered at them.

As she looked at Jazmine's body, she wanted her again. She slid her hand down Jazmine's arm and then back up to her shoulder, then to her collarbone and down her side, careful to avoid the scars. She then smoothed her hand over Jazmine's lower torso and abdomen, then slid her hand up over perfectly rounded breasts, her thumb sliding over her nipple. Just touching Jazmine was getting her further aroused.

Jazmine stirred, and turned over on her side, facing away from Dakota. Dakota slid her hand over Jazmine's waist and pulled her gently back, closing the gap between them so she could hold her closer. Dakota moved her head, to nuzzle Jazmine's neck, her lips kissing and sucking gently, her hand between Jazmine's breasts brushing back and forth on her skin.

Jazmine woke to the feeling of Dakota kissing and caressing her. Her body was already alive with sensations. She moaned softly, and pressed back against Dakota who pulled her closer. She continued to touch her, getting her more and more excited, until she finally slid her hand downward, touching Jazmine and sliding a finger inside her. Jazmine gasped out loud and pressed closer to Dakota. She reached her hand back to grasp at Dakota's body, pulling her closer, moaning louder. Within minutes Jazmine was climaxing and holding tight to Dakota's hip.

Immediately after her orgasm, Jazmine turned over to kiss Dakota deeply, her hand sliding up from Dakota's hip to her shoulder and then down to caress her nipples. She pressed Dakota back on the bed and moved over her. She positioned herself between Dakota's legs, and moved her body against Dakota's. As a dancer, she had very strong hips and the ability to move them in very enticing ways. Dakota's hands were on those hips, guiding her, and grinding Jazmine down against her. Jazmine's lips kissed her skin, sucking gently, then harder as she felt Dakota getting more and more excited. Within minutes Dakota was crying out, holding onto her, sending Jazmine over the edge again as well.

"And good morning…" Dakota said, grinning as they both lay panting.

Jazmine chuckled. "I'll say."

Jazmine positioned herself on her side facing Dakota, and put her hand on Dakota's shoulder. Dakota looked over at her, grinning.

"This is actually kind of nice…" Dakota said, sounding surprised.

"Guess you don't usually do this either, huh?" Jazmine asked, her eyes sparkling with amusement.

"Nope," Dakota said, shaking her head.

"So is this hard for you?" Jazmine asked, not wanting Dakota to be uncomfortable.

Dakota looked back at her for a long moment, as if trying to decide, then she shook her head. "No," she said, smiling in wonder. "I guess I've never tried it before…"

"Well maybe I'm not the only one who needs to try new things," Jazmine said, grinning as she winked at Dakota.

"Uh-huh," Dakota said, grinning.

Jazmine sat up and stretched with Dakota watching her appreciatively "You are one seriously spectacular looking female, you know that?"

Jazmine glanced back at Dakota, looking surprised by the compliment. She leaned down and kissed Dakota's lips.

"Thank you," she said, smiling.

Dakota pulled her back down and kissed her again. Within minutes, they were making love again. Afterward they lay together and got to chatting again. After a while, they got up and got dressed. The hotel had cleaned the clothes they'd driven to Vegas in.

They went down to the hotel restaurant and had breakfast. While eating they decided to stay another day and night. Dakota wanted to check out the night clubs in an area of Las Vegas called the Fruit Loop.

Jazmine agreed, but wanted to buy something less flashy for going to a club. This time she insisted on using her own credit card. They went back to Diesel, a trendy punk rock style store. She bought a pair of opaque black slim fit jeans and a shirt that was see through black tulle with a blue, gray, and white leopard print on it and pockets strategically placed to cover her breasts. Dakota insisted on buying her a pair of rocker style boots that had three-inch heels.

"They look like you," Dakota told her, grinning.

Dakota ended up buying a sleeveless denim shirt and a edgy black bra with stud accents.

They spent the rest of the day gambling. Dakota hit another winning streak and was able to not only settle the hotel bill and charges, but had an addition $20,000 to spare which she pocketed.

That night they hit the bars. Jazmine looked really sexy with her shirt open to just below her breasts. She had on Dakota's wide studded belt with a Harley Davidson belt buckle, her rocker boots, and Dakota's leather biker jacket. Dakota also wore the new clothes she'd bought earlier, keeping the shirt open to her waist. At the first club they went to there were a lot of butch women who flirted outrageously with Jazmine. They asked her to dance, asking if she and Dakota were together. Dakota made a point of not being possessive, not wanting to interfere with Jazmine's good time. She did, however, keep a watchful eye on the goings on, making sure the other butches weren't getting too pushy. Jazmine would look over at Dakota whenever a woman was being too forward, and Dakota would intervene, strongly if necessary. One woman got to see the nasty side of Dakota when she wouldn't give up her effort to corner Jazmine. She quite literally had Jazmine backed into a corner when Dakota returned from the bathroom. Dakota immediately stepped up behind her, looking down at the slightly shorter woman.

"Back up off her now…" Dakota growled lowly.

"She said you ain't her thang," the woman muttered over her shoulder.

"Well, neither are you, so back up," Dakota said, clamping her hand around the woman's forearm.

"Back off!" the woman snapped, apparently used to being in charge.

Dakota used strength it never appeared she had, to whip the woman around to face her. Then she grabbed the woman by two handfuls of the jean jacket she wore and backed her up against the nearest wall, her blue eyes blazing.

"I told you to leave the lady alone," Dakota said, her tone still low. "Now you either listen, or I'm gonna make you listen. You got me?"

The woman stared back at Dakota and sensed the violence simmering just under the surface in the younger woman. Finally, she held up her hands in surrender. Dakota let her go, and turned back to Jazmine.

"You okay?" she asked, her eyes scanning Jazmine's face.

Jazmine smiled. "I'm okay."

Dakota put her hand out and Jazmine took it. She led her back to the bar and bought her a drink. The rest of the time at that particular club, Jazmine only danced with Dakota, making it very obvious to everyone that they were indeed together. There were a few deep long kisses on the dance floor, but it was fun and drinking.

The second club they went into had a lot more femme lesbians and they were like a swarm of locusts on the quite handsome and sexy Dakota. Jazmine hung back, watching Dakota work her magic. She had women panting over her left and right. It was undeniably interesting to watch. Jazmine was very careful to keep any feelings of jealousy out of her eyes and out of her comments when Dakota made her way to her after each brief encounter.

Jazmine keeping out of Dakota's way didn't go unnoticed. She found it very interesting. She was used to either extremely jealous women, or women that didn't care at all. She could tell that Jazmine was watching her, but she didn't feel like Jazmine was trying to build a case against her. She'd found over the years that women would sometimes watch and wait, and then hit her with all the bad acts she'd done. They'd foolishly thought it would work to make her feel bad. She never felt bad. Jazmine didn't seem to be doing that though.

At one point Dakota walked over to where Jazmine sat at the bar with her back to her. Dakota slid Jazmine's shirt off her shoulder, and kissed the exposed skin softly. She held her empty bottle up the bartender, giving her a wink, then leaned on the bar facing Jazmine.

"So how're you doing?" Dakota asked.

"Good," Jazmine said, smiling. "That one is cute." She nodded back toward the girl Dakota had just danced with.

Dakota looked over at the girl. She was a very tiny blond Barbie doll type. Then she looked at Jazmine. "Not as cute as you," she said, winking at Jazmine.

"Uh-huh," Jazmine said, grinning.

Dakota looked back at Jazmine thinking that she was definitely the hottest woman in the place. She pushed off the bar and positioned herself between Jazmine's legs so they were eye to eye. She leaned in, kissing Jazmine's lips deeply, her hands sliding around Jazmine's waist to pull her closer.

"Come dance with me," Dakota said.

Jazmine smiled, "Okay."

They danced for a couple of fast songs. Dakota really loved to watch Jazmine dance, the girl definitely had the hot hip hop dancer thing down. She could easily see why Jazmine was popular for the music videos. She had the body and the moves and the look to stand out, and she did. Even the femmes in the place were attracted to her. As the song slowed down, Dakota moved in, taking Jazmine in her arms and moving with her, her body molding to Jazmine's.

Jazmine enjoyed dancing with Dakota, she had good rhythm, and now during the slow song, with Dakota's body pressed close to hers, she felt her body getting excited. By the time the song was over, she was aching for release.

As the song ended and another started, Jazmine leaned into Dakota. "I need you..." she whispered into Dakota's ear, her tone unmistakably horny.

Dakota looked down at her, seeing the look in her eyes. She grinned, and dropped her hand to take Jazmine's. There was a quick walk to the bathroom and they had sex in the larger stall, their screams covered by the loud music of the club.

Chapter 6

Raine was sitting on the bed in the room she was staying in at Cat's house. She'd just gotten out of the shower after getting back from work. She had her music on and was listening to Justin Timberlake's "Cry Me a River." It was hitting way too close to home at that point. The lyrics talked about how she was everything to him, and they just threw it away and now they were sorry. It went on to sarcastically suggest that the girl "cry a river" indicating that it wouldn't do any good to do it.

The problem was that she knew she couldn't be as callous at this. Part of her wished that she could be, because it would probably hurt less, but wishing didn't make it happen. Natalia had finally stopped calling and texting. Raine knew she needed to make a decision and do what she needed to do. She couldn't hide out at Cat's house forever.

She was sitting on the bed, her knees up to her chest when there was a knock on the door. It was half open and she looked up to see Natalia standing hesitantly in the doorway. Raine couldn't believe the way her heart lurched at seeing Natalia again. There had never been a way to get over how beautiful how Natalia was with her dark eyes and bright smile that made her eyes sparkle. Even as she stood looking almost afraid to talk to Raine, she was beautiful. Her dark hair was pulled back in a messy ponytail and her eyes red from crying.

Raine steeled herself and motioned with her hand for Natalia to come in. Natalia walked in, closing the door behind her, and then walked over to the bed and sat down right next to where Raine's feet were. Raine looked at her, seeing the sadness in Natalia's entire presence. It struck a chord in Raine, but she filed it away, not wanting to let it make her weak right now.

"Can we please talk?" Natalia pleaded.

Raine thought about it for a moment, then nodded. "Okay."

Natalia took a deep breath, expelling it slowly to try and calm her nerves. "Raine, I am so sorry for what happened, I would give anything to change it, but I can't. You need to know that I love you so much and I will never love anyone the way I love you. Nothing will ever change that."

Raine looked at Natalia, her eyes searching Natalia's as she talked. When Natalia finished her statement, Raine narrowed her eyes slightly.

"Tell me what happened that night," she said to Natalia. "The truth."

Natalia winced at the last. The fact that Raine now didn't trust her to tell the truth bothered her no end. She knew that she'd destroyed Raine's trust and that it was what was keeping them apart. She just didn't know if she knew how to fix it at this point.

"I was drinking too much that night," Natalia said. "And I'd gone to the bathroom feeling sick and emotional. I was mad that you'd come late again that night, and that you were working so much… I was crying in the bathroom and was just coming out of the stall when I ran into Dakota. She saw that I was crying and I tried to wipe away my tears so she wouldn't see, but I got makeup in my eyes. She helped me over to the sink to try to clean up. When I thought I'd gotten it all, she saw more and wiped at it with her thumb. That was when we kissed."

"Did you kiss her?" Raine asked, remembering what Dakota had said.

Natalia hesitated, but then shook her head. "No, she kissed me, but I should have stopped her and I didn't."

"Then what?" Raine asked, doing her best to steel herself against the rest.

"Raine…" Natalia said, her voice pained.

"I need to hear it," Raine said evenly.

Natalia looked down, afraid to see Raine's eyes when she told the rest of the story. When she got to the part about what Dakota had done, tears fell from her eyes.

"So she left, you didn't…" Raine said. Her voice trailed off as she felt sick at the idea of Natalia touching Dakota sexually.

"No," Natalia said, shaking her head vehemently.

Raine drew in a deep breath and expelled it slowly. Natalia's account of what had happened matched Dakota's.

"You said you were mad at me…" Natalia nodded, looking sad still. "You were working so much, and I just felt like we were drifting apart. With the studio deal I was really excited by the idea and I wanted to share it with you, but you were so tired all the time. You'd come home, take a shower and go to bed… I just felt like you weren't even a part of this great opportunity that I was getting. I guess I resented you a bit."

Raine closed her eyes for a moment, nodding and grimacing at the same time. She blew her breath out, pressing her lips together.

"I heard that you're pulling out of the studio," Raine said then, surprising Natalia by the change in direction of the conversation.

Natalia nodded. "I just can't be there right now, knowing that what happened with Dakota did this to us and... This mess has shown me what is really important to me, and it's not the studio. It is and has always been you, Raine. If I don't have you, I don't want anything."

Raine gave her a pained smile. Then she surprised Natalia by reaching over to the nightstand and picking up an envelope, which she handed to Natalia.

The envelope was addressed to her at the apartment and even had a stamp on it already.

"What is this?" she asked, her eyes searching Raine's face.

"Open it," Raine said softly.

Natalia opened the envelope. It was a single thing, a check made out to her. Then she read the amount.

"Fifty thousand..." she whispered. "Raine, what is this?"

"It's why I was working so much overtime," Raine said, "because I wanted you to have something to buy into the studio with."

Natalia's mouth opened in surprise. "You did this for me?" she asked, her tone aghast.

Raine nodded, looking somber.

"Aye dios mio..." Natalia whispered as new tears began.

She'd been so mad at Raine for working so much. She'd thought that Raine had just wanted to stay away, or didn't care about the studio. It had made her believe that Raine really didn't love her, and it had made her just taciturn enough to allow Dakota to do what she'd done.

"Raine…" she said through her tears. "I had no idea… Why didn't you tell me?"

Raine smiled sadly. "Well, it's not really a surprise if I tell you…"

"I can't take this," Natalia said, handing the check to Raine.

"Why?" Raine said. "It's what it was always meant for."

Natalia shook her head. "I meant what I said, Raine, if I don't have you, I don't want the studio, especially knowing that ultimately it was the studio that brought Dakota into our lives, and it's what happened with Dakota that ended us."

"I talked to Dakota," Raine said after a long pause.

"You did?" Natalia asked, looking worried.

"She came to apologize to me."

Natalia blinked a couple of times, looking surprised.

"What happened?" Natalia asked.

"I didn't deck her if that's what you're asking," Raine said.

"Did you accept her apology?" Natalia asked.

"Not really," Raine said, "but I heard her out, which is why I wanted to hear you out too."

Natalia nodded, looking sad.

Raine looked back at Natalia for a long minute, then sighed. "There was something else."

"Something else?' Natalia asked, not understanding what Raine was saying.

"That was supposed to go with that check," Raine said, her lips pursed in consternation. "Maybe if I give you that, you'll take the check and use it for what I worked all that overtime for."

"I don't understand," Natalia said, shaking her head.

"I know," Raine said. She leaned over and opened the nightstand drawer. She pulled out a small box and handed it to Natalia. "I wanted to give you this too."

Natalia was sure her heart stopped at the sight of the box.

"Raine…" she breathed, not wanting to even dare to hope.

"Open it," Raine said.

Natalia did and was stunned.

Nestled inside was a rose gold ring, with a round diamond in the center. It had a split band that had round baguette diamonds running down both sides, and three round stones in a triangular shape. It was an incredibly beautiful ring and Natalia was once again in tears.

"Oh Raine… It's so beautiful."

"Then put it on and say you'll marry me," Raine said smiling.

"Yes, yes, of course I will!" Natalia said, as she hugged Raine jubilantly.

"Let's go home," Raine said, getting up off the bed.

An hour later, they were back in their apartment making love.

***

Jazmine and Dakota got back to Los Angeles on a Thursday night. Dakota dropped Jazmine off at Rayden's, kissing her on the cheek chastely. Jazmine grinned at the action, but figured Dakota was trying to remind her that nothing had really changed. She didn't need a reminder, she knew who Dakota was, and was okay with that. It had been a wonderful couple of days and she'd enjoyed herself. It didn't need to be any more than that.

As she got out of the car, she winked at Dakota who smiled blithely. Jazmine turned and walked to the front door and went inside. It was around seven in the evening, but it was quiet in the house. Jazmine walked around to the garage and looked inside, Rayden's car wasn't there. She pulled out her phone to check to see if she had any messages from Rayden, but she didn't. She sent Rayden a message, just letting her know that she was home, and asking where she was. She set her phone down on the counter, opened the refrigerator and looked inside, thinking she definitely needed to go grocery shopping. She pulled out a container of yogurt and stood in the kitchen eating it. Her phone buzzed and she checked it, finding a message from Rayden.

It said simply, "Upstairs."

"What?" Jazmine said out loud, confused.

She walked upstairs and stuck her head in Rayden's open door. Rayden was lying on her bed in a tank top and shorts. As Jazmine walked in, Rayden turned her head, and that's when Jazmine saw the cuts on the side of her face.

"Ray! What happened?" she asked, moving to sit on the side of the bed, reaching out to turn Rayden's head so she could see the cuts.

Rayden grinned. "Had a little bit of excitement on the way home from work today," she said, her tone matter of fact.

"Why does that sound really ominous?" Jazmine asked.

"Well, someone took a shot at me tonight," Rayden said.

"What!" Jazmine exclaimed. "Who, do you know? What happened?"

"Well, the 'who' is your friend Jeremy," Rayden said, "and what happened is that fortunately he's a lousy shot, especially when he's driving his big black Escalade. Unfortunately, it's a big black tank of a vehicle that did a pretty good job of forcing me off the road. So…"

"God, Ray… you could have been killed…" Jazmine breathed. "Is that why the Viper isn't in the garage?"

"It's totaled," Rayden said bluntly.

"Ray… I'm so sorry, if I hadn't come here with you… If—"

"Jaz, stop," Rayden interrupted, pulling Jazmine down to hug her. "If you hadn't come here with me you'd probably be dead by now. It's not all bad news, okay? Because he's a dumbass and used his own vehicle and a gun that's not registered to him, the cops picked him up in short order. He's going to be sitting in jail with the added charges of attempted murder of a peace officer, and attempted vehicular manslaughter. He won't get out before the trial, okay?"

"Okay… but are you alright Rayden?" Jazmine asked, looking worried.

"I'm okay," Rayden said.

"You went to a hospital, right?"

Rayden grinned. "Yes, I went to a hospital. They said I have a concussion and I'm bruised and cut up, but that's it."

"Thank God!" Jazmine exclaimed, putting her hand to Rayden's cheek. "I'm so glad you're okay."

Rayden smiled at her.

"So did you have fun?" Rayden asked then, her tone teasing.

Jazmine opened her mouth in surprise, but then saw the amusement in her eyes.

"Yes, I did," she said, her tone chiding.

"Good," Rayden said, nodding her head, her lips twitching slightly as she did.

She sighed then and turned over on her side, wincing slightly as did.

"Is there anything I can do?" Jazmine asked, seeing Ray wince in pain.

"No, I'm okay," Rayden said quietly.

Rayden put her hand on Jazmine's side and closed her eyes. Jazmine kicked off her shoes, moving to at least try comfort Rayden. When Rayden was asleep Jazmine got up and went to shower and change. She climbed back into bed, careful not to wake Rayden. She was happily surprised when Rayden moved to hold her close.

The next morning Jazmine got up and made coffee, checking on Rayden to see if she wanted anything. She saw that the doctors had given Rayden pain meds and she asked if she needed one. Rayden agreed to take a painkiller and even agreed to breakfast. Jazmine spent the next couple of days taking care of Rayden. She was surprised and happy that Rayden let her do just that. It felt like Rayden was finally letting her in a bit and she enjoyed the feeling.

Dakota had texted at one point, just saying, "Hi," and Jazmine had responded. A light conversation had ensued. Jazmine had told her about Jeremy taking a shot at Rayden. Dakota had responded with asking if she needed anything. It seemed that she and Dakota were actually going to manage to be friends. She was very happy about that.

For six months after Grayson had returned to the States, she and Rayden had emailed, texted, talked on the phone, and even Skyped a few times. As Rayden's tour came closer to ending, Grayson nervously anticipated the news that Rayden had been re-upped for combat in the Middle East. Things in the Middle East were always destabilizing, and she was afraid that a recent upswing in violence would definitely mean that Rayden would get held back.

She also knew that even if Rayden didn't get held in Iraq, it wasn't likely that she'd end up on the east coast either since there were no naval bases nearby with SEAL team placements. She got increasingly worried about what would happen next. She missed Rayden desperately; Rayden said she missed her too.

Then suddenly there was a four day time period when she didn't hear from Rayden. By the fourth day of calling and texting with no response, Grayson started thinking every possible thing. She thought maybe Rayden had been hurt, or, God forbid, killed. Then she thought that maybe she'd just gone on a mission, but four days was long time for a "sudden" mission. Her mind churned constantly trying to figure out what happened. She replayed in her head the last few conversations and reread emails looking for clues that Rayden had been pulling away. She really couldn't find anything.

On the fourth day of not hearing from Rayden, Grayson arrived home to the house she was renting. As she walked in, she was surprised to hear music coming from her room. She figured she'd just forgotten to turn it off when she'd left in the morning. She put down her keys and took off her shoes. She walked into her bedroom, intent on turning off the radio. Walking around the corner she was surprised to see someone sitting on her bed, and then she saw who it was. Rayden was sitting, leaning against the headboard, one jean clad leg extended in front of her, the other bent with one arm thrown over it casually. She wore a black button up shirt and black boots. Her hair was loose and she looked so absolutely amazing that Grayson actually forgot to breath.

"Rayden!" she cried, practically throwing herself into Rayden's arms.

"Whoa!" Rayden exclaimed, laughing as she did.

"You're here! How are you here?" Grayson asked, her face pressed against Rayden's neck and inhaling the scent she wore, a rich ocean scent.

"There are these things called planes..." Rayden said, grinning.

"Oh stop..." Grayson said, looking up at Rayden.

Rayden bent her head moving back so she could capture Grayson's lips with hers. Touching her cheek, she deepened the kiss until Grayson was grasping at her shirt. Rayden took her time removing Grayson's uniform, exciting her beyond all reason. Then she removed her own clothes, and made love to her. Both of them reached their release at the same time, crying out and grasping at each other.

Afterwards they lay facing each other, with Rayden's arms wrapped around Grayson who had her face pressed against Rayden's neck.

"I still can't believe you're here," Grayson said her tone awed.

"Well, I'm here," Rayden said, smiling.

"How long can you stay?" Grayson asked, biting her lip worriedly.

Rayden shrugged. "Well, that's going to depend on how quickly I can find a place to live."

"Well, when do you report?" Grayson asked.

"Uh," Rayden stammered, "what day's today?"

"September fifth," Grayson said.

Rayden grimaced. "Three days," she said. Seeing the sad look in Grayson's eyes she said, "I'm sorry babe, but the damn transport from Iraq took forever, and we had like three stops. I swear I got here as fast as I could… I'm sorry…"

Grayson clamped down on her disappointment. She had Rayden here with her at that moment, and at least she was back in the States. *I hope that her new base wasn't ridiculously far.*

"What base did you get?" Grayson asked, trying not to sound too desperate.

Rayden looked back at her for a long moment, her look hesitant. Grayson waited, holding her breath.

"Annapolis," Rayden told her.

Grayson's mouth dropped open, then she narrowed her eyes. "You got Annapolis and that's not the first thing you told me?"

Annapolis, the Naval Academy was literally thirty-three miles from Grayson's base at Andrews, and about fifteen miles from where they were lying.

Rayden chuckled, a deep warm sound. "Well, I kinda wanted to surprise you… And there is the matter of a place to live…" she said, her voice trailing off.

Grayson actually punched her shoulder softly. "You better plan on living here, woman…"

"Ohhhh…" Rayden said, grinning, "I wasn't sure if you'd want me to, I might cramp your style or something…" her voice trailed off as Grayson shoved her to her back and moved to lay over her.

"You will be living here, with me, Rayden Black Wolf, do you understand that? I'm not letting you out of my sight again!"

"Well, if you insist," Rayden said, grinning.

Then her eyes focused on the pendant dangling between them. It was Rayden's pendant.

"You wear that all the time?" Rayden asked her look fond.

"Yes ma'am, all the time," Grayson said, inclining her head.

"Even with your uniform?" Rayden asked.

"Yep," Grayson said, her eyes shining in the semi-darkness of the room. "It's my girlfriend's, you see, and it's very important to her, so I can't let it out of my sight."

"Hmmm," Rayden said, nodding slowly, "but you know that's not regulation, Airman."

"And you know I don't give a shit, SEAL," Grayson replied with a sweet smile.

"Well, I'm gonna want that back," Rayden said, her eye staring up into Grayson's.

"I know," Grayson said, smiling.

"I did bring you something to trade for it though," Rayden said, smiling.

"You did?" Grayson asked, smiling. "Like you aren't present enough for me? Because believe me you are."

"Well, give me my necklace back and I'll give you what I brought you."

Grayson unhooked the necklace and turned it around put on Rayden's neck. Rayden in turn reached over into her duffel bag, which was leaned up against Grayson's nightstand, and pulled out a small box. She held it up to Grayson.

"Rayden..." Grayson said hesitantly.

"Yes?" Rayden asked her smile serene.

"What is this?" Grayson asked.

"Gonna have to open it to find out," Rayden said, her dark eyes sparkling.

Grayson opened the box, and inside sat a diamond ring. It had a round diamond in the center, and was surrounded by what looked like petals with smaller round diamonds dotting the petals. The diamonds were set in white gold.

"Rayden is this..." Grayson began, not wanting to overthink it.

"Yes it is," Rayden said, looking up at Grayson. "Marry me, Gray."

Grayson stared down at Rayden, completely shocked and over-whelmed. She couldn't even formulate a response for a couple of long minutes.

"That isn't exactly an answer..." Rayden said, looking a bit nervous.

"No it's not... I just," Grayson said, then saw Rayden's shocked look and shook her head vehemently. "I mean, yes, yes, I'll marry you, yes!"

Rayden blew her breath out in relief, and then hugged Grayson to her, smiling.

After a couple of minutes, Rayden said. "These last four days, when you didn't hear from me... what were you thinking?"

Grayson didn't answer for a few moments.

"At first I thought that maybe you'd been hurt, or God help me, killed... But then I started thinking..." Her voice trailed off as she shrugged helplessly.

"You started thinking I'd found someone else," Rayden said evenly.

Grayson nodded, her eyes lowered.

"Hey," Rayden said, touching Grayson's chin to get her to look at her. "You should know that wolves mate for life," she said, smiling. "And you are my soul mate, Gray. No one else has ever been to me what you are. I love you."

Grayson smiled brilliantly. "I love you."

Three days after Vegas, Dakota drove up to the Falco home. She'd been summoned once again for a "wound check." She wondered if it was really a welfare check, but she didn't mind.

Lyric was out front washing her car, and Dakota approached her, running an admiring eye over the car once again. Lyric glanced over at her.

"Another wound check?" she asked.

"Yeah," Dakota said, grinning. "She's pretty much all doctor on this kind of thing, isn't she?"

"You can say that again. Savanna's very good at taking care of people," Lyric said, grinning. "After Cody and I were hurt, she's been a bit more protective."

"Was it at the same time?" Dakota asked.

"Yeah, pretty much," Lyric said.

"Aw," Dakota said, nodding. "Still lovin' this car..." she said, smiling. "Ya know if you have any other spare Ferrari's hanging around..."

"Oh, I think something could be arranged if you wanted to do some work on it," Lyric said, moving to soap the other side of the car.

"Why would you want to do that?" Dakota asked looking suspicious.

"Why wouldn't I?" Lyric asked, her tone reasonable.

"You don't really know me."

"No, but you seem like you need more in your life. Maybe building something would be a good thing."

"What's wrong with what I have?" Dakota asked, gesturing to the Bugatti.

"Don't you want something that belongs to you that can't just be taken away if the mood strikes?" Lyric asked.

"Technically my name is on the pink slip of the Bugatti," Dakota said, with a grin. "But I know what you're saying. I still don't get why you'd want to do that for me though."

"Jesus, Dakota, do you ever trust anyone?" Lyric asked her tone astounded.

"Not really, no," Dakota said.

"Well, I think you know enough about me to know that you can trust me, don't you?"

Dakota thought about it for a long moment, but then nodded slowly.

"So, trust me when I tell you that if you'll let us, Dakota, we'd like to be here for you."

"Why?" Dakota asked again suspiciously.

Lyric sighed. "Dakota, you and Cody are so much alike, she was just as suspicious as you at one point in time." She looked over at Dakota as she rinsed her car off. "The fact of the matter is, Savanna and I wish you would have stuck around when you came to see how Cody was way back when at the group home. We honestly feel like you would have maybe had an easier time of things."

"You're saying you would have adopted two street kids?" Dakota asked sarcastically.

"That's what I'm saying, yeah," Lyric said.

Dakota just stared back at her for a long moment her look almost hopeful. Then Lyric saw the cynical mask drop over her face again.

"Who says that's what I want anyway?" Dakota said.

"Well, I think if it wasn't what you wanted, we wouldn't still be talking about it," Lyric said, winking at her.

Just then the door to the garage opened, and Savanna stuck her head out.

"Lyric, have you seen… Oh, Dakota, hi!" she said smiling.

"Hi," Dakota said, smiling brilliantly at Savanna.

Lyric recognized Dakota's look, it was the same one Cody used to get when she would arrive at the group home to pick her up. Savanna's eyes connected with Lyric's who raised her chin slightly and then canted her head toward Dakota as the younger girl was walking toward Savanna. Savanna caught the message, almost telepathically, and smiled again at Dakota as she motioned her inside.

"Let me know what you decide on the car," Lyric called.

"Will do," Dakota said, grinning.

"What? Car? Huh?" Savanna asked as they walked into the house. "She's not trying to trade you for that Bugatti is she?"

Dakota laughed. "Her car's pretty awesome, but it's not even close to being worth what the Bugatti is."

"So, then…" Savanna asked, her tone leading.

"Oh, Lyric said she'd help me work on restoring a Ferrari of my own if I wanted to do that."

Savanna nodded. "Oh, yeah… Be careful there though, Lyric really makes you do the work. She's all about the work being yours."

"That's cool, I think it would be fun," Dakota said, grinning.

"Well, I know she and Cody definitely bonded over Cody's car. They spent hours out there working on it, and going to the yard to pull stuff or pouring over the computer to find the right do-hickey to go with the thingamajig. And yes, I know I'm being very technical, but I've had a lot of practice," Savanna said, winking at Dakota, even as she looked at her arm. "This looks really good," she said, smiling.

"Uh-huh," Dakota said, grinning.

"What?"

"Did I really need to be checked again?"

"Well, it isn't a bad idea," Savanna said, looking chagrined.

"But it wasn't necessary," Dakota said, not looking displeased.

Savanna grinned. "Okay, you caught me. I just wanted to check in with you, see how you are."

Dakota smiled softly, somehow completely disarmed by this woman's kindness. She didn't want to be open to these people, but something kept compelling her to be just that. It was really frustrating.

"I'm alright," Dakota said, smiling.

"Good," Savanna said, smiling too.

Dakota spent another hour at the Falco house talking to Savanna about whatever came to mind. She found that she really liked Savanna. She asked questions, but didn't push too hard about anything. It was obvious she was used to dealing with damaged and skittish kids. Dakota never got the feeling she was being 'handled' though, she felt like Savanna honestly cared. It was an odd feeling.

Chapter 7

Rayden was in her office, it was an insanely busy day. There'd been an officer involved shooting that morning and there were meetings to go to and people to meet with. Rayden was on her fourth cup of coffee of the day, and she'd been in the office for four hours. She was typing furiously on her computer, muttering to herself about, "Budgets being blown all to hell," when there was a light knock on her open door.

"Hold on," she said, with her back to the door as her phone rang. "Black Wolf... Yeah? Well what the hell are they doing there? No, no, you can't let them past, it's still a crime scene... Jesus Christ, seriously? No, tell them that... They what? Oh like I care about their rights at this point. No... Just tell them no. Okay, okay, good. Thanks."

She hung up the phone and went back to typing. She heard a clearing of a throat and only then remembered that someone had knocked on her door.

"What is it?" she said as she turned around.

Then suddenly she couldn't breathe. In her doorway stood a dead woman, and she simply stared.

Grayson stared back at Rayden, her slate-blue eyes shining with unshed tears, her hands held out slightly from her sides plaintively, like she had no idea what to do or say.

"Gray?" Rayden breathed, as if not wanting to say it too loud, lest what she was seeing disappear.

Grayson nodded woefully.

Rayden blew her breath out loudly, putting her hands on her knees and bending forward in an effort to catch her breath. It was obvious she was going into shock. Grayson closed the office door and then strode around Rayden's desk. She got down on her knees, looking up into Rayden's face. Rayden's eyes were open, but she was closing them every so often, looking like she was about to pass out.

"Ray..." Grayson said gently. "You need to breathe slower or you're going to pass out... And that won't be good at all."

Rayden was shaking her head. "How... how..." she started to say through gasping breaths.

Grayson reached up and touched Rayden's face. Rayden closed her eyes, breathing out slowly, her lips trembling. When she opened her eyes again, there were tears in them.

"I buried you..." Rayden said, her voice tremulous.

"No..." Grayson said shaking her head slowly. "No you didn't..."

Rayden let out a sob then, and Grayson hugged her, holding her tightly as Rayden grasped at her as if she was drowning. Grayson held Rayden in her arms, her own tears falling on Rayden's hair. When Rayden finally moved back, she kept her hands on Grayson's arms.

"Come... sit..." Rayden said, moving her gear bag off the chair near her desk and pulling it forward.

Grayson got up and sat in the chair. Rayden moved her chair to sit right in front of her, putting her hands on the arms, and just stared down into Grayson's eyes. She had a million questions but no idea where to start.

"Tell me how you're here," Rayden said, still in total disbelief.

Grayson took a deep breath. "When my plane went down, I didn't go down with it," she said. "I got out… I was badly hurt, and honestly was sure I was dead… I got to the surface, but then I blacked out."

Rayden lowered her head, putting it against Grayson's chest. Grayson smiled fondly and put her hands to Rayden's head, stroking her hair as she told the story.

"From what I could understand some fisherman got me out of the water and took me back to his island. It was some island off of Madagascar. I was in a coma for more than eleven months. No one there seemed to know what to do about telling anyone, so they didn't."

Rayden raised her eyes. "Eleven months?" she asked. "Then…"

"It took some time until I could leave," Grayson said. "And when I got back to D.C. I tried to find you… The house… The Service… I even tried to get ahold of Tyler and Shenin… Your former commander in the Service was finally the one that could tell me where you were."

"Shenin and Tyler are here," Rayden said, feeling a sense of absolute surrealism at that moment. "They came here about two months after…" Her voice trailed off as she swallowed convulsively.

"Oh," Grayson said, nodding. "I guess I have a little bit to catch up on."

Rayden nodded, still looking completely shell-shocked. She sat back in her chair and stared at Grayson.

"So how long have you been back in the States?" Rayden asked.

"About two weeks," Grayson said.

Rayden nodded, looking like she wanted to ask a question.

"You want to know why I didn't contact you sooner," Grayson said.

Rayden nodded her look grave.

"This needed to be in person, Ray…" Grayson said. "What was I going to do? Call you and say 'oh hey it's Gray, I'm alive.' You'd have hung up on a nut."

Rayden grinned. "True," she said. But then she shook her head. "God… I can't even… this is going to take me some time…"

Grayson bit her lip, her slate-blue eyes shining. "I'm not going anywhere."

Rayden sat and stared at her for at least fifteen minutes. The ringing of her phone dragged her out of her trance. Even then, as she reached for her phone, her eyes were on Grayson, like taking her eyes off of the woman would make her disappear.

"Black Wolf," Rayden answered. "Hey Jericho, yeah… I'll be there… I know, I have it… I, uh… Yeah…" she said, stammering as she grinned at Grayson who was watching her closely. "Hey, is Shenin around anywhere up there?" she asked then, winking at Grayson who started to grin. "Great, can you ask her to come see me? Perfect, okay, yeah, I'll see you there."

Rayden hung up the phone, tilting her head at Grayson. "This ought to be interesting…" There was a knock on her office door a couple of minutes later.

Rayden looked at Grayson as she called. "Come!"

"Ray, Jericho said…" Shenin began as she walked into Rayden's office. Then she stopped dead in her tracks as she saw the woman sitting in the chair near Rayden's desk.

"Oh my God…" she breathed. "Gray!" she exclaimed moving to hug Grayson, who stood up to do just that.

Rayden smiled, watching the two hug. They'd been pretty good friends back in D.C.

"How is this possible?" Shenin asked.

"Long story," Grayson said. "Suffice it to say, I'm not dead."

"That's an understatement," Shenin said, beaming.

Shenin looked over at Rayden, smiling sadly. She knew what Rayden had been through, and knew that she needed to tell Grayson that part of it, but she also knew now was not the time.

"I'm gonna leave you two alone, you probably have a lot to talk about," Shenin said, hugging Grayson again. "I'm so happy to have you back."

Grayson smiled. "Thanks."

As Shenin left, Grayson sat back down and just stared at her wife. Her beautiful wife who she'd fought so hard to get back to. For a few minutes they both just sat, watching each other, almost as if they were examining each other, making sure everything was still the same. Rayden just couldn't believe she was looking at her wife. She'd dreamed of this moment every night since she'd 'died.

Rayden's phone rang again, bringing them both back into the present.

"Damnit!" she growled, reaching over she picked it up.

Grayson watched Rayden talk on the phone. She knew that Rayden was having a really hard time with everything. She couldn't begin to imagine how she'd feel in Rayden's position. Grayson's eyes moved over Rayden; she'd lost weight, she could see that much. She was wearing jeans and boots, and a blue button up shirt; it was a really good color on her. Her long black hair was loose and it was obvious she'd run her hands through it a number of times already, but it still look like black silk. At one point during the call, Rayden stood up with her back to her, and Grayson could see the holstered weapon at her back. She'd already seen the badge clipped to her belt. It was so strange to know that a year had passed and things with Rayden had changed and she didn't know about every minute of it.

When Rayden hung up, she looked over at Grayson apologetically.

"I'm sorry, today is absolutely crazy, and I have a meeting later I can't get out of… We can go have lunch somewhere…"

Grayson nodded. "We can do whatever you have time for."

Rayden looked at her watch, another new thing Grayson had never seen.

"Yeah, let's go now," she said, standing up and reaching for her jacket that was slung over the back of her chair.

As they walked out to Rayden's car, Grayson was looking for the Copperhead. She was surprised when Rayden walked over to a blue Jaguar.

"Uh…" Grayson stammered, as Rayden opened the passenger door for her. "What happened to the Viper?"

Rayden rolled her eyes. "It's a long story. I'll tell you, promise."

"Okay," Grayson said, nodding.

Rayden started up the car and music flooded the interior. It was Rayden's usual rock music. She turned it down with a grin.

"Good stereo system," Grayson said, smiling.

"Oh yeah," Rayden said, nodding.

As she pulled out of the parking lot, she looked over at Grayson, still unable to believe that she was alive. As she drove down the road, her mind kept turning over and over the incredible news.

Grayson watched Rayden drive the sports car, and remembered the day that they bought the Viper.

"Am I about to be sorry I let you get this?" Grayson asked, one eyebrow raised at her wife.

"What? Why?" Rayden asked, grinning.

"'Cause you're already a major speed demon, now you've got a really fast car..."

Rayden laughed, her eyes sparkling as she drove the brand new Copperhead Viper. She stopped at a light and glanced over at her wife.

"Oh, and that..." Grayson said, making a face.

"What?" Rayden asked, looking perplexed.

"Coming up on your left," Grayson said, her eyes narrowed.

Rayden glanced to her left as a red Mustang pulled up. The woman was looking over at her with very definite interest. Rayden stuck her hand out the window of the Viper, and waggled her left ring finger with the black wedding band on it. The woman shook her head ruefully and blew Rayden a kiss before she drove off.

"What?" she asked, as Grayson gave her a disapproving look. "It's not like I can control women looking at the car..."

Grayson pressed her lips together. "They aren't just looking at the car, Ray, they're looking at the hot woman driving it too... I don't know about this..."

"Stop it," Rayden told her. "I've mated for life, babe, no one else exists."

Grayson nodded, her slate-blue eyes sparkling. "You better remember that."

"I always do," Rayden said, smiling.

Rayden's phone rang then. She put her Bluetooth in her ear and answered it.

"Black Wolf," she said.

Grayson could only hear her side of the conversation, and she watched her wife closely, always astounded by the incredibly beautiful strong woman she was lucky enough to be married to.

"I, yes, yes sir..." Rayden was saying. "I am, yes... You do? Okay... I... Yes, yes I'm very interested... You'd... I'm what?" Rayden asked, her eyes widening slightly. Then she was nodding, glancing over at Grayson. "Yes, I can, of course sir..." she said, smiling. "I will be there... thank you." She disconnected the call then and looked over at Grayson.

"What was that?" Grayson asked.

Rayden looked at her for a long moment, then a slow smile spread over her lips. "That was the Secret Service... I got it..."

"Oh my God, you did?" Grayson asked, her eyes shining with excitement.

Rayden nodded. She'd applied with the Secret Service as she was due to get out of the SEALs at the end of the month. She really hadn't expected to get it, but she had and there was more than that.

"Babe, I got Obama..." Rayden said then, her tone awed.

"Are you serious?" Grayson asked.

"I am," Rayden said, looking shocked herself.

"Oh my God, Ray, I am so proud of you..." Grayson breathed, reaching across the console and grabbing Rayden's hand to squeeze it.

Rayden was smiling from ear to ear. Things were looking up.

Grayson was very surprised when the song on the iPod changed and the next one that came on was an Adele song. She looked at Rayden, shocked.

"Yeah..." Rayden said, wincing slightly. "The last time I updated my iPod it loaded your playlist too... I couldn't delete it... I just couldn't."

Grayson grimaced. She could see and hear the pain Rayden had been in and was so sorry for it. She took Rayden's hand in both of hers.

"I'm so sorry, Ray..." she said quietly.

Rayden squeezed her hand slightly, nodding.

When they reached the restaurant, Rayden got out and strode around to open the door for Grayson. Inside they ordered some food, and Rayden also ordered a shot and a beer. She drank the shot as soon as it arrived and Grayson noticed that her hand was shaking. She reached out and touched Rayden's arm, her slate-blue eyes searching Rayden's face.

"What happened there?" she asked, gently touching the still heal-ing cuts from the accident.

"Same thing that happened to the Viper," Rayden told her.

"Tell me," Grayson said.

Rayden blew her breath out, knowing there was a lot to tell her, and not sure how to do it.

"Some guy took a shot at me, missed, but shattered the driver's side window... he then forced me off the road, which totaled the Viper."

"How long ago was this?" Grayson asked looking shocked.

"About two weeks," Rayden said.

"But you're okay..."

"Yeah, bruised up, but fine otherwise."

Grayson nodded with relief. "Why was he trying to take a shot at you?"

Rayden looked back at her for a long moment, blowing her breath out.

"He doesn't like me dating his ex," Rayden said, her lips twitching slightly.

Grayson was doing her best to understand.

Rayden lifted the beer to her lips, draining the bottle and signal-ing the waitress for another. She set the bottle down and looked over at Grayson. She had her eyes down and was biting her lip.

"Gray..." Rayden said, feeling aggrieved.

"It's okay, Ray," Grayson said tearfully, still not looking at Ray-den. "It's been a year, and I know that... I knew that this was possible."

Rayden grimaced, wishing that she could make things easier, but she had no idea how to do that. So she waited, knowing that Grayson would ask questions.

"So, who is she?" Grayson asked softly.

"Her name is Jazmine," Rayden said. "I knew her from before I ever went to Iraq."

"So you came back here to be with her?" Grayson asked, feeling knives stabbing her heart as she did.

"No," Rayden said immediately. "No, babe, no..." She could see the pained look on Grayson's face and wanted desperately to take it away. "It was pure coincidence that I ran into her. I kind of had to rescue her from some guys who were trying to hurt her."

Grayson smiled sadly, nodding. "Always saving damsels in distress, aren't you?"

Rayden didn't answer, pressing her lips together in consternation.

"Gray..." Rayden said, shaking her head, her eyes reflecting the turmoil in her head.

Grayson shook her head again. "It's okay," she told Rayden. "Like I said, I knew that this was possible... Do you love her?"

Rayden looked back at Grayson, shaking her head. "No, I care about her... but I've never gotten over you, and I never intended to..." She held up her left hand showing Grayson the black wedding band.

Grayson looked at the wedding band, wondering why she hadn't noticed it before.

"You're still wearing it?" Grayson asked her tone awed.

"I never took it off, Gray, and I never plan to. My heart and soul always belonged to you." Tears gathered in Grayson's eyes then and

Rayden moved around the table to sit next to her. She put her arms around Grayson and whispered in her ear.

"I love you, Gray that never changed... I was completely lost without you... You are never leaving my sight again..."

Grayson cried then, and Rayden held her, not caring who was looking or what they thought. When Grayson had calmed down, Rayden leaned back, looking down at her.

"You okay?" she asked softly.

Grayson nodded, doing her best to wipe at the tears and not mess up her makeup. Rayden saw what she was doing and grinned.

"So what other questions do you have?" Rayden asked.

They spent the better part of an hour going over everything that had happened since Grayson's "death" and Rayden brought her up to speed.

"So you're an actual peace officer now," Grayson clarified.

"Yeah," Rayden said, nodding.

"Wow," Grayson said, her eyes sparkling. "That's kinda hot..." she said then, sounding like her old self suddenly.

Rayden laughed out loud at that.

"And the house..." Grayson asked.

"I sold it, I couldn't be there," Rayden said, "not without you."

Grayson nodded. "Is that why you left the Service?"

"No." Rayden shook her head. "There was an incident," she said, her look pained.

"What happened?" Grayson asked, knowing it wasn't going to be something she wanted to hear.

Rayden blew her breath out. "Someone took a shot at POTUS," she said, using the acronym for the president, in case anyone was listening.

"Was he hit?" Grayson asked.

"No, I blocked the shot," Rayden said.

"Oh God, Ray..." Grayson said, knowing what that meant. "How badly were you hit?"

"To my way of thinking then, not bad enough," Rayden said her look pointed.

"Oh Ray," Grayson breathed, shaking her head, a grimace on her face.

Rayden shook her head. "Anyway, it was enough for me, so after I recovered I put in my resignation."

Grayson nodded, knowing how hard that would have been for Rayden. She'd loved working for the Secret Service and she'd loved protecting Obama. It said a lot about how much Rayden had changed after Grayson's "death."

"So we live here now..." Grayson said, her voice trailing off as she looked around the restaurant.

Rayden nodded. "I bought a house," she said. "Hopefully you'll like it."

Grayson chuckled. "Well, fortunately you have good taste, so it's highly likely."

"So what happens with the Air Force?" Rayden asked then.

"Well, as of right now I'm discharged," Grayson said. "Apparently being dead causes that kind of thing."

Rayden rolled her eyes, nodding.

"I have the option of going back in. They said they'd reinstate me pending a medical clearance... I'd get my wings back, and be right back to normal..."

"And God knows where..." Rayden muttered.

Grayson looked at her for a long moment. "What do you want me to do, Ray?" she asked, her tone completely open.

Rayden looked back at her. "I don't want you to go back into the Air Force," she said, her tone strong. "They could station you anywhere. I really don't want you anywhere but here with me."

Grayson bit her lip, trying not to cry again at the words Rayden used. She nodded.

"But is that going to be okay with you?" Rayden asked.

Grayson touched Rayden's cheek tenderly. "After what you've been through for the last year, anything you want is okay with me, Rayden."

Rayden closed her eyes slowly, breathing a sigh of relief. Grayson smiled sadly at the gesture. She had a feeling Rayden had been through a lot in the last year.

She found out more later that afternoon when she talked to Shenin.

Ray was a mess," Shenin said, shaking her head. "You know how strong she usually is, but there was no consoling her. She stayed with us at first, but then she moved back to base."

"She hates the dorms," Grayson said.

"She hated being at the house without you more," Shenin told her. "I had to practically drag her there just to get clothes and stuff. It was really awful."

Grayson shook her head. She was surprised to hear how openly distraught Rayden was. It made her feel worse about everything.

"How badly was she hurt with the Obama thing?" Grayson asked.

"God, I don't know, Gray, I was already here. So was Ty by that time."

"So she really had no one…" Grayson said, her tone sad.

"I'm sorry, Gray," Shenin said. "We should have taken better care of her, but there was so much going on with us at that point…"

"No, it's okay, Shenin," Grayson said. "I just feel so awful about all of this."

"It isn't exactly your fault, Gray. I seriously doubt you meant to crash and be in a coma for eleven months…"

"No," Grayson said, shaking her head, "but it doesn't change the fact that Ray suffered so much from it."

"So," Shenin said, shrugging, "you spend the rest of your lives making it up to her."

Grayson grinned. "You're right about that."

Shenin reached out and hugged Grayson again. "I'm so glad you're okay, Gray."

"Thanks, it's really nice to know I have at least a couple of friends here," Grayson said. Then she gave Shenin a hesitant look.

"What?" Shenin asked.

"How well do you know the girl Rayden is dating?"

"I really don't," Shenin said. "I mean I've met her, but I don't know her at all."

"What is she like?" Grayson asked.

Shenin frowned, wishing like hell that she could tell Grayson that Jazmine was awful. "She's actually pretty nice."

Grayson nodded. "Is she pretty?"

Shenin winced and nodded.

"Well, Rayden doesn't do things halfway, does she?" Grayson asked.

"I know she was staying at the house with Rayden for a while... I don't know if she still is though."

"Well, that'll be awkward," Grayson said, rolling her eyes.

"You can stay with us..." Shenin said her tone conciliating.

"I may have to take you up on that," Grayson said. "I don't want to cause a big scene."

"You are Rayden's wife, Gray," Shenin said, her tone strong.

"Technically I'm not anymore," Grayson said. "They dissolved the marriage to settle the estate and pay Ray death benefits."

"Oh," Shenin said, grimacing. "This is a real mess."

"Yeah," Grayson said, nodding.

"Well, did Ray say she wanted to stay with Jaz?" Shenin asked.

"Jaz?" Grayson asked.

"Yeah, that's what most people call her," Shenin said, knowing that Grayson was particularly sensitive right now, and understandably so.

"Rayden says she loves me, and that she always has."

"Okay," Shenin said, nodding, "then she just needs time to break the news to Jazmine."

Grayson shook her head. "I just don't know what's the right thing here…"

"Well, what do you want, Gray?" Shenin asked.

"I want my wife back," Grayson said without hesitation.

Shenin smiled. "Then let your wife do what she needs to do to handle things and trust her."

Grayson nodded.

***

At three that afternoon, Jazmine walked out of the building where the dance studio was being built, and saw Rayden standing by her car smoking. Rayden had texted her to tell her that they needed to talk. Jasmine had hoped it would be a good thing, but if Rayden was smoking, something she rarely did, then it wasn't likely to be good.

"Well, this doesn't bode well…" Jazmine said, smiling at Rayden as she reached up to kiss her cheek.

Rayden hugged Jazmine with one arm, extending the hand with the cigarette in it away from her. When Jazmine stepped back, she saw the look of regret in Rayden's eyes.

"Did you hear about Raine and Natalia?" Jazmine asked.

"No, what about them?"

"They're back together and getting married," Jazmine said, smiling wistfully.

"Oh, that's great," Rayden said, smiling. "Does that mean Natalia is back in?"

"Yeah," Jazmine said, smiling. "Yeah she is."

"Good," Rayden said, smiling. "That's a good thing."

Jazmine nodded, knowing that Rayden was trying to gain her nerve to tell her something.

"What is it, Ray?" Jazmine asked her look searching.

Rayden blew out a stream of smoke. "I got kind of a shock today…"

"Okay…" Jazmine said her tone leading.

Rayden looked at her unsure of how to say it. "Jaz… Grayson is alive."

"What!" Jazmine exclaimed, shocked.

"Yeah," Rayden said, nodding. "Trust me it shocked the hell out of me too. She showed up at the office today. I just about passed out," she said her voice strident.

"Wow," Jazmine said, shaking her head. "Where has she been?"

"Apparently in a coma for like eleven months on some tiny little island somewhere," Rayden said looking as shell-shocked as she sounded.

It was clear to Jazmine that Rayden was struggling with everything and trying to break up with her was just part of it.

"That's amazing news, Ray," Jazmine said, smiling, even as her thumbnail dug into the palm of her hand.

Rayden nodded, looking pained.

"Hey," Jazmine said, moving to touch Rayden's face gently. "Don't worry about me, okay? This is Grayson, the love of your life... It's amazing."

Rayden blinked a couple of times, and then narrowed her eyes slightly at Jazmine.

"What?" Jazmine asked, careful to keep her tone perfectly normal, and her expression light.

"You're okay with this," Rayden stated warily.

"Ray, it's Grayson, she's your wife. I know how you feel about her, of course I'm okay."

Rayden was pleased but surprised by Jazmine's reaction. She watched as she spoke, trying to see if there was anything she wasn't saying. Jazmine was very careful to keep her eyes on Rayden's, knowing if she looked away Rayden would know how she was really feeling. Finally, Rayden nodded, as if accepting what Jazmine was saying.

"Jaz, if you need me..." Rayden began, her voice serious. "You know I'll be there for you, right? No matter what."

Jazmine smiled, nodding "Yes, I know that."

"Okay," Rayden said, her look still wary.

"Okay, I gotta get back in there before Dakota and Cassandra kill each other." She reached up to hug Rayden, kissing her on the cheek again. "I'm very happy for you." With that she turned and walked back into the building without a backward glance.

Rayden watched her go and shook her head slightly.

She didn't see that Jazmine never went back upstairs to the studio. Instead, she went out the back door and waited until she heard the Jaguar start up and leave. She then went to her car, got in, and drove away.

Three hours later, no one had heard from Jazmine. Dakota had texted Rayden and said she'd never come back to the studio. Rayden was sick with worry. She called Jericho and had an APB put out on the silver Honda that Jazmine drove.

"Goddamnit!" Rayden cussed, as one more person said they hadn't heard from her. She was still in her office, and Grayson was sitting watching her wife freak out, over another woman. "I knew she was upset, but I let her fucking sweet talk me... Damnit!" she yelled, throwing a stapler across the room.

Grayson jumped at the violence Rayden was exhibiting. She hadn't seen Rayden violent too often, so it always shocked her to see her temper. She was doing her best to keep out of the way and not ask too many questions. She knew that Rayden had gone to see Jazmine and that Jazmine had accepted Rayden breaking up with her quite easily. Things were fine until an hour later when Rayden had gotten a text from someone named Dakota. Then things had gone south quickly.

"Ray..." Grayson said hesitantly.

Rayden looked over at Grayson and saw her uncertainty. She blew her breath out and knelt down in front of where her wife sat.

"I'm sorry honey," she said. "I'm just worried."
"I know," Grayson said, nodding.

"And you think it's because I'm in love with her," Rayden guessed easily.

Grayson blinked a couple of times, looking sad as she nodded.

"Oh babe…" Rayden said, moving to take Grayson in her arms. "No, it's not that, okay? It's not… I just feel like shit, I screwed her over once before, and now this… And I just feel like hell right now, okay?"

"How did you screw her over before?" Grayson asked.

"When I left for Iraq, I literally left her a note, six months' rent and a kind 'I'll call you' kind of bullshit. And I never talked to her again."

"Ouch," Grayson said, grimacing at what Rayden said.

"It's how I was then," Rayden said, shrugging. "But I was hoping not to do that to her again, and here I am… doing it again."

"I think the circumstances are a bit different this time, Ray…" Grayson said.

Rayden blew her breath out. "I know, you're right, but if something happens to her, I'll never forgive myself."

"I know," Grayson said, feeling better about the situation now she understood why Rayden was so upset.

Rayden's phone buzzed. She looked at it and sighed in relief.

"Dakota found her," she said.

"Good," Grayson said, smiling.

Rayden nodded, looking immensely more relaxed suddenly.

"I think it's time we go home, Mrs. Black Wolf," Rayden said, standing up and putting her hand out to Grayson.

Grayson bit her lip, smiling up at Rayden as she stood up taking Rayden's hand.

Rayden drove into the garage at her house, still feeling a sense of unreality. Grayson looked over at her as she turned the car off and Rayden smiled softly.

Rayden got out of the car and walked around to open the door for Grayson. Then she led the way into the house and turned off the alarm. Grayson walked into the house and looked around. She smiled, seeing some of the things they'd had together in their old house. There were other things that were new, that were very much Rayden's style. Rayden reached into the refrigerator for a beer, looking over at Grayson in askance.

"Yes," Grayson said, smiling.

Having a beer when they got home from work together was always a routine for them.

Rayden took out two beers and opened them both, then handed one to Grayson. She leaned against the kitchen counter watching Grayson look around their house.

"There are two other floors," Rayden told her.

"Okay," Grayson said, smiling as she took a drink of her beer. "Which floor is the bedroom on?" she asked simply.

Rayden's mouth dropped open. Then she grinned.

"This way," she said, motioning with her head for Grayson to follow her.

Grayson followed Rayden upstairs. In the master bedroom, Grayson put her beer down and slid her hands over Rayden's shoulders. Rayden slid her arms around Grayson, pulling her to her and kissing her lips gently. Grayson promptly wrapped her arms around Rayden's neck, and moved closer to her. Rayden deepened the kiss and Grayson moaned against her lips.

Grayson unbuttoned Rayden's shirt, pulling it open as Rayden pulled Grayson's blouse off over her head.

Grayson's hands stilled Rayden's movements as she stared at Rayden's chest, where the tattoo with the "Gray" was.

"Ray…" Grayson breathed, seeing the peace symbol tattooed next to her name.

Rayden looked down at her, there were tears in Grayson's eyes. She put her hand to Grayson's cheek, her thumb brushing from her cheek to her temple.

"I lost you," Rayden said simply. "I needed to keep you close somehow."

Grayson bit her lip, tears dropping from her eyes as she shook her head. Rayden pulled her into her embrace then, hugging her, and kissing her temple and cheek. Grayson wrapped her arms around Rayden tightly, her head resting against the tattoo.

"For as long as I live," Grayson said, her voice a whisper, "I'll never fully know what this did to you, will I?"

Rayden hugged her tighter, closing her eyes for a long moment. Then she leaned back and looked down at Grayson.

"It doesn't matter," she said. "You're here with me now, Gray, and that is all that matters."

Grayson nodded, trying to take in what Rayden was saying, not wanting to spoil their reunion with her remorse. It was clear Grayson was struggling with feeling bad about what her "death" had done to Rayden. But she was also trying to be in the moment with her wife.

She captured Grayson's lips again and kissed her until she was breathless and unable to think of anything other than their bodies together. Minutes later, they were lying on the bed making love and remembering how much sexual chemistry they'd always had.

As they lay together afterwards, Rayden's eyes looked over every inch of her wife's face. She reached out and touched her cheek, her eyes reflecting amazement and wonder.

"I love you so much…" Rayden said. "And my God I have missed you every second of every day… But you're here now, Gray, really here and I wouldn't give that up for anything."

Grayson smiled at Rayden, knowing that Rayden was trying to help her get through her guilt.

"You know how I think," Rayden said then. "And you know that I always feel like things happen for a reason… the Spirit did this for a reason… We don't know what it is, but I think we will someday. Until then, let's just be happy that she saw fit to put us back together now."

Grayson nodded, knowing that it was exactly how Rayden would see things. She always believed that everything that ever happened, good or bad, happened for a reason. Somehow, it felt good to know that Rayden hadn't changed, and hadn't abandoned her beliefs when it would have been so easy to do just that.

She shook her head in wonder, looking back at the proud, beautiful Cherokee warrior she was lucky enough to be loved by. Her eyes reflected all the love and pride she had in Rayden. They spent the entire night just staring at each other, touching at times, other times just looking into each other's eyes. It was nearly midnight when

Grayson remembered they hadn't eaten anything. They went downstairs to the kitchen and made omelets from the few things that Rayden had in the house. It was the perfect night.

***

Dakota was frantic by the time she circled back to the studio, just in case… and there sat Jazmine's car. She parked the Bugatti and jumped out, then checked the Honda but Jazmine wasn't in it. She ran up the stairs to the where the studio build was going on and found the door open. She pushed the door open slowly and saw the mess. There were floorboards strewn everywhere, there was drywall knocked over, nails thrown everywhere.

Then she saw Jazmine lying on the floor curled into almost a ball.

"Jaz!" Dakota called, running over to her, and sliding to a stop on her knees on the floor. "Jaz?" she said again. "Come on, hon, talk to me…" Dakota said, moving to touch Jazmine's face, checking to make sure she was breathing.

Jazmine stirred, and Dakota could smell the tequila. She glanced around saw a broken bottle nearby.

"Okay, we're drowning our sorrows… Why?" Dakota asked.

Jazmine moaned and shook her head. Then she sat up, bursting into tears immediately upon seeing Dakota. Dakota immediately took her in her arms. As she held Jazmine, she pulled out her phone and texted Rayden that she had found her. "Okay, okay…" she said over and over again, holding Jazmine and doing her best to soothe her. "What's going on Jaz, huh? What's wrong?"

Jazmine took gasping breaths. "Ray… Ray's… wife… she's not… dead…"

"Oh Holy Hell really?" Dakota asked. Jazmine started to cry again. "Okay, honey, okay, let's get you out of here, okay?" Dakota stood up, helping Jazmine to her feet slowly.

Jazmine looked around and then cried out. "Oh God, Dakota, I'm so sorry!"

"It's okay, honey, I can fix it," Dakota said, grinning. "Come on." She helped Jazmine walk toward the door, careful to avoid nails and glass.

In the Bugatti on the way to Jazmine's apartment, she sat huddled in the seat, looking extremely drunk and miserable.

"Jaz? You with me?" Dakota asked.

Jazmine nodded.

"How much of that bottle did you drink, babe?" Dakota asked gently.

Jazmine just looked back at her.

"I'll take that as all of it… Jesus Jaz…Why didn't you just come back upstairs?"

Jazmine shook her head. "Cassandra was there, I couldn't fall apart in front of her."

"Okay, so why didn't you text me. I would have come down."

Jazmine shook her head again. "She's already so mad at you over Vegas…"

"She doesn't know you were with me in Vegas, Jaz," Dakota said. "And I can handle her, okay?"

Jazmine just shook her head again, but stayed silent.

At Jazmine's apartment, Dakota sent a quick text to Cody to ask Savanna to come over if she could. Then she got out of the car and helped Jazmine out, and took her up to her apartment. Jazmine opened the door and turned to Dakota.

"Thanks," she said, mumbling.

"Yeah, I'm not leaving you here alone," Dakota said. "Go on." She motioned for Jazmine to go into the apartment.

"Dakota…" Jazmine started to say but Dakota just stood and waited, her look impassive.

Jazmine finally shook her head and walked inside. Dakota followed her, kicking the door closed and locking it.

"Go take a shower. I'm going to find something for you to eat to soak up some of that alcohol," Dakota told her.

Jazmine nodded and walked toward her bedroom. Ten minutes later Dakota walked into the bathroom.

"Jaz?" she queried.

Looking in the shower, she saw Jazmine sitting under the water with her arms wrapped around her knees, crying.

"Oh babe…" Dakota said. She kicked off her shoes and took off her jacket, shirt, and pants.

She climbed into the shower behind Jazmine, bent down, and wrapped her arms around her. "Come on honey…" she said softly.

Jazmine only cried harder. Dakota reached out, turning off the shower.

"Jaz... honey... come on..." Dakota said softly, pulling Jazmine into her arms.

Jazmine turned in her arms and put her head against Dakota's shoulder still crying.

"Okay... just stay here with me. Okay... just stay here..."

She gathered Jazmine against her, and grabbed a towel off a hook to wrap around Jazmine who was now shivering.

"Okay, we're good..." Dakota said, her tone still gentle.

When Jazmine finally calmed again, Dakota helped her stand, assisting her out of the shower. She walked her into the bedroom, putt her in bed, and covered her up making sure she was warm. She sat next to Jazmine on the bed, and Jazmine snuggled against her. Dakota put her arm around her and Jazmine huddled closer. Dakota lay down, pulling Jazmine into her arms, she held her until she was finally asleep.

Dakota got out of bed carefully, not wanting to wake Jazmine. She did her best to dry off her bra and underwear then put her clothes back on. She went down to her car, got her iPad out, and went back up to the apartment. She checked her phone and saw that Cody had texted back for the address to Jaz's apartment. Dakota sent it, and got a text back saying Savanna would be there in an hour or so.

An hour later there was a knock at the door. Dakota got up and walked to the front door. She checked the peephole and saw it was Savanna. She opened the door and smiled.

"Thanks for coming," Dakota said.

"No problem," Savanna said, stepping inside. "What's going on?"

"It's Jazmine," Dakota said, gesturing toward the bedroom. "She drank an entire bottle of tequila and I'm just worried that she might have way over done it, you know?"

Savanna nodded. "Let me see her."

Dakota led the way into Jazmine's bedroom. Savanna checked her over carefully, as Dakota more or less paced looking worried. When she was done, she motioned to the living room and they both left Jazmine to sleep.

"Is she okay?" Dakota asked.

"She seems fine, but you need to watch for a few things, okay?" Savanna said.

"Keep checking her breathing; if it slows down or becomes shallow you need to call 911. Also I want you to wake her up every half hour to make sure she wakes up. If she gets hard to wake up, call 911, alright?" Savanna put her hand out to Dakota. "She's probably okay, Dakota, but you being here is really important, okay?"

Dakota nodded, her eyes wide. She looked scared.

"Are you okay?" Savanna asked, seeing the fearful look in Dakota's eyes.

"Yeah," Dakota said, nodding. "I'm just worried, that's all."

Savanna smiled. For someone who didn't want attachments, Dakota sure seemed to be forming them left and right these days. Impulsively, Savanna took Dakota into her arms and hugged her.

"You are a good friend, Dakota. I'm so proud of you," Savanna said against Dakota's head.

Savanna felt Dakota's hands squeeze her gently; she took it as a thank you. When Savanna stepped back, she was sure she saw a sheen of tears in Dakota's eyes. She purposely looked around the apartment to give Dakota time to compose herself.

"She'll be fine, Dakota," Savanna said then, smiling. "Just keep an eye on her, okay?"

"Okay," Dakota said, nodding. "Thank you Savanna, I really appreciate you coming."

"If you need anything call me, or Lyric," Savanna said and she pulled a pad of paper out of her purse and wrote down their numbers.

"Okay," Dakota said again, taking the paper and tucking it into her pants pocket.

Savanna left then and Dakota walked back into Jazmine's bedroom. She sat on the bed again, looking down at Jazmine who was sleeping with her hand curled under her cheek. She smiled fondly; Jazmine looked just like a little girl when she slept.

Dakota spent the next twelve hours checking on Jazmine and waking her up every half hour like Savanna had told her. Jazmine woke every time, much to Dakota's relief. While Jazmine slept, Dakota worked on her iPad, playing with some ideas she'd had for the studio.

When Jazmine woke on her own, Dakota got her to eat some toast and drink some water, then Jazmine went back to sleep. Dakota spent the next day and a half much the same way. She'd texted Cassandra and told her that "Something came up." She was assailed with a number of threatening texts from Cassandra but she ignored them all.

Jazmine had been right about Cassandra being pissed about Vegas. Dakota had taken off and not let her know where she was or where she was going. Cassandra tried to play it off that she'd been worried about Dakota, but Dakota knew better. What Cassandra didn't like was that Dakota had been out of her control and she had no idea who she'd been with. Dakota had told her that she'd gone alone, that she'd just needed time to "blow off steam." Cassandra knew better than that, and knew that at the very least Dakota had whored her way around Las Vegas. It pissed her off no end.

Things had gotten loud and almost violent when she'd returned. Dakota had warned Cassandra off telling her that if she tried the same bullshit she'd done before, that she would fight back and Cassandra would have to explain to her friends why she had a black eye. Cassandra had backed off then, but Dakota had a feeling she hadn't heard the last of it.

Jazmine woke up and noticed that Dakota was sitting next to her on the bed. She sat up and leaned against Dakota's arm to see what she was doing. Dakota had her iPad on her lap, and was working with a stylus on a schematic drawing. Dakota glanced over at her, grinning.

"What is that?" Jazmine asked.

"The studio," Dakota said, moving things around on the screen.

"Show me," Jazmine said, moving closer.

"This is just some of the ideas I had," Dakota said, pointing to the side of the screen. "Okay, these are the windows here and here… and this is where we have the mirrors right now… If we move this… and this… we can open this up…"

As Dakota moved things, Jazmine's eyes grew wider and wider. "Oh my God, Dakota, that would be fantastic!" she exclaimed, hugging Dakota's arm ecstatically.

Dakota smiled. "Glad you like it…"

"I really do," Jazmine said, smiling. "You really have a great eye, Dakota. You see things the way they could be, not just the way they are, and how you can work around it."

Dakota looked over at Jazmine and saw her sincere look. It made her feel good that Jazmine thought so highly of her work.

Later that evening Dakota ordered dinner for them and they sat eating and chatting.

"You know," Jazmine said. "You've been here all this time, and you haven't made one pass at me..." she said, her grin wry.

"Is that a compliment or a complaint?" Dakota asked, grinning.

"It's an observation," Jazmine said.

Dakota looked back at her, narrowing her eyes slightly, but then shook her head. "It probably has something to do with that conscience thing I've been cultivating, it's really messing with my game..." she said, winking at Jazmine.

Jazmine laughed softly. "Uh-huh..." she said, her voice trailing off as she shook her head.

Dakota's phone buzzed again, ringing this time. Jazmine saw Cassandra's name on the display. Dakota hit ignore and set the phone aside.

"Dakota..." Jazmine said. "I'm okay if you need to go."

"It's fine," Dakota said.

"She's just going to get more pissed off," Jazmine said. "Just go."

"Okay, I will, after dinner."

"Okay," Jazmine said, feeling better.

A half an hour later, Dakota was at the front door. Jazmine hugged her tight.

"Thank you for being here for me," Jazmine said. "I don't know how I would have even gotten home."

"Well, that's what friends do," Dakota said, smiling.

Chapter 8

Things between Raine and Natalia had improved more and more since their reconciliation. They'd talked for hours on end about what had happened, and how each of them felt.

One Saturday afternoon, they were sitting in their living room, discussing ideas for the wedding.

"We can do whatever you want," Raine said, smiling.

"You don't care?" Natalia asked.

"All I care about is that we get married," Raine said, reaching out to touch Natalia's cheek, her look tender. "I just want you to be mine."

Natalia smiled warmly, her eyes misting with tears. "I am yours Raine, siempre... always."

Raine nodded, smiling brightly. "Good, as long as we have that settled."

Natalia laughed and put her head on Raine's shoulder. "I love you," she said, glancing up at Raine.

"And I love you," Raine said, her look sobering a bit, "and I never want to go through that again."

"You never will," Natalia assured her. "I will never let us get to that point again. I should have talked to you, I should have asked you questions. I was stupido and assumed too much."

"Well, I should have noticed that I was losing you, babe, and I should have told you what I was doing. We're both guilty in this."

Natalia pressed her lips together, feeling like she was still mostly at fault, but knowing it would do no good to argue with Raine. It still amazed her that Raine was so willing to let everything go, and even willing to take some responsibility in what had happened. She knew, now more than ever, that Raine was who she'd been meant for all along.

Hugging Raine closer, Natalia once again thanked the powers that be that she still had this wonderful woman.

***

Jazmine texted Dakota for the fourth time in an hour, she was getting worried. She'd received a text from Dakota when she'd gotten back to Cassandra's house the other night. It said simply, "She's not even here! LOL!" with an emoticon of someone rolling their eyes. That was the last time she'd heard from Dakota. She knew it was possible that Dakota was just busy "making it up" to Cassandra, but her mind veered away from that thought. She knew she was becoming far too attached to Dakota, and that was likely to end as badly as her relationship with Rayden had.

By this time, everyone had heard about Grayson Black Wolf being alive and back in Rayden's life. Jazmine had received a few texts, one from Natalia asking if she was okay. Another text she'd received was from Shenin, again asking if she was okay and offering to 'talk' if she needed to. Jazmine thought she might take Shenin up on her offer, since Shenin knew Grayson. She wanted to talk to Dakota about the idea, but she couldn't get ahold of her.

Finally, she just answered Shenin's text and asked if Shenin had time to meet for lunch. Shenin agreed and they planned to meet at a local café near the office. Jazmine got there early and found a table that was private enough for them to have a conversation.

"Hi," Shenin said when she arrived. She smiled and hugged Jazmine.

"Hi," Jazmine replied hugging Shenin back.

"So, how are you?" Shenin asked, after they'd ordered drinks.

Shenin had been fully aware of the APB Rayden had put out on the girl and that she'd just disappeared for a while after Rayden had told her about Grayson being back. She had hoped that Jazmine would be willing to talk to her, if for no other reason than for her to tell Rayden if Jazmine was okay or not.

Jazmine was slow to answer, considering what to say. "I'm okay," she said softly. "I guess I just…" She shrugged. "I just don't know how to deal with this, you know?"

Shenin nodded. "Yeah, they really don't write Cosmo articles on how to deal with things when your girlfriend's dead wife shows up."

Jazmine laughed, nodding her head. "Yeah, why don't they have that one?"

"I don't know, maybe you should write it," Shenin said, grinning.

"I'm betting Cosmo wouldn't agree with 'drink an entire bottle of tequila and trash the dance studio you're working on…' " Jazmine said, grimacing.

Shenin grimaced as well. "Yeah, that's probably not considered very healthy," she said, her tone chagrinned.

Jazmine sighed. "I know," she said, shaking her head. "But it's what I did and I can't undo that fact."

Shenin nodded. "That's true. But you can control how you handle things from here."

Jazmine looked back at Shenin, trying to decide if she was trying to help her or if she was really trying to help Rayden and Grayson.

"I'm not planning to make any trouble for them, you know," Jazmine said evenly.

Shenin blew her breath out. "That's not why I'm here, Jazmine," she said, shaking her head. "I'm not here to tell you to leave them alone, okay? I'm here because I want to make sure you're okay."

Jazmine thought about it for a long moment. "Why?"

Shenin looked somber. "Because I know what happens when people get too far down with no one to break their fall..." she said, turning her arm over, exposing the scars on her wrists from a suicide attempt.

Jazmine looked at the scars and widened her eyes, shocked. Shenin had always seemed so strong. She was married to Tyler and they seemed to be so in love, it didn't make any sense. Her eyes searched Shenin's.

Shenin smiled. "Are you looking for what caused this?" she asked, nodding at her wrists. "Trauma," she said simply. "Undealt with trauma."

Jazmine drew in a deep breath and blew it out slowly, nodding her head.

"You think I'd do that?" Jazmine asked her voice holding no derision or judgment.

"I don't know," Shenin said, "But I've learned the hard way that sometimes we don't ask the questions we need to ask to make sure people we care about are okay."

Jazmine nodded slowly. "Well, I appreciate your concern, but I'm okay."

"Okay," Shenin said, nodding. "Did you want to ask me anything?"

Jazmine's look flickered, and Shenin knew that she'd hit on Jazmine's reason for accepting the invitation.

"Ask," Shenin said simply.

"What is she like?"

Shenin smiled. "Gray asked me the same question about you."

"She did?" Jazmine asked, looking shocked.

"She's just as curious about you, as you are about her."

"Why? She's got Rayden, she wins," Jazmine said, sounding defeated.

Shenin winced at not only Jazmine's words but her tone as well.

"Jazmine, you have to see it from her side. She's been gone for a year, 'dead' as far as Rayden knew. Now she shows up here in LA, Rayden has moved on with a beautiful dancer, how do you think she's going to feel?"

Jazmine looked back at Shenin for a long moment. "Rayden loves her, she never stopped loving her," she said, her tone flabbergasted. "How can she not see that?"

Shenin smiled sadly. "We women can't always see what's right in front of our faces. We look at ourselves and tell ourselves all kinds of crazy shit to justify our feelings of insecurity. It's a birthright of women."

"So you think she's telling herself that Rayden really loved me?" Jazmine asked.

"I think it's in her head, yes," Shenin said.

"That's crazy," Jazmine said, shaking her head.

"Is it?" Shenin asked. "You and Rayden were together before, right?"

"Right," Jazmine said.

"Here in LA," Shenin said.

"Yeah," Jazmine replied.

"They lived in D.C., Grayson 'dies' and Rayden moves all the way across the country, and ends up with you again. What do you think Grayson is thinking?" Shenin asked.

"But Ray didn't move here to be with me, she moved here for a job."

"Right," Shenin said. "But she's with you. What part do you think Grayson is seeing?"

Jazmine blew her breath out, shaking her head. "Jesus, we women are fucked up messes aren't we?"

Shenin laughed, nodding her head. "Yes, we are."

"So maybe I should talk to Grayson."

Shenin looked pensive. "That would be up to you."

"Do you think she'd talk to me?" Jazmine asked.

"We can ask."

"We?"

"I can text her right now, if you want me to."

"You'd do this with me?"

"If you want me to, yes."

"Text her," Jazmine said, wanting to get things resolved.

To Shenin's surprise, not only was Grayson willing to talk to Jazmine, she wanted to do so as soon as possible.

"Do you want me to invite her down here?" Shenin asked Jazmine.

"Yeah, do it."

In Rayden's office, Grayson was surprised when she got the text from Shenin asking if she would meet her and Jazmine for lunch.

"What?" Rayden asked seeing the surprise on her wife's face.

"Uh," Grayson stammered.

"Who is that?"

"Shenin," Grayson said. "She's having lunch with Jazmine and they want me to come down there."

"Aww…" Rayden stammered, looking like she thought it wasn't a good idea.

"What?" Grayson asked.

"Why would you go down there?"

"Because Jazmine and I need to talk, Ray."

"Why?"

Grayson stared back at her, a little surprised Rayden didn't understand why. "If the roles were reversed, wouldn't you want to talk to the person I'd been spending time with?"

"I'd want to kill the person you'd been spending time with," Rayden said her dark eyes glittering with malice.

Grayson laughed softly at that. "Okay, but, in this case…"

Rayden looked pensive, then shook her head. "I don't like it," she said simply.

"Why?"

Rayden's eyes searched hers. Grayson could see she was conflicted. "Tell me why, Ray," she said softly.

Rayden blew her breath out, shaking her head. "I guess I'm afraid you'll be too hard on her, or she'll be too hard on you, or both."

Grayson tilted her head slightly. "Why don't you trust that the two women you love can be adults about things?"

Rayden narrowed her eyes, not liking that Grayson had just referred to Jazmine as one of the women she "loved." But the fact was, she did love Jazmine, she just wasn't in love with her, not the way she was with Grayson. The fact that Grayson had put them together in that category bothered her. It also told her that there was something that Grayson needed to work through and she needed to let her do that her way.

Finally, she nodded. "Okay, go," she said. "But if I have to send armed agents down there to break up a fight, I'm not bailing either of you out."

Grayson laughed, standing up as she sent Shenin a text accepting the offer. Then she leaned down to kiss Rayden's lips.

"I'll try not to get into trouble," she said, smiling.

"Uh-huh," Rayden said, shaking her head ruefully.

Ten minutes later, Grayson was walking into the restaurant and out onto the patio where Jazmine and Shenin sat. The very first impression Grayson had of Jazmine was, *Oh my god she's hot!* Jazmine wore an emerald-green lace up off the shoulder blouse that exposed her perfectly smooth and tanned leanly muscled shoulders. The blouse exposed the slight rounding of breasts, cleavage that Grayson only ever dreamed of having. The color of the blouse set Jazmine's rich auburn hair off perfectly. Her hair cascaded in waves halfway down her chest. She had a brilliant white smile with perfect makeup that complimented her eyes. She looked like a goddamned Victoria Secret model!

Jazmine saw in Grayson an athletic, leanly muscled woman with beautiful slate-blue eyes and honey-blond hair pulled back into a messy ponytail. Grayson had the sporty, sexy look that Jazmine had always envied. She was slim, but Jazmine could see from her arms, exposed by her blue Air Force tank top, that she was strong. She suspected Grayson was the type of woman that had perfect abs, and not an ounce of fat on her. She had very little makeup on, but was beautiful all the same.

"Hi," Grayson said, looking at Jazmine, and extending her hand to the other woman. "I'm Grayson."

Jazmine took Grayson's hand. "I'm Jazmine," she said, knowing it was unnecessary.

She appreciated that Grayson hadn't used her last name Black Wolf. She felt it indicated that Grayson wasn't trying to shove it in her face that she was Rayden's wife. Jazmine knew full well that Grayson could have used it like a weapon. The fact that she didn't put Jazmine at ease.

Grayson sat down in a chair, glancing up as the waitress came over.

"Can I get a beer?" Grayson asked, then grinned at Shenin and Jazmine "And I don't know about you two, but I need a shot of something, what do you say?"

"Love it," Jazmine said, grinning. "Just not tequila please…"

Shenin chuckled. "How about Jack? That's always safe."

Grayson glanced at Jazmine, who nodded agreement. "Three shots of Jack, and if you have Shocktop that'd be great."

"We have it on tap," the waitress said, winking at Grayson flirtatiously.

"Perfect," Grayson said, grinning engagingly.

When the waitress walked away and Grayson turned back to the other two women. "You get that a lot here?" Grayson asked, looking surprised.

Shenin laughed. "Not here. But I guess we're just not her type," she said, winking at Grayson.

"Oh, God, stop it," Grayson said, shaking her head and rolling her eyes.

"Gray, that was a definite 'call me' wink," Shenin said, grinning delightedly.

"It was a flirt, I'll give you that," Grayson said, looking amused.

"I bet you get that kind of thing a lot," Jazmine said, smiling at Grayson.

"Why do you say that?" Grayson asked, looking surprised but smiling.

"You've got that sexy sporty thing going on," Jazmine said, waving her hand in Grayson's direction.

"I've got that, I don't have any clothes anymore thing going on," Grayson said, laughing.

"Ouch," Shenin said. "That would be the worst part for me…" she said, shaking her head.

"Bullshit," Grayson said, her look serious. "The worst part for you would be the same as it is for me, thinking that you'd fucked Ty up forever."

"No, I did that a whole other way," Shenin said, rolling her eyes as she grimaced.

Grayson canted her head. "What happened, Shen?" she asked, her voice concerned.

"Gave in to the demons," Shenin said, looking pained.

"Oh God…" Grayson said, reaching out to take Shenin's hand. "Are you okay now?"

Shenin nodded. "But we're not here to talk about me," she said, looking over at Jazmine.

Jazmine had watched the two women talk, and knew that they'd been good friends for a while. She missed that closeness with someone. She never had good friends for long, there was always some jealous crap over a guy or a job, and the friendship ended.

"You're right," Grayson said, "but you and I need to talk later," she said, giving Shenin a pointed look.

"Okay, okay," Shenin said, waving her hand in surrender.

The three were silent for a moment, and the waitress arrived with the beer and the shots.

"To Girl Power," Shenin said, grinning.

"Here, here," Grayson said.

"Amen!" Jazmine said.

They clinked glasses and did the shot, grinning at each other afterwards.

"So, Grayson," Jazmine said.

"Call me Gray," she said. "Grayson always sounds so snobby."

Jazmine smiled. "I think it sounds sophisticated."

"I'm not that either," Grayson said, grinning.

"Okay," Jazmine said, chuckling. "Gray," she began again, "Shenin said that she thinks you might think that Ray is in love with me."

Grayson looked surprised, but then nodded. "She's right."

Jazmine grimaced. "Gray, I don't know how much you know about Rayden's past," she said, "but if you know anything about her from before, you'd know that she doesn't commit to just anyone."

Grayson looked back at Jazmine, her look speculative, but then she nodded. "You're right about that."

"So if you know that, you should know that Rayden is in love with you, and she has been, even when she thought you were dead."

Grayson blinked a couple of times. It was obvious she was almost afraid to accept that answer.

"But what about you?" Grayson asked then.

"What about me?" Jazmine asked, her tone somewhat caustic. "Rayden was rescuing me yet again, it doesn't mean she was in love with me."

"Rescuing you again?" Grayson asked. "I know Ray said that she had stopped some guys from hurting you when you met again, but there was another time?"

"Yeah," Jazmine said, grinning. "The first time I met Ray she rescued me from some guy I was dating who was getting rough with me."

Grayson laughed. "Yeah, that sounds like Ray. That's how I met her too."

"Seriously?" Jazmine asked her eyes wide like her grin.

"Yep," Grayson said, smiling.

"She does have an MO doesn't she?"

"That she does," Grayson said, nodding.

"Well, she knocked my guy out with one punch, what did she do to yours?"

"Picked him up by the throat and slammed him into a building," Grayson said, grinning.

"Wow," Jazmine said, looking surprised.

"Yeah," Grayson said, her eyes shining with remembered awe. "She was all bad assed Navy SEAL... It was so hot."

Jazmine laughed out loud, nodding as she did. "Yeah, that was this time too."

"Gotta love her for her chivalry," Grayson said.

"Oh yes," Jazmine said, nodding. Then she looked serious. "Don't get me wrong, Gray, I love Ray, I really do, and your sudden appearance definitely put me into a tailspin. But I knew in my heart of hearts that she was never going to love me, not like she loved you."

Grayson looked back at Jazmine. She could see nothing but open sincerity in the other woman's eyes. A visible weight lifted off her as she finally let herself believe what Rayden had been telling her all along. She'd never stopped loving her.

"Thank you," Grayson said. "It's really hard to think that the person you love desperately might not love you the same anymore."

"Well, I think you can rest assured that Rayden does," Jazmine said.

Grayson looked back at Jazmine, astounded by the empathy she saw in Jazmine's eyes. She couldn't say that she'd be so gracious if the roles had been reversed.

"So what happens now?" Grayson asked, her look sympathetic. "For you, I mean?"

"Well," Jazmine said, her look contemplative. "The one thing that I've kind of figured out from being with Ray again is that I really need to stop dating men altogether."

"Amen!" Shenin said, grinning.

The three laughed.

"Is Ray really different from the other women you've dated?" Grayson asked.

"That's the thing," Jazmine said. "Ray is the only woman I've ever dated."

"Wow, really?" Shenin asked, grinning. "Ty's the only one I ever dated too."

"Really?" Jazmine asked. "You two are so perfect together, that's really amazing."

"Oh, trust me, it took a lot of convincing on my part," Shenin said, rolling her eyes.

"Convincing Ty? Of what?" Jazmine asked.

"That I really wanted to be with her," Shenin said. "This was during Don't Ask, Don't Tell, and we were both Air Force."

"Oh," Jazmine said, curling her lips in derision. "Another great idea of men, huh?"

"Tell me about it!" Grayson said, shaking her head.

"Well, for me, it was Ray that told me I should try out more women."

"She told you that?" Grayson said, her look deadpan. "While you were dating her?"

Jazmine laughed, nodding her head. "Yeah, I think she really knew that I was going to get hurt dating her again, and she was trying to get me to find someone else."

Grayson shook her head, rolling her eyes. "How'd that go over?"

"I wasn't really happy with her when she said it, trust me," Jazmine said.

"I would say not," Grayson said, thinking her wife needed to learn a thing or two about how to deal gently with hearts. Although she'd never had that problem.

It was one more thing that solidified what Jazmine had told her about Rayden not being in love with her. Rayden was a very possessive person, she would never have told someone she was in love with to go out looking for other women.

"So, is that what you're going to do?" Shenin asked.

"Well, I kind of did already," Jazmine said, biting her lip and grimacing.

"What! When?" Shenin asked.

"Like almost a couple of weeks ago…" Jazmine said looking embarrassed.

"With who?" Shenin asked, but then she knew. "It was Dakota wasn't it?"

Jazmine's mouth dropped open. "How the hell…?"

"Dakota's the one that found you a few nights back," Shenin said. "And you said that you were at the studio, and she's the one doing the work there…"

Jazmine pressed her lips together. "You're too damned smart, Shen," she said, grinning then.

Shenin waggled her eyebrows. "Well, was she as awesome as everyone thinks she is?"

"Oh yeah," Jazmine said, her look radiant.

Shenin wrinkled up her nose in excitement. "So… then…"

"No," Jazmine said, shaking her head. "Dakota's so much worse than Rayden, Sorry Gray, I mean the old Rayden."

"No worries, I know what you meant," Grayson said, smiling. "But just like I was for Ray, maybe you're the exception for Dakota…"

Jazmine made a face. "I don't think so," she said, shaking her head.

"Why not?" Grayson asked. "You're beautiful, you're smart, you're sexy as hell,"

"Really now?" Jazmine asked, grinning at Grayson.

"Don't tell Ray I said that," Grayson said, grimacing as she grinned.

"Well, what happened when she found you the other night?" Shenin asked.

"She was a complete gentleman," Jazmine said.

"Well, but that's different for her, isn't it?" Shenin asked. "I mean after the Natalia thing we all know she's a major player."

"Natalia thing?" Grayson asked.

"Long story, I'll tell ya later," Shenin said, smiling.

"Well, we're kind of friends," Jazmine said. "So it makes sense that she was respectful, and maybe says that that's all she wants to be now, you know?"

"Or it means that she respects you too much to take advantage of you when you're vulnerable," Grayson said.

"That's true," Shenin said. "Ty was like that. I swear I tried to get her to kiss me when she was drunk and so was I... She wouldn't do it."

Jazmine looked back at both women, her look considering. Then she shrugged.

"She's with Cassandra," she said then.

"That old bat?" Shenin said, rolling her eyes. "What kind of attraction could she hold?"

"Her checkbook," Jazmine said simply.

"Oh," Shenin said, looking circumspect then grimacing.

"Yeah," Jazmine said her look dejected.

***

Two days later Jazmine still hadn't heard from Dakota and was worried sick. She'd tried over and over to get ahold of her but to no avail. She would have written it off to Dakota blowing her off, but when she'd spoken to Cassandra, she had given some lame excuse about Dakota being 'under the weather.' That had set off all kinds of alarms in Jazmine's head. She'd even gone to the house to see Cassandra, who had pointedly kept her downstairs and then finally told her she needed to go to an appointment and had ushered Jazmine out of the house. She'd seemed nervous.

By the third day, Jazmine was done waiting around, so she went to the DOJ offices and straight to Rayden's office. She walked through the open door without knocking.

"Ray, I need your help," she said without preamble.

Rayden turned around surprised to see her, but then saw the worry in her eyes. Grayson was in the office and saw it too.

"Jaz, what's wrong?" Rayden asked, as she got up from her desk and walked to where Jazmine stood.

"It's Dakota, I can't get ahold of her, and I'm worried. Cassandra is a violent bitch and I'm worried she's done something crazy…"

"Okay, okay, slow down…" Rayden said, walking Jazmine over to the chairs at her table and sitting her down.

Rayden kneeled in front of her. "Okay, tell me what you mean by Cassandra being violent."

Jazmine took a deep breath. "She's hurt Dakota before."

"What! When?" Rayden said.

"About three weeks or so ago, Cody knows about it. Savanna dressed it for her. Cassandra cut her arm open and hit her, and raked her nails down her chest."

"Jesus!" Rayden exclaimed. "Okay, so why do you think something's happened now?"

"Cassandra's been mad at her since Vegas and she was really short with me when I asked about Dakota," Jazmine said, grimacing.

"She knows it's you that went to Vegas with Dakota?" Rayden asked sharply.

"No," Jazmine said, shaking her head. "Well, I don't think so. Dakota told her she went alone… Anyway, she stayed with me for a couple of nights after…" Her voice trailed off as she shook her head.

"After what?" Rayden asked.

"Ray, you just need to help," Grayson put in. She sensed that it was something Jazmine didn't want Rayden to know and guessed it had to do with when Dakota had 'found' her at the studio.

Grayson caught Jazmine's grateful smile and nodded, winking at her.

"Okay." Rayden nodded.

"I want Cody there too," Jazmine said. "She knows Dakota the best."

"Okay," Rayden said, as she walked to her office door. "Someone get me Falco," she called.

"Which one?" someone called back.

"Both!"

An hour later Rayden, Lyric, Cody, and Jazmine walked up to Cassandra Billings' front door.

"Cody, you ask for Dakota," Jazmine said. "She's already put me off."

Cody nodded. She was worried sick about her friend too, as was Lyric. It was everything she could do not to punch the woman out for the first time she'd hurt Dakota. She rang the bell.

Lyric and Rayden exchanged a look, both of them worried, but doing their best to stay calm.

When the butler opened the door, Cody smiled and said. "Hi, I need to see Dakota."

The butler's eyes went to the other three people standing there, then back to Cody. "Miss Dakota is not feeling well at this time. If you will give me your name I will let her know you came by."

Cody narrowed her eyes slightly. "Maybe you didn't hear me, I said I need to *see* Dakota. That means I need to see her in person," she said her tone all cop at that point.

"I'm sorry, Miss, but she is not accepting visitors at this time," the butler said, and actually had the temerity to start to close the door in Cody's face.

Rayden's hand on the door stopped that from happening.

"Go get Dakota, now," Rayden told the man, her dark eyes glittering dangerously.

"I… but… ma'am!" the butler stammered, flustered.

"Fuck this," Cody said, shoving the door open and stepping inside the house. "Dakota!" she yelled, her voice carrying in the open foyer. "Dakota!" she yelled again, glancing back at Lyric who was grinning and shaking her head.

Cassandra came sweeping down the stairs looking at Cody and the rest of them like they were armed robbers.

"What is going on here!" she screeched. "I'm going to call the police!"

Cody, Lyric, and Rayden held up their badges.

"Well... I will not stand for this intrusion!" Cassandra huffed.

"Cassandra, where is Dakota?" Jazmine asked, moving to stand in front of the others. "We just need to see that she's okay."

Cassandra's eyes widened as she looked at Jazmine, then they narrowed. "Just because she's been fucking you doesn't mean she cares about you Jazmine, you should know that by now..." she said, her voice pure acid.

"Tell me where she is!" Jazmine yelled.

Cassandra merely smiled icily crossing her arms in front of her chest.

Cody, who was well past being patient, strode toward the stairs.

"You can't do that!" Cassandra snapped moving to intercept Cody and putting her arm on Cody's arm.

"You better remove that," Cody said, her eyes glittering with malice. "Or I'll break every one of your bony ass fingers."

Cassandra snatched her hand back like she'd been burned. "I will not tolerate this invasion of my privacy! Douglas, call my lawyer!"

"Good, you're gonna need him," Cody said and then she started up the stairs.

Jazmine, Rayden, and Lyric followed her. It took a while to find the right room but then they stepped up to a door that had Cassandra throwing herself in front of it.

"You can't go in there! This is my home! You don't have a warrant!"

"We don't need a warrant," Lyric said. "We believe Dakota Blair to be in grave danger, and have probable cause to search these premises to locate her since you failed to produce her to verify her safety."

"Wait!" Cassandra said, staying in front of the door.

"Lady, if you don't move, I'm gonna move you, and I guarantee you it's going to hurt," Cody growled.

Rayden reached out, gently taking Cassandra's arm and pulling her out of the way. Cody tried the handle to the door but it was locked. Without hesitation, she stepped back and kicked the door open. She strode inside but stopped dead in her tracks when she looked over to the bed. All she could see was red and Dakota lying in the middle of it. She reached out blindly, and Lyric was there supporting her as her knees weakened.

"Dakota!" Jazmine screamed, running over to the bed. She climbed onto it, her hands shaking as she reached out to touch Dakota's hair. "Dakota?" she queried, terrified that they were too late.

She could see cuts and scratches everywhere. Dakota wore only boy shorts underwear and an exercise bra. There was blood everywhere and it was impossible to tell where the blood was coming from.

Dakota looked pale, her eyes were closed, and her face slack. Jazmine called her name over and over again, with no response.

"Ray…" Jazmine breathed tearfully.

"Okay," Rayden said. She reached over and put her finger to Dakota's neck feeling for a pulse. "She's got a pulse, Lyric call an ambulance now!"

Jazmine jumped off the bed, strode over to Cassandra, and slapped her so hard that Cassandra fell to the floor. Cody picked her up and turned her around, holding her hands behind her back and pulling out her handcuffs.

"You are under arrest for assault and battery," Cody said, her voice shaking, but sure. "You have the right to remain silent, anything you say can and will be held against you in a court of law. You have the right to an attorney…" Cody marched Cassandra out of the room, unable to look at Dakota's body again for fear she'd kill this woman she had in cuffs.

Chapter 9

At the hospital, doctors told Lyric, who had stepped as Dakota's "guardian," that Dakota needed blood and that she was a rare type O Negative. As luck would have it so were Cody and Lyric. They both donated as much as they were allowed, which fortunately was enough for what Dakota needed. It had been determined that Dakota had lost twenty to thirty percent of her blood due to the numerous cuts, some quite deep. It had been further determined that had Jazmine not insisted that they go to get Dakota, she would have likely have died due to the blood loss within eight hours.

Savanna arrived at the hospital as Lyric was being given an update of Dakota's condition.

"How is she?" Savanna asked, looking frantic.

"She's okay," Lyric told her, looking relieved. "She'll be okay."

"We need to get her out of here as soon as possible," Cody said.

"What?" Savanna said. "Cody, she needs to be here."

"Mom, she hates hospitals, why do you think I had you look at her arm? 'Cause she wouldn't set foot in a hospital. She had some major trauma when she was a kid." She put her hand on Lyric's arm. "Trust me, Mom, she wakes up in a hospital and there's going to be a problem…" Her voice trailed off as they heard a ruckus down the hall. "Shit, too late!"

Jazmine had been sitting in the room where Dakota was lying hooked up to an IV and various machines. Jazmine hadn't noticed when Dakota woke up, but she noticed a minute later when Dakota sat up and started yanking the IV out her arm and pulling off the monitor.

"Dakota! Stop!" Jazmine yelled, trying to get through to her.

"Get me out of here, Jaz," Dakota said trying to get off the bed, weaving dangerously as she did.

"Whoa!" Lyric yelled as she came through the door, just in time to catch Dakota as she slid out of the bed, and started to fall when she couldn't support her own weight. "Hold on Dak, hold on…" Lyric said, supporting Dakota's weight as Cody and Jazmine helped her back into the bed.

"I'm not stayin' here…" Dakota said mutinously, even as she gasped for breath.

"Okay, okay," Lyric said, as Savanna came into the room.

"I need to go…" Dakota said, her voice rasping, looking at Savanna.

"Okay, honey, we'll get you out of here," Savanna said soothingly. "Just let me talk to your doctor first, okay?"

Dakota looked like she wanted to argue.

"Dakota, please," Jazmine said, putting her hand on Dakota's arm.

Dakota looked over at Jazmine, seeing how worried she was, she sighed. "Okay, but just long enough for Savanna to talk to the doc."

"Right," Jazmine said, nodding, glancing over at Cody who only grinned.

Two hours later it had been discussed, argued, and eventually Dakota signed out AMA (against medical advice) allowing her out of the hospital. Jazmine had offered her apartment for Dakota to recover at. Cody had given her mother's silent signal to agree with that option. Dakota hadn't said anything, but certainly didn't argue with the idea of staying at Jazmine's.

They got Dakota settled in Jazmine's room on one side of her bed. Savanna went over all the instructions that they'd been given by the hospital with Jazmine. Savanna and Lyric then went shopping for groceries, and Cody and Jazmine sat in the living room while Dakota slept.

"I'm really glad you were keeping tabs on her," Cody said sincerely.

"I just wish I would have gotten there sooner," Jazmine said. "I should have beaten the shit out of Cassandra the first time I went over there."

"I should have ignored Dakota and arrested her ass the first time she cut her," Cody said, her lips twitching.

"Do you think she's going to be okay?" Jazmine asked Cody.

Cody drew in a deep breath, then blew it out. "I think that she's gonna have a rough time for a bit…"

Jazmine nodded. "Well, she can stay here as long as she wants."

Cody smiled. "I'm really glad she has you."

"Well, we're friends," Jazmine said, her tone conciliatory.

Cody nodded, her eyes showing that she didn't really believe they were just friends.

A little while later Lyric and Savanna got back with groceries and after Savanna had checked on Dakota again, the three of them left. Jazmine walked into her room and sat down on her bed looking at Dakota. She'd been terrified when she'd seen Dakota lying in her own blood, she'd been sure she was dead.

She saw the tiny cuts on her face, it seemed like Cassandra had avoided doing too much damage to parts of Dakota that would be visible. It drove Jazmine crazy to know that Cassandra had done all this damage to Dakota, and then just left her to bleed to death. Every time she thought about it, she just wanted to go down to the jail and kill Cassandra Billings painfully and slowly, like she'd tried to do to Dakota.

She'd received all kinds of texts from everyone, telling her to tell Dakota to get well fast.

Jazmine took a shower and got ready for bed. She climbed into her bed, next to where Dakota slept and lay with her hand on Dakota's shoulder, so she'd feel it when or if Dakota woke up and needed something. She slept all night, Dakota never even stirred. The hospital had given her some heavy-duty painkillers. Savanna had explained to Jazmine that, between the painkillers and the blood loss, Dakota was likely to sleep a lot over the next few days.

The next morning Jazmine got up and went into the kitchen to make some coffee. When she walked back into the bedroom, she sat on the bed with her coffee, tucking her feet up under her. She spent the day reading and started to reach out to her contacts to try to line up more dancing jobs. With Dakota out of action, she'd need to find some work for the time being.

At one point, Dakota stirred, opening her eyes and staring up at the ceiling for a long minute. Jazmine turned to look down at her. Dakota blinked a couple of times, then she looked over at Jazmine, her eyes searching Jazmine's face.

"You came for me…" Dakota said, her voice barely audible.

"Well, me, Cody, Lyric, and Rayden," Jazmine said smiling softly. "And of course I came for you, I always will," she said, her eyes staring down into Dakota's.

Dakota looked back at her for a long moment, and Jazmine could see she was trying to decide how to take what Jazmine had just said. Finally she reached out her right hand, and touched Jazmine's hand, sliding her fingers over Jazmine's. Then she closed her eyes again and was asleep again moments later.

Later that day Savanna came to check on Dakota to make sure she was doing alright. Dakota barely woke as Savanna checked her more serious cuts on her left side and up near her collarbone.

"They look good right now," Savanna told Jazmine when she walked back out to the living room. "Just keep an eye on them, and check with her to see if they hurt or are feeling hot, okay?"

"Okay," Jazmine said, nodding.

"We've got to watch for signs of infection, we have no idea what that bitch cut her with," Savanna said, her eyes narrowing dangerously.

It was another three days before Dakota was feeling better. Unfortunately that was the same day Lyric heard that Cassandra had been released from jail. Her lawyers had gotten her out on bail. She'd already tried to file charges against Lyric, Rayden, and Cody, and she was threatening charges on Jazmine for "assault." Jazmine tried to keep all of this information away from Dakota, but Dakota saw the shadow in her eyes the minute she walked back into the bedroom.

"What's wrong?" Dakota asked her blue eyes searching Jazmine's face.

"Nothing, it's okay," Jazmine said, shaking her head and smiling at Dakota as she sat down on the bed.

Dakota levered herself to sit up wincing slightly as she did.

"Careful..." Jazmine said, seeing Dakota's wince.

"Tell me what's going on," Dakota said her voice stronger now.

Jazmine drew in a breath, shaking her head. "It's no big deal."

"Jaz..." Dakota said, her tone and look serious.

"Okay, okay," Jazmine said, seeing that Dakota was getting irritated. "Cassandra is out of jail and threatening everyone with charges."

Dakota froze for a moment. "They arrested her?" she asked, her tone shocked.

"Yeah, Dakota, Cody did," Jazmine said her tone indignant. "She almost killed you!"

Dakota let out a sarcastic sound. "People like Cassandra don't pay for shit like this."

"Shit like this?" Jazmine repeated disbelievingly. "What does that mean?"

Dakota shook her head, her look disdainful. "For hurting someone like me," she said, her tone full of derision.

"Someone like you," Jazmine repeated her face a mask of incredulity. "What exactly do you think 'someone like you' is, Dakota?"

Dakota gave a cynical snort. "Some fuckin' street kid that isn't worth shit."

Jazmine stared at Dakota open mouthed as she shook her head. "Do you really believe that?"

Dakota didn't answer, seeing the look Jazmine was giving her.

"You do, don't' you?" Jazmine asked sadly.

Dakota shook her head, looking away. "It doesn't matter, she'll win, she always wins."

"She won't this time," Jazmine said, shaking her head.

Dakota looked back at her for a long moment. Jazmine could see she didn't believe her.

"I'm guessing that she's pulled the funding for the studio too, right?" Dakota asked then.

Jazmine shook her head. "I don't know, but I don't care, I would never do business with her again anyway."

"Jaz…" Dakota said, her tone imploring. "This was your dream."

Jazmine shook her head. "It was never part of my dream to be in business with someone that sadistic and cruel, Dakota."

Dakota curled her lips in derision. "They're all like that," she said, her tone matter of fact. "They just don't show it so blatantly most of the time."

"Why would you want to be around people like that, Dakota?" Jazmine asked shaking her head in disbelief.

Dakota didn't answer, her eyes dropping from Jazmine's.

"It doesn't have to be that way, Dakota," Jazmine said, her look pointed.

"What doesn't?" Dakota asked raising, her eyes to look at Jazmine, her look scornful.

"Your life," Jazmine said. "You don't have to be around people like that."

Dakota gave a short laugh, shaking her head.

"What?" Jazmine asked, pinning Dakota with a look.

Dakota gave her a narrowed look, like she was looking for something in Jazmine's eyes.

"You don't get it, do you?" Dakota asked.

"Get what?" Jazmine asked her eyes searching Dakota's.

"I'm like them," Dakota said. "I'm just like them I just don't have their money."

"Oh my God, no you're not!" Jazmine said. "I've seen who you are Dakota, and you're not going to make me believe that you're like them, like her."

"What have you seen?" Dakota asked, her voice quiet suddenly.

"I've seen you unguarded. I've seen you gallant and charming, and I've seen you remorseful and apologetic, I've seen you kind and considerate… Those people, people like Cassandra, they aren't any of those things," Jazmine said softly.

Dakota blinked a couple of times, her lips trembling at Jazmine's assessment of her. In truth she hadn't realized she'd revealed that much to Jazmine, or that Jazmine had actually been paying that close attention. And she had absolutely no idea how to respond to what Jazmine had said.

Jazmine could see that Dakota was surprised by what she'd told her, and she could also see that Dakota was searching for a response. Because she was afraid Dakota would close up on her, she leaned in, kissing Dakota's lips softly.

She pulled back and looked into Dakota's eyes. "I love you."

"What?" Dakota breathed, looking almost terrified.

Jazmine pressed her lips together, tears coming to her eyes. "I love you, Dakota," she repeated.

Dakota started shaking her head, averting her eyes. "No, you don't, you can't," she said, her tone strident.

Jazmine put her hand to Dakota's cheek, stilling her movement, turning Dakota's face back to hers.

"I do, I can, and I love you," Jazmine said.

"But, Ray… You love her," Dakota said grasping at anything at that point, not willing to believe that Jazmine loved her and speaking her biggest fears at the same time.

Jazmine nodded. "Yes, I do, but when I saw you lying there… With all that blood… The idea of you being dead…" She shook her head, her look devastated. "I knew I was in love with you then. I knew I couldn't lose you, not like that."

Dakota looked back at Jazmine, her eyes still searching Jazmine's face.

"You're looking for signs that I'm lying to you," Jazmine said. "You're waiting for the other shoe to drop, right?"

"I'm waiting for the cost," Dakota replied simply.

"The cost," Jazmine repeated. "That's simple," she said, touching Dakota's chest with her fingertip. "Give me your heart."

Dakota opened her mouth, and Jazmine could see the smart-ass reply forming. She stopped it by kissing Dakota again. Every time Dakota opened her mouth to say something smart, Jazmine kissed her.

"I can do this all day long," Jazmine said, her grin making her eyes sparkle mischievously.

Dakota pursed her lips, narrowing her eyes at the other woman.

Jazmine gave her a delighted look. Dakota tilted her head slightly.

"You love me?" Dakota asked.

"Yes."

"You're sure?""Yes."Dakota looked at her for a long moment, her look measuring, and Jazmine could see her mind churning. Finally she nodded slowly, as if agreeing to some decision she'd just come to in her head.

"How much money was Cassandra putting toward the studio?" Dakota asked unexpectedly.

"I…" Jazmine stammered. "I think about a million, why?"

Dakota nodded, obviously doing some sort of calculation in her head. Then she looked back at Jazmine.

"I want to buy into the studio," Dakota said.

Jazmine looked stunned, shaking her head. "Dakota… we can't do it, it's too much. Between Natalia and I, we only have about a hundred thousand. Cassandra was the principle on this…"

"I know, and I mean I want to become the principle," Dakota said.

"How?" Jazmine asked, surprised by this completely off topic conversation.

"I'm going to sell the Bugatti," Dakota said.

"How can you do that?"

Dakota laughed. "My name is on the title... the only name on the title."

Jazmine stared back at her openmouthed, but then she shook her head. "No, you love that car, I can't let you do that."

"I do love that car," Dakota said, with a mysterious smile on her lips. "But I love you more, so... the car goes."

Jazmine gave a slow blink, her mouth open in surprise again. "I'm sorry... Say that again?"

Dakota smiled lovingly, putting her hand to Jazmine's cheek. She then slid it to the back of her head to draw her forward, and kissed her lips softly.

"I love you," Dakota said simply.

"Now that's more like it," Jazmine said, smiling brightly.

Epilogue

The line of cars shocked drivers as they weaved in and out of traffic. There were muscle cars, old and new as well as sleek sports cars. It was an auto show on the freeway. There were three Ferrari's: a red one, a black one, and a dark gray one. There was a blue Maserati, a black Mercedes, a black Hummer, a red Challenger Hellcat and a classic dark blue Mach 1 Mustang. Lastly, there were two Nissan 370Zs, one white Nismo edition and another blue one. The cars moved together and around each other, some going faster than others, on the open freeway.

"Hey Jet! That's cheating!" Skyler called over the two-way radio as she laughed.

"Only if a cop catches you doing it!" Jet called back over the radio.

"You are a cop, dumbass!" Cat replied, causing a lot of the group to grin.

They were on their way to San Francisco. They'd decided as a group to attend the San Francisco Pride parade. They were making the trip as a group and had reserved a block of thirteen rooms at the Fairmont Hotel in San Francisco. They had every intention of making it a great weekend.

"Comin' up on yer left," Quinn said into her radio.

"Who's left?" Kashena asked.

"That was my left," Jericho said, laughing as Quinn's Mach roared past her.

"Someone is watching for CHP, right?" Sebastian asked, glancing over and winking at Ashley who sat in the passenger seat. This was their first weekend away since their baby had been born, and the last thing they needed was a speeding ticket.

"Yeah, yeah, daddy!" Kashena chimed in with a laugh.

"Not me," Lyric said in answer to Sebastian's question.

"Me either," Cody said.

"Someone was supposed to be watching for CHP?" Jericho asked.

"I didn't get that memo," Rayden said, grinning.

"No memo received here either!" Skyler added.

"Well, this is a mess," Dakota put in, winking at Jazmine.

"Listen here youngster..." Jericho said, grinning.

"Yes dear?" Dakota queried.

"Watch it!" Quinn yelled, laughing.

A conversation ensued about ages, and how much it mattered and why it was all about experience.

Suddenly a black 370Z with red racing stripes and stickers that identified it as a Stillen Supercharger began weaving its way through the group. It zipped past Rayden's Jaguar, Sebastian's Hummer, and Kashena's Mercedes easily. Then it slid to the right and passed Cat's Z and Dakota's Ferrari.

Dakota looked over at Jazmine, her eyes sparkling with the challenge the other driver had just thrown her.

"Damnit, I really want to do it…" Dakota said.

"Don't even think about it, Dak!" Lyric called over the radio, having seen the black Z pass Dakota. "We're still tuning that engine. If you blow it out we're gonna spend weeks rebuilding!"

Dakota was driving a 1955 Ferrari 250 GT, but it was a special and rare body style called a Panin Farina Berlinetta. Lyric and Dakota had searched for weeks for the car and finally found it across the country. They'd spent four months on it already, trying to get it back in good condition. This was the first trip the Ferrari had been on.

"I knew I was gonna miss the Bugatti," Dakota said, grinning.

"Oh sure, you say that now," Jazmine said, smiling over at Dakota.

"Only kidding, babe, promise," Dakota said, winking at Jazmine again.

"Who the hell is that?" Jet asked as the black Z moved up on her bumper, even as she dropped the hammer and zipped ahead, the 454 horsepower engine of her Maserati surged forward.

To her surprise, the black Z caught up quickly and passed her.

"Son of a bitch…" Jet muttered, glancing over at her wife who was shaking her head at her.

As the black Z zipped up to Lyric and Cody in the black and red Ferraris, they gave the Z a little bit of a challenge, but still the Z overtook them and passed them. Shortly after that, it passed Jericho's red Hellcat and zipped up to Skyler in her Nismo edition Z.

The driver of the black Z paced the Nismo. Skyler glanced over but couldn't see the driver, due to the heavily tinted windows. She accelerated, grinning, and the black Z did the same.

"That's a fuckin' Stillen Supercharger," Skyler said. "Who the hell is that?"

Devin looked speculative, and just as she was about to say something the black Z zipped ahead and paced Quinn's Mach 1.

"Oh this fecker wants to play…" Quinn's Irish accented voice came over the radio. "Let's go!" Suddenly the Mach 1 surged ahead, and the black Z took a few moments to catch up, but catch up it did.

Over the two-way radios, Def Leppard's "Let's Get Rocked" started to play with the first line "Do you wanna get rocked?" Everyone knew then that whoever was in the black Z was on their frequency. The song played on as the black Z challenged Quinn's Mach to a race.

As things got a little too dangerous and they came close to Buttonwillow, Jericho cut in on the radio.

"Quinn, back it off a bit, you're getting to town!"

"Got it!" Quinn called back. Then to her opponent, she asked, "Draw?"

There was silence on the radio for a full minute, everyone waited to see who would respond or if they even would. They did notice with relief that the black Z was also backing down on their speed.

"Rematch?" came the reply, a very definite female voice.

"Hell yeah!" Quinn said, laughing.

"Draw!" said the woman who drove the black Z.

Ten minutes later, they all pulled into a Denny's parking lot. The last to pull in was the black Z and as everyone got out of their cars, they all waited to see who would get out of it. The woman who climbed out had white-blond hair pulled up into a ponytail and there were two long skinny braids that were colored in a rainbow. She wore black jeans and a black tank top that had a circle with a Z in it, with the words "Livin' Z Life" around it. She wore black heeled boots and a thick black studded watch on one arm and a series of bracelets on the other arm that were a myriad of colors and textures and went four inches up her arm. She also wore mirrored sunglasses, but she took them off as she walked up to the group.

"Sorry I'm late," she said, grinning. "I'm Harley."

"There you are!" Devin called, just having gotten out of the car. She walked over to hug the other woman.

Devin turned to the group. "I thought this might be who that was," she said, grinning. "But I figured she could introduce herself."

Skyler walked up to Harley and extended her hand. "Helluva a nice Z," she said grinning. 'I'm Skyler."

Harley smiled, glancing at Devin.

The rest of the group crowded in and introductions were made all around.

When she got to Rayden, Rayden canted her head. "Davidson?"

"Yeah," Harley said, grinning.

"I think I'm your new boss."

"You're Black Wolf?" Harley asked.

"How many Raydens do you think there are in LA?" Devin asked, grinning.

"Probably not too many," Harley said, glancing at Rayden again. "Good to meet you, ma'am."

"Call me Ray, everyone else does," Rayden said, smiling. "This is my wife Grayson."

Harley smiled at Grayson, extending her hand to her.

Grayson took the proffered hand smiling. "That was some fancy driving."

"I do like to play," Harley said, nodding.

"Wait, your name is Harley Davidson?" Quinn asked as she walked over.

Harley grinned, rolling her eyes. "Yeah, my dad was a biker and my mom thought she was being cute."

"Sucks to be you," Quinn said, grinning. "I'm Quinn."

"That's a nice Mach," Harley said, her eyes on the dark blue Mustang.

Quinn inclined her head.

The group headed into the Denny's restaurant then, flustering the waitresses with their sheer size. In total, there were twenty-seven of them. It was a large group, not what the Denny's in Buttonwillow was used to.

Lyric, Savanna, Cody, McKenna, Dakota, and Jazmine sat together at one table, with Natalia and Raine pulling a small table over as well.

"So are you sure you want to go with wainscoting in there?" Dakota was asking Lyric.

"You think it's a bad idea?" Lyric asked.

"I think it'll be hell to clean with a kid," Dakota said.

Lyric looked at Savanna. "It's up to you babe, this is your thing."

"How much more time will it take?" Savanna asked, her hand on her baby bump that was just barely showing.

Dakota closed her eyes doing calculations in her head. "I'd say an extra month, and I'm tellin' ya, it'll be a pain in the ass... Why don't you go with like a chair rail, you can do the two colors that way."

Lyric and Savanna had hired Dakota to work out a master suite with a baby's room for the house. Savanna was now five months pregnant and she and Lyric were beyond thrilled.

Lyric and Savanna had officially and legally adopted Dakota. To their surprise and delight, Dakota had taken Lyric's last name. She was officially Dakota Falco now. Cody and Dakota constantly joked about being blood sisters due to the blood Cody had donated, and that she was officially Lyric's kid because of Lyrics blood that now ran in her veins as well.

Jazmine watched the three talk about the baby's room, and smiled. She was happy to see Dakota so happy and settled. The studio was up and running, and even though Dakota had put in a million dollars exactly as she'd said she would, she remained a silent partner. She'd sold the Bugatti for 2.7 million dollars. She'd given Jazmine and Natalia the one million and had bought a house with another million. She'd used the remaining money to set herself up in a business.

Jazmine had quickly discovered that a settled and happy Dakota was a very astute businesswoman. She had not, however, lost her wild edge in the slightest, and they went out every weekend. Dakota was forever getting hit on, but she always turned to her redheaded dancer. She was also always having to step in when too many butch women went after Jazmine. Rayden often assisted in that area. Jazmine and Rayden had become good friends, as had Jazmine and Grayson.

Dakota and Jazmine had gone with Rayden and Grayson to Las Vegas so that the Black Wolfs could get legally remarried. Rayden and Dakota had gambled after that, and Grayson and Jazmine had gone shopping and hung out at the pool. It had been a fun weekend.

As Dakota had expected, Cassandra beat the case against her for Dakota's assault. She'd actually had the temerity to contact Dakota afterwards wanting to see her. Dakota had told her to take a hike. Fortunately, Cassandra had taken the hint and disappeared.

At another table Jericho, Zoey, Rayden, Grayson, Kashena, Sierra, Sebastian, and Ashley were discussing the direction of the department.

"Well, with Rayden in charge of Crime Prevention, I'm expecting to get an up in my budget for some of the new programs," Jericho was saying.

"The paycheck for Davidson alone is going to kill my budget," Rayden said, grimacing.

"Well, Midnight is aware of the step up of the tech side," Sierra said. "So I'd bet you she's got a plan."

"She usually does," Kashena said, grinning.

"So is Davidson a consultant?" Sebastian asked, glancing over at the blond who was sitting with another group.

"Yeah," Rayden said. "Devin Boché recommended her. She's supposed to be really good."

"That's what I've heard too," Jericho said. "Which is why I approved her hire."

"Well, if Devin recommended her, I can imagine she's good. Devin's dangerous she's so good," Kashena said.

"So speaking of hires," Jericho said, looking over at Grayson. "I'm told you're a pilot."

"I was a pilot, yes," Grayson said hesitantly.

"Ever consider flying again?" Jericho asked.

Grayson looked at Rayden who raised an eyebrow.

"In what capacity?" Grayson asked.

"For DOJ," Jericho said. "We need fixed-wing pilots."

"What kind of aircraft?" Grayson asked.

"Babe, they use Air Force aircraft," Rayden said, starting to grin. "That's what Shenin's doing, remember? She coordinates the planes and the pilots for missions…"

"Oh, well, that's handy," Grayson said, grinning.

"That's right, you were an Air Force pilot," Jericho said, suddenly remembering.

Grayson nodded.

"So? Would you be interested?" Jericho asked.

Grayson looked at Rayden. "What do you think?"

"I think it would get you back in a plane where you're completely at home," Rayden said, smiling.

Grayson bit her lip, smiling. Rayden knew her so well. She looked back at Jericho then.

"Yes, I'd be interested," she said.

"Let's talk when we get back next week," Jericho said.

"Okay," Grayson said.

At another table Shenin, Tyler, Jet, Fadiyah, Skyler, Devin, Cat, Jovina, Quinn, Xandy, and the newcomer, Harley sat at another table.

"So what body kit is that?" Skyler was asking Harley, looking out the window at Harley's Z.

"It's an Amuse kit," Harley said.

"Woah, that probably set you back," Skyler said, grinning.

"Not as much as the Stillen did," Harley said.

Skyler closed one eye, grimacing. "Go ahead, give it to me."

"The body kit was two thousand, the Stillen was eight."

"Dayum…" Skyler said, whistling. "And you have Sparcos in there too."

"Sparcos?" Devin queried, lost when it came to most of the car stuff.

"Racing seats," Jet supplied.

"Yup," Harley said, grinning. "Yeah, they're Sparcos, the set cost me about fifteen hundred."

"That's one bad ass ride…" Quinn said, grinning. "But I'm gonna have to hand you yer ass on the next match."

"You can try," Harley said, grinning.

Quinn chuckled, nodding.

"I feel bad for my poor little sport now…" Cat said sighing.

"Oh we can set you up," Harley said. "You got a great base, it just needs some work."

Cat grinned, glancing at Jovina who shook her head rolling her eyes.

"Well that's a nice Mas you got out there," Harley said to Jet.

"Yeah, I love that car… Almost as much as my wife," she added, winking at Fadiyah who smiled.

"I am not too sure about that," she said, her accent still clear even after almost a year in the States.

"Where are you from?" Harley asked Fadiyah. "If you don't mind me asking."

"I do not mind," Fadiyah said, smiling. "I am from Iraq."

Harley nodded slowly, glancing at Jet and obviously trying to make the connection.

Jet looked back at Harley and let her stew on it for a bit, waiting to see if she'd ask. She didn't, and it was surprising to Jet. Most people found they needed to satisfy their curiosity of her and Fadiyah. She liked that Harley seemed willing to accept things as they were.

"So, Quinn," Harley said, looking at the Irish woman. "What part of Ireland are you from?"

"Northern Ireland, Belfast," Quinn said.

"Cool," Harley said, nodding.

Two hours later, it was time to get on the road again. They had another two hundred and fifty miles to go. As everyone got in their cars and turned on the radios, people in the nearby parking lots turned to stare at all the muscle and beauty of the cars. They all pulled out of the parking lot and entered the freeway again.

As the black Z took the lead yet again, they all heard Harley's music blasting on her radio as she keyed the mike.

"Last one to Coalinga buys the first round tonight at the bar!" With that, she punched it and surged ahead.

The race was definitely on!

You can find more information about the author and series here:

www.sherrylhancock.com

www.facebook.com/SherrylDHancock